Access All Areas

TEDDIE DAHLIN

Other titles by the author

A Vicious Love Story: Remembering the Real Sid Vicious

Fast Living: Remembering the Real Gary Holton

ACCESS ALL AREAS

ACCESS ALL AREAS

First Edition

Published 2013
NEW HAVEN PUBLISHING LTD
www.newhavenpublishingltd.com
newhavenpublishing@gmail.com

Front cover photograph © Melanie Smith
Back Cover photograph © Tina Pammer

Cover designs © Pete Cunliffe
pcunliffe@blueyonder.co.uk

TABLE OF CONTENTS

ACCESS ALL AREAS

PROLOGUE 1983

Bill and Delphine Graham stood together at the entrance to their country home, welcoming their guests to the biggest party of the year. It was not a formal event and people had not dressed up, but some of them had certainly taken the 'smart/casual' recommendation on the invitation as far as they could.

Bill spotted Drusilla White place one well-shaped leg out of her sports car, followed by the rest of her. She is one beautiful woman, he thought, as he watched her throw her car keys to the valet, shake her long raven hair, and walk elegantly towards him. Bill greeted Drusilla with a kiss on each cheek, the smell of her perfume wafting over him from her tanned, athletic body, before she turned to Delphine to repeat the ritual. His wife wore an icy smile on her lips as she gave her own greeting before quickly turning her attention to the next guest in an almost dismissive way.

Was that a little jealousy, Bill wondered with a smile? Drusilla was at least ten years older than his wife, but much more attractive in his opinion. Delphine could not hold a candle to her effortless elegance and style.

Bill's band, The Sticks, was number six in the UK singles music charts and their album had gone straight into the top forty. Events like that needed to be celebrated, although he and his wife never needed much of an excuse to throw a party. The royalties from the single, 'Leggy Blonde Bombshell' alone were a staggering amount, even for an old rock band like The Sticks who'd had their fair share of hits over the years. It was more than enough to allow him to stop working, but Bill enjoyed touring, so retirement was not an option.

Besides, why would he want to retire at the age of forty-two? Bill still had a lot of living to do. He enjoyed the adoring fans and the attention, and it took him away from Delphine for a while. Not that he needed an excuse to spend some time by himself, but the added excitement of a world tour was what made Bill love the music business. The rush he felt when fifty thousand screaming fans shouted his name was addictive.

Delphine never accompanied him on his tours. Well, she had done so once, and Bill made sure it never happened again. To be honest, he didn't want her there. She could do what she wanted when she wanted, but just not come on tour.

Grinning like a Cheshire cat, Bill could not remember when he last felt this good, and he would be feeling even better next week when his lawyers worked out the divorce papers he was planning to hand to Delphine as soon as possible, ensuring she got very little in the settlement. He was looking forward to turfing her out of his life completely. What a stupid mistake it had been to marry the stick insect, blood-sucking junkie. He had not known about the drugs and the extent of her addiction at the time.

Of course, Bill enjoyed a couple of mandies himself from time to time, and the odd line or two of coke to keep him going. It was all in the name of good fun, but he never used smack. That was a big no-no in his book. Tell a lie, Bill had tried it once. Well, he had tried just about everything once. It was his philosophy in life: don't regret what you haven't done when you are too old to do anything about it.

That happened in the late 70s when heroin became the drug of choice in the music business. It had always been around, but suddenly gained popularity when the iconic Johnny Thunders and Jerry Nolan arrived in London with the infamous Nancy Spungen in tow.

Bill remembered it well. The whole music scene changed overnight, and you had these people like Sid and Nancy acting like the coolest kids in town, with their shite excuse for music. Bill could not stand punk, but he had to admit it did have a huge impact on everything back then. Luckily, it hadn't been popular for long.

He remembered the time he met Sid Vicious, an obnoxious twat; well, that was his first impression. Then he started talking to him and found he quite liked him. The real obnoxious twat was his girlfriend, Nancy. Thank God there were not many like her around.

Bill remembered how he'd been out on the town in London with a crowd of the usual people. They started off at the Roebuck pub, which was a punk hangout he detested, but his girlfriend, Gina, wanted to go, so he tagged along. It was quite hot that summer, and as they went from one club to the next, he started feeling drunk and reckless. Later that night they all trooped into Gina's smart apartment on Kings Road, just down the street from Malcolm McLaren's and Vivienne Westwood's trashy shop, Seditionaries.

Gina and her friend, Anne, immediately got out a leather pouch containing the equipment for shooting up heroin. Bill was fascinated as he watched the girls wash a dirty spoon with a slice of lemon and heat the brown powder with a lighter. Anne took the syringe and drew some of the liquid into it while Gina tied some rubber tubing around her upper right arm. As Anne moved closer, the two girls giggled and started kissing each other passionately.

Bill observed them, but found he wasn't aroused. He had seen this happen a million times, and was not really bothered that Gina liked both men and women, preferably at the same time, which was never a problem.

He watched in silence as Anne helped Gina to find a vein by slapping her skin and then she expertly injected some of the liquid into her arm. Gina smiled sheepishly at Bill before she let Anne release the rubber band and slide backwards on the comfortable leather sofa with a look of utter pleasure on her face. Anne then turned to Bill and laughingly tried to tie the rubber band on his arm whilst he feigned protest.

"Come on, Billy, let me help you. I know you don't like needles. Are you a man or a boy, Billy?" Anne teased him.

Bill considered it for a few seconds. As he was drunk and feeling a buzz from the lines of cocaine he had taken a few minutes earlier, he replied, "What the hell. Come and give me a little. Just make sure you don't give me too much." He let Anne tie the band and inject a tiny amount of the substance into his left arm.

First Bill felt nothing. Then it was as if someone had poured a bucket of boiling hot water over his head and he could taste the smack running through his veins. He had never felt as good as this before in his entire life; so at peace and he didn't care about anything. Everything was suddenly just great, and even if someone had told him they wanted to remove one of his limbs with a rusty knife it would have been perfectly fine with him.

He didn't feel Anne remove the rubber band or the needle. Nor did he see her inject the rest of the substance into her own arm. Bill was too far away in the most pleasurable place he'd ever been.

Later, when he came around as the effect of the drug was wearing off, Bill vowed to himself that he would never ever touch heroin again. He now knew why it was so addictive, and he realised that if he ever took it again that would be his fate and he would never be able to stop—he would die a heroin addict. Bill kept his promise to himself and never took it again, though a few of his friends and some band members were not as disciplined. His bassist, Tiger, had a huge heroin problem, verging on the impossible, and he was an inch away from getting sacked.

ACCESS ALL AREAS

When Bill met Delphine, he knew she liked her drugs. Everyone did a little; it was a fact of life. He was impressed by her at first. She had made her own money modelling and had been quite successful in her early twenties. Later, wise investments had turned her into a successful businesswoman with her own line of jewellery. Bill had liked the fact that she didn't need his money, only himself... well, to begin with.

It was not until after he stupidly, in a second of pathetic weakness, married Delphine that he discovered the real woman behind the façade—the weak junkie who could not do anything without a fix. It was unnoticeable to begin with, because she lied, covered her tracks and hid her gear. She concealed her addiction so well that Bill did not notice until it was time to go on tour.

At the time, Delphine had protested and refused to go on tour with him, using all sorts of weak excuses. Bill could not understand why she didn't want to go with him and he had to force her to travel to the States. It was only after landing at Los Angeles airport that he noticed Delphine acting strangely. She looked desperate and edgy, and a little worse for wear, having drunk herself to sleep on the flight.

They checked into the Beverly Hilton on Wilshire Boulevard and their suite was available straight away, much to the relief of Bill, who was extremely tired. The hotel was well situated, being not too far from the concert venue, but not close enough for there to be a problem with fans. The executive suite offered a stunning view of Downtown Beverley Hills from the wide floor-to-ceiling doors leading from the living area to the step-out balcony. Bill took in the panoramic view whilst Delphine, unbeknown to him, was waiting anxiously for the arrival of one of his roadies who had befriended her.

Bill had just entered the bathroom when there was a knock on the door of the suite. Surprised, he was just about to see who it was when he thought better of it. Instead, he waited quietly where he was and observed a guy handing Delphine a packet. As she grabbed it eagerly, her hand shaking slightly, Bill noticed a thin line of sweat on her forehead. She glanced around the room to make sure no one could see her, not noticing that the bathroom door was cracked open.

Bill watched as Delphine, trembling and acting erratically, filled a syringe with heroin and injected herself through her shirt, not even taking the time to roll up her sleeve. It was at that exact moment that Bill knew his whole marriage was based on a lie, and he realised he did not love this woman—this junkie.

***

Originally from France, Delphine Graham looked the archetypical rock-chick wife of The Sticks' front man and vocalist. Fittingly, she was wearing figure-hugging faux-leather trousers, a tight black top with zips on the shoulders and towering heels. Her dog-collar belt hung carelessly loose off her small hips while her long, black hair was big; the fringe pulled back from her face, as was the trend.

ACCESS ALL AREAS

Delphine had met Bill the previous year and
fallen in love with him, despite the ten-year age gap.
There was just something very sexy about him that
women found appealing, she reflected, but she
would have to keep her eye on that bitch, Drusilla.
Delphine had quickly learned that if she was going
to keep Bill, she had to accept his hedonistic
lifestyle of groupies, drugs and hangers-on. But that
was a small price to pay.

Having to share Bill had not bothered Delphine
one bit. She had the status of wife, so what did it
matter if he fucked a groupie from time to time? It
didn't mean anything and she actually loved having
an open marriage, regularly enjoying her own little
flings and affairs. But with ladies like Drusilla, it
was a completely different kettle of fish altogether.

Drusilla was serious competition and she would
never accept being the mistress or one-night stand.
The woman would pursue Bill until she got what she
wanted and Delphine was not going to let that
happen. She saw how Bill looked at her, but she
couldn't understand what he saw in the old cow.
Still, he seemed to find her attractive, so Delphine
was wary and made a note to hire a private detective
to check her out. She always liked to know who she
was dealing with.

Delphine never travelled with The Sticks on tour,
preferring the company of her London and Paris
friends instead of the hassle of travelling, late-night
concerts and endless hotels. Besides, drugs were
always a problem when flying great distances. She
needed to have her fix on time, before she felt

unwell, and long-haul flights were not good for you if you wanted to stay well. Delphine did not look upon herself as a drug addict, defining herself as user, not a junkie. She didn't think she had a problem, so long as her dope was always readily available.

Like most of their friends, her and Bill dabbled in recreational Grade A drugs to escape the tedium of everyday life. Delphine had started using in Paris when she was working as a model for the large couture houses and needed to stay thin, but later it became a habit. Everyone was using, so she didn't see a problem. It was no worse than smoking a cigarette or getting drunk, she reasoned; just a fact of life, if you could afford it.

'Visions of China' by Japan was playing loudly in the main reception room as the house filled up quickly with an array of celebrity faces. Malcolm Reynolds, The Sticks' manager, arrived with a very young girl in tow. Delphine guessed that she could not have been more than fourteen years old, at the most. Malcolm liked his girlfriends young; very much so, and the younger the better. There had even been talk of him preying on extremely young girls and boys while touring in Thailand the previous year, but Delphine did not listen to gossip, and she certainly didn't spread any herself. Bill had not discussed what Malcolm got up to with her, so she decided to do the same and keep quiet.

The girl looked like she could take care of herself and was here of her own free will, so where was the harm? Besides, she must know what was expected of her; she couldn't be that stupid, Delphine thought, as she eyed the youngster's fresh face and pert bosom squeezed into a low-cut floral dress. Her tanned legs had been pushed into a pair of suede ankle boots that looked expensive.

A lot of girls her age were sexually active and preyed on rich, well-connected older men like Malcolm. Delphine had seen it many times. Groupies would hang out at the backstage entrance of venues, waiting to get a glimpse of The Sticks whenever they played. They would be there in droves as the band left after a concert and a few of them would get to go to the after-party. It was always the roadies who chose who would be allowed backstage and who got left outside. Hence a few of them saw a little action too. It was all meaningless fun in Delphine's opinion.

"Yay, Bill, good to see you. This is Mandy," Malcolm announced in greeting and his guest held out her small hand for Bill to shake.

"Oh my God, I am such a fan of yours and The Sticks! I have all your records and a poster on my bedroom wall. I can't believe I'm here," said Mandy, giggling nervously.

Bill shook her hand politely and raised an eyebrow at Malcolm, who in turn just laughed and shrugged his shoulders. Malcolm then pulled Mandy away to find some much needed booze and a line or two of cocaine, if there was any going. They entered the house through the large oak front doors and made their way towards a pair of double glass doors that opened on to a balcony overlooking the garden at the back.

People had gathered on the lawn around the swimming pool. Stopping on the wide stone balcony, Malcolm pulled Mandy backwards into his arms as they looked out over the fifty or so people who had arrived before them.

The summer air was warm and a light breeze carried the sweet smell of flowers up from below, along with the sound of laughter. Malcolm pawed Mandy's tight buttocks beneath her thin, cotton dress and felt himself getting aroused. She giggled and pulled away, and they made their way down some steps into the garden. Mandy would definitely be losing that prissy attitude tonight, he thought with a devilish smile on his face.

Malcolm had picked Mandy up from her parents' house earlier that night, like so many times before. He had met her after a Sticks concert a few weeks earlier and asked whether she would like to visit him in his studio. She was an innocent child; just the way he liked them—untouched. Well, she had certainly been touched now and he knew she liked it.

Mandy had not protested when Malcolm had placed his hand between her legs in the back of his limousine one night while taking her home. His driver had parked outside her house, and knowing her parents could appear at any time made it all the more exciting. Malcolm had placed his hand in their daughter's knickers, making her climax only metres from their front door while they were inside, too impressed with his money and fame to even think he was, in fact, abusing their underage daughter. Would they even care if there was a chance of them being accepted into that closed circle that was the music aristocracy? Malcolm very much doubted it.

He had taken his time in gaining their trust and Mandy's, pushing her a little further each time they met. She had not wanted to go the full distance yet, but she was very close. Malcolm knew she wanted it. He could see how aroused she became when he kissed and touched her; she loved it. But Malcolm did not mind the wait, as long as the hand jobs in the back of his limousine were taking the pressure off. However, he had different plans for her tonight, and he smiled to himself again.

As the final guests arrived, Bill and Delphine made their way into the garden to join them. Tables and chairs had been set out under white parasols to provide shelter from the sun, but equally to stop any sharp paparazzi lenses from picking up who was there, and what they were doing. Security was always tight at Bill's parties and invitations were like gold dust.

The security team they had hired for this event were under strict instructions to keep unwanted guests out and their own mouths shut. The catering company had been carefully vetted, and anyone working at the house had to sign a contract, forbidding them from talking to the media. Nothing whatsoever was to be leaked to the press.

Large tarpaulins had been hung between the trees in the woodland surrounding the mansion. If

any paparazzi wanted photographs from Bill
Graham's party, they were going to have to risk life
and limb to get them. There was the added risk of
getting caught by the security guards, who were
known for their brutality.

The party was well under way when Delphine
decided she needed something to take the edge off
her bad mood, which was threatening to ruin the
evening for her. She also had a feeling there was
something her husband was not telling her. Bill
seemed different lately—aloof and secretive—and
she instinctively knew there was something going
on, although she couldn't put her finger on what it
was exactly. He could be having another affair, but
then he had always been very open about such things
before. The other women never meant anything;
they were just a bit of fun.

Delphine sensed it was something serious this
time and she didn't like that. Outwardly, Bill was
playing the role of loving husband and host, but
there was a sharper edge to his personality lately,
which made her uneasy. She could not remember the
last time they had sex and he didn't even want to
take her out any more. Their lives were sliding
further and further apart.

Delphine went to look for Simone, her drug
dealer and closest friend. They had been best mates
and models together when they shared an apartment
in Paris ten years earlier. Simone did not do as well
as Delphine when it came to modelling jobs, but she
found she had a talent for the murkier side of the
industry in providing a service to the other girls who

needed it. She had contacts all over the world and there wasn't anything Simone could not get you within a matter of minutes. Cocaine, uppers, downers, E or smack; whatever you needed, she could supply it—at a price.

Delphine did not expect to be treated any differently from any of Simone's other buyers. Her friend had to make a living, and she knew and respected that. Besides, Delphine didn't give money a second thought anyway and would normally order large quantities of heroin as there could be times when it was difficult to come by. It was better to be safe than sorry in a drought.

Delphine found Simone in deep conversation with a young, very good-looking guy by the pool. "Hi, sweetheart, you are looking very pretty tonight. Are you enjoying the party?" she asked, greeting Simone with a kiss on each cheek, and making sure she air kissed so as not to get lipstick on her face.

"Hi, Delph, yes, thank you," Simone replied. "Lovely day for it. This is Kevan. He's a model with our old agency in Paris."

The man looked a little unsteadily at Delphine, clearly feeling a little worse for wear after binge-drinking champagne. He was young and muscular with a very pretty face, which she liked. Blonde and tanned, he was almost angelic—cherub-like even.

"Gooday!" Kevan answered in a broad Australian accent. He smiled at Delphine as he took her hand in greeting. "Love the house. You must be very happy here?"

Delphine smiled back, not answering his question, but giving Simone a little wink with one eye.

"Perhaps we can show you a little more of the house. We have a little business to take care of, but you are welcome to tag along," Simone added, and Delphine smiled knowingly before they made their way up the steps and into the house.

The three of them walked silently up a flight of stairs to the first floor of the mansion, the sound of music and people's voices barely reaching them as they entered Delphine's suite. She and Bill had separate bedrooms, at his request. Well, it had never been a request: he simply showed her to her room when he bought the house the previous year. Delphine was fine about it. Bill snored, and she preferred her beauty sleep alone and undisturbed.

Simone took a brown leather pouch out of her bag, from which she removed a plastic bag containing the brown powder that her friend had ordered. She threw it on the bed in front of her. Delphine pulled a similar pouch from the drawer of her night stand. It contained a small spoon, a lighter, a syringe and rubber tubing—everything you needed to feed the habit.

"You do it darling. I'm feeling a bit edgy tonight," Delphine suggested.

Simone nodded and expertly prepared the heroin before handing the syringe to Delphine, who quickly shot a dose into her arm, during which time Simone had prepared a second and handed it to Kevan, who eagerly took it.

Simone was careful with syringes, and made sure her clients knew they could catch HIV/AIDS from sharing, which had just become known. It had been a shock to the music industry when the news emerged that there was a deadly disease out there, and that it was not only gay men who could contract it, but also addicts who shared needles. Simone wanted to protect her clients and anyone dying would be bad for business.

Delphine leaned back on the bed and looked at Kevan, suddenly realising that she could not even remember his name. She didn't care. As the heroin started to take effect, she lay down on her back with her hands spread out at her sides, her body making a cross on the white bed linen.

She glanced at the beautiful boy before closing her eyes. Kevan was sitting in the chair, the needle still in his arm. That was strange, Delphine considered. *Why hasn't he removed it?* His head was resting on the back of the chair with his face angled towards the ceiling. *His beautiful face.* She made a note to fuck him when she came down from her trip. Yes, she would do that, definitely, she thought as the familiar sweep of the drug ran through her veins towards her head.

Simone removed the syringe from Kevan's arm and placed the remainder of the drugs on the nightstand, so Delphine would see them when she came down. She then left the room, closing the door quietly behind her.

It was dark outside and getting late, in contrast to the brightness of the ceiling lights in the hall. The party had quietened down and many guests had left already. Lit candles were arranged on tables around the pool, and lanterns had been hung here and there, giving the garden a peaceful ambience. The remaining guests had gathered around one of the larger tables, sitting together in small groups, talking and drinking.

Simone saw Bill as she passed a window, and she stopped to look out and observe, unbeknown to the people below. He was deep in conversation with Tiger, The Sticks' bass player. Simone watched as Tiger flinched at something Bill said, and the conversation became heated. Looking extremely angry, Tiger got up abruptly. Turning his back on Bill, he started to make his way towards the exit, pulling his girlfriend, Tracy, by the arm, and practically dragging her out of the garden and into the house.

Simone wondered what it was all about. Tiger had been in the band from the early seventies when they started. She walked further down the hall and was startled by the sound of someone talking loudly from one of the bedrooms. It sounded like an argument. Simone stopped and listened quietly, not wanting to alert the people in the room to the fact that she was there, and listening.

"Now stop wiggling about, Mandy. Fuck it! Did you think it was all free? That I've brought you here to meet your idols out of my good nature?" Malcolm said angrily.

Simone could hear Mandy weeping, and she imagined her struggling or fighting with him. "No, please, don't! I don't want this. Please, Malcolm, take me home. You are hurting me." Mandy wept louder now, but her voice sounded a little slurred.

"Shut the fuck up, bitch. Hold her down, Darren. She is going to learn the hard way. I will not let a piece of groupie shit tease me and then not follow through. Hold her, for fuck's sake!" Malcolm shouted, and Simone recognised an edge to his voice. He was definitely panting and clearly aroused.

She realised then what Malcolm and Darren, his assistant, were up to. There was the sound of a loud slap, followed by Mandy's scream. Then there was silence for a few seconds before Simone heard the girl sobbing, "No, no, no." Simone started to move away from the door, but as Malcolm called out in pleasure, she stopped again.

"She's all yours, Daz. It's a bit messy. She's bleeding a bit. Just get some baby oil from the bathroom. Come on now, Mandy, spread them for Daz. Be a good girl," Malcolm said in a soft voice as she continued to sob.

"I've got some painkiller, Mandy. You can just take it like before. Just sniff it up your nose. It will make you feel much better. But you have to be a good girl and let Daz fuck you, because I've promised him, and you know I never break a promise."

"Turn her around, Malc, you know I like the back entrance better," Darren panted, clearly aroused in anticipation of what he was about to do.

Simone listened again, placing her ear closer to the door, and glanced at her hand. One of her nails needed filing and the nail varnish was chipped; she would have to see to that straight away. The room seemed to have gone silent, so she made her way towards the staircase. Suddenly, Mandy let out a loud wail of pain. Simone kept walking, down the stairs and into the garden below.

The breeze brought the smell of flowers towards her, accompanied by a slight whiff of chlorine from the pool, as she made her way over to where Bill was sitting and sat down beside him. She could really do with something to drink.

Chapter 1
30 Years Later

Right, it's official. My mother's worst nightmares have come true—I'm a nymphomaniac. There, I've said it. It doesn't sound that bad, now the truth is out. I'm not sure how it happened. One day I was fine and the next I'm thinking about sex all the time. But then I got married, and the next day I'm back living with my parents in my old room, thinking about sex all the time. It's doing my head in, to be honest.

Can you be a nymphomaniac without actually having sex? Are there certain grades of nymphomania; say, due to the severity of each case? Perhaps I'm a nymphomaniac-light, or since I don't actually have sex, but fantasize about it all the time, then I could be a virtual nymphomaniac. You know, like those online worlds that my nephew plays in on his computer, only mine's in my head; the type who is always thinking about sex, but never actually has any. I might evolve and become a medium/rare nymphomaniac who has sex once in a while. I'll let you know if that happens.

Anyway, I'm Charlotte Hart; Charlie to my friends. I was happily married a couple of weeks ago, and if the sex wasn't all that great, it was certainly always readily available. I say 'happily' married, but I mean bored stiff; not totally unhappy, just bored. My husband, James, the lying bastard, is still living in our nice house in Sussex while I'm in my old room here at my parents' place. The lying bastard also has his company and the cars, and all the money. And I'm in my old room... Yeah, well, I'm beginning to repeat myself now, but you get the gist of it.

James swept me off my feet a couple of years ago, and we had a fairy-tale, romantic wedding in Barbados. Well, that was what we planned, but it didn't really turn out that way. James is rich and also fifteen years older than me, making him forty-one to my twenty-six. James makes his money helping other rich people invest their cash in restaurants and real estate, so they can save and not pay taxes, so making them even richer.

Wealthy people seem to appreciate people who can save them money, and James is the best at what he does for a living. I was impressed with him too, in the beginning, because he's successful and I was dazzled by the lifestyle. I'd only just graduated from university and was offered an internship at his company, and that was it really. He pursued me from the first day I arrived, and I was too flattered to go with my better instincts and turn him down, or at least take it slowly.

James didn't want me to work and said it would look bad. He said it would be better if I was on the payroll at his financial investment company, but stayed at home, looking after my nails and going shopping. Stupidly, I agreed. Well, I used to love shopping and doing nothing, so the suggestion sounded like a fantastic offer... to begin with.

ACCESS ALL AREAS

I decided it was the perfect time to write a bestselling novel. I had an expensive computer and the software to go with it—everything I needed to create a fantastic book, except that I didn't have a clue what to write about. Whenever I sat down to do it, I couldn't think of anything. I would stare at the computer screen for hours and opt to read *The Daily Mail* online instead.

I'd write a few lines and then decide to have a bath or go to lunch. I think I quickly realised this great bestseller just wasn't going to miraculously appear on the screen in front of me. I didn't have it in me, and I can honestly say that I had never been so bored in my entire life before.

James was out at the office all day and sometimes entertained clients in the evening, so I was alone for much of the time we were married. He worked long hours in London during the week and sometimes there were restaurant openings to attend at the weekend.

James used to encourage me to shop in London, and make sure my wardrobe was always new and up to date, ready for those occasions where I would have to accompany him to social gatherings. Soon, I found that I hated it. While I used to love shopping for clothes and dressing up, I started to think of it as just another boring chore.

Looking back, I was just another thing my husband owned: a possession; an accessory like his car or his watch. James loved to introduce me as "his wife, the writer". He couldn't say author, because I hadn't yet produced anything that would elevate my position in life to profess to 'author-dom'.

What happened to spoil everything, this Stepford wife existence, was pretty much the lying bastard's fault. I'm sure I would have come to my senses at some point and left him, but as it was, James managed to open my eyes to the fact that I could no longer be his wife sooner rather than later.

One day he came home and told me, out of the blue, that he wanted us to have an open relationship. Just like that! I didn't even know what one was until I Googled it. Bloody hell, I thought, no way was I interested in an open relationship. It went straight up there on my list of things I would never do, along with dogging and swimming the English Channel. James must have taken some drugs, or lost his mind or something, I reasoned, so I didn't say anything to begin with. Then he told me that he'd met another woman and he wanted her—and her husband—to be part of our relationship.

This woman runs an establishment in Ealing that specialises in intimate massage and breathing techniques to maximise your climax, he told me, matter-of-factly. It turned out that James had been visiting this place a couple of times a week for the whole two years we were married, and now he wanted me to be part of it. He called it "an alternative lifestyle", and said I would feel free and much more spiritual if I only gave it a try.

Apparently, the woman's husband would supply us with drugs to make us feel free of our inhibitions and more open to trying new things, once we'd shed our initial shyness, James said. I didn't know what to say. I mean what do you say to your husband when he wants you to have sex with a prostitute and her drug-dealing husband?

I'm not a prude. Each to his own is my motto, but this was totally ridiculous. I didn't want to become more spiritual; I had an adversity to all things spiritual, and I had never felt the need to look into my soul. God could fuck off in my opinion and a spirit was something that came in a glass.

James claimed you can make contact with the spiritual world through drugs and meditation, but I had never believed in any of that wish-wash. Did he mean inner spirituality or ghosts? Both were a load of rubbish. When I was at school this girl in my class told everyone she had seen a ghost in the cemetery from her bedroom window. She told us in minute detail how it had been wearing a veil and was dressed in seventeenth-century style clothes. It all became a joke when I asked her, "Who sells ghosts their frocks in the afterlife?"

How could a ghost appear to be wearing a long dress? Had the dress died too? As far as my own clothes went, they had never been alive, with the exception of an old jumper I lost in the garden one summer and a whole colony of ants took up residence in the strawberry jam stain on the sleeve.

James then went on to tell me about 'the spirit of place', which meant that absolutely everything around me was alive and had a spirit. That's when he lost me completely. I got bored and my mind started to wander. I drifted away, wondering what

Mum had decided to make for dinner on Friday night; probably something really good with roast potatoes and gravy.

Meat was always something my mother was good at. I fancied a big portion of roast beef and Yorkshire pudding. You can't get proper Yorkies in Sussex. Not like my mum's. Perhaps there would be apple crumble and homemade custard, and not that crap in a tin, for dessert.

My husband went on talking as if I'd already consented to this open relationship. He told me it had to be a secret since this couple were not the kind of people we should be seen to know. James likes to think of himself as very conservative, but I think there is only one word that describes him and that is jumped-up snob. Okay, so that was three words, but you know what I mean.

Looking back, I don't know what on earth I saw in the lying bastard in the first place. Okay, so he's really good looking and has a lot of money. Oh, and he does know just about everyone that's famous, rich or royal, in the whole world. I must have been mad to have fallen for him. Oh well, I plead insanity; it's the only explanation I have.

So, anyway, I told him I'd think about the open relationship and let him know the following day, when I'd slept on it. I made up something about this being an important, life-changing decision, which shouldn't be taken lightly, and said I would give it my full attention the next day. I secretly decided that I needed a cunning, but subtle plan. James seemed to accept my answer, and we went to bed on seemingly

amicable terms, whilst I was planning what to pack
and wondering how fast I could get my things
together.

As soon as James left for work the following day,
I packed my belongings into three huge suitcases
and stuffed them into my very smart Range Rover.
James had insisted on buying me a white one before
we married. I would have preferred a smaller
vehicle, but he insisted we have 'his and hers' cars,
like a lot of people who lived in our area. I thought it
was a stupid idea and didn't really give a toss what
my neighbours thought, but I gave in, as it was
important to him. It seems I did that a lot.

While I was married I never stood up for myself
and let James have total power over who I was. I
come from a small village in middle England. My
family is by no means poor, but compared to James'
wealth we are small fry. I think I let him make so
many of my decision for me because I wanted to fit
in and I was afraid of looking like a country yokel in
front of his friends. So I allowed James to guide me,
and before I knew it, he had taken over most of my
life.

I made sure to pack everything that was mine; all
the items I had bought with James' money whilst we
were married. I felt it was only right that I should
have my clothes and handbags. What would he want
with my clothes anyway? Although after the
previous night's revelations, anything was possible.

James was totally off his rocker. I think that
massage place was just a front for some sort of
spiritual cult following, for people who wanted to

shag others they were not married to. I mean
couldn't they just go to a swingers' party or
something? I'd read about wife-swapping parties,
which was also on my list of things I would never
do.

I worked hard all day as I knew James wouldn't
be back until late. I placed my wedding ring on the
kitchen table, but then I picked it up and put it on
again. That felt wrong, so I took it off. It was such a
beautiful ring that it was a shame to give it back to
him, but I couldn't continue wearing it. That would
be saying I still cared and wished to stay married
when it was the last thing I wanted.

I stared at the beautiful, two-carat diamond ring
with two wavy, gold lines on either side, covered in
smaller diamonds. James had bought it for me at a
very exclusive shop on Worth Avenue in Palm
Beach. The diamond was shaped like a peanut, and I
had loved the ring as soon as I set eyes on it. Picking
it up again and placing it on the third finger of my
right hand, I had second thoughts. No way was I
leaving that ring—I deserved it for being with him
for so long and putting up with his lies, right?

While I knew that I wouldn't miss this Stepford
wife lifestyle, I had no idea what I was going to do,
beyond going back home to live with my parents and
trying to get my head together. And there was dinner
to look forward to, if I didn't get stuck in the rush-
hour traffic. I really hoped Mum was making
Yorkshire pudding.

It took a few hours to drive to where my parents
still live in the house I grew up in. Strangely, the

time just whizzed past. My head was empty of all thoughts. I was neither sad nor happy; I had no feelings at all. Instead I felt numb and shocked, possibly traumatised, but, overall, I was mostly hungry. I phoned my mother on the way, so she would expect me, and I asked what was for dinner and whether she could please make my favourite dish since I was feeling traumatised and needed comfort food.

My mother is a worrier. She lives with my father and her mother, my Grandma Blue. My dad was the local doctor until he retired a few years ago, and Mum was his receptionist and nurse. Now he drives a taxi some evenings a week and at weekends. Dad says he does it to help out an old friend who owns the taxi company, but I'm pretty sure it is to get out of the house and away from Grandma Blue.

She moved in with my parents when Granddad died two years ago. It was at the same time as I was getting married in Barbados and my family couldn't attend the wedding because of the funeral. James refused to delay the ceremony, saying it would disrupt the lives of the guests.

With tears running down my face, I went through with the wedding so as not to upset James' guests, who had paid a lot of money for their flights and hotels. It was certainly not the fairy tale event I had hoped it would be. Talk about a bad start; it couldn't have been worse. The marriage was doomed.

My grandparents had always lived close to us, but Grandma Blue sold the house as soon as Granddad was buried and moved into the guest room on the ground floor of our home. It isn't a small house and there is plenty of space. I find it strange though that Grandma Blue is my mother's mother; that they are related at all seems impossible. My grandma often jokes that there must have been a mix-up at the hospital when Mum was born, because she couldn't possibly have produced this child. I think my mother probably agrees with her.

Grandma Blue isn't really called Blue. Well, she is, but it isn't her real name. She is called that because she has blue hair. My grandma dyed it that way by mistake a few years ago. She bought some dye at the local chemist, being too tight-fisted to go to the hairdresser, and it was supposed to make her grey hair blonde again.

Grandma Blue is in her late seventies, but refuses to wear glasses as she thinks they make her look old. So, she misread the instructions on the bottle, and instead of leaving the mixture in her hair for twenty to thirty minutes, she left it overnight. When she woke up the following morning, she looked like a Smurf. She actually likes it, and says it's cool and makes her stand out in a crowd. So, from that day on, she has dyed her hair blue. This is not a blue rinse that gives a tinge of colour, mind you. I'm talking deep, shocking, turquoise blue. Trust me to have a grandmother who is having her teenage rebellion in her seventies.

Apart from the colour of her locks and clothes, Grandma Blue looks like all other grandmas. She has short hair that gets a monthly perm to make it tight and curly. Sometimes, if there is a funeral to go to, she will let the hairdresser put her permed blue hair into curlers and backcomb it to within an inch of its life, recreating the sort of style that was popular with old ladies in the sixties; a beehive, I think it's called, but I could be wrong. Definitely not the sort of hairdo you want to be sitting behind at the cinema, if you know what I mean.

Grandma Blue has taken to wearing a tracksuit and Nike trainers lately, and even has her own Facebook page with about a million friends and followers. She refuses to grow old gracefully, and is never tactful or quiet, in stark comparison to my quiet humble, peace-loving parents.

After Granddad died, Grandma Blue decided she was too young to be the grieving widow. Despite being over seventy-eight, she won't admit to more than sixty-nine, which is impossible. She was always controversial and opinionated when Granddad was alive, but she went completely off the rails when he died; suddenly enjoying her newfound freedom, she says.

So, instead of sitting in the house pining for Granddad, she is off out every evening, looking for another man. I somehow doubt she would know what to do with one, should she ever be successful in her search. I think she just gets off on the excitement of the chase, mostly. She's like a cat that catches a bird and then drags it into the house to show it off without ever actually devouring it.

Actually, there are a whole gang of the old ladies; six in total. Their hobbies consist of chatting up men on Facebook, going to the pensioners' club and attending funerals. Grandma Blue loves a good old burial, but won't set foot in church.

We have a large wrought-iron gate that opens on to our front garden and garage area, and the entrance also has a smaller one at the side. Both gates squeal in protest every time they are opened. The larger ones open electrically and seem to object vigorously every time they are disturbed from their dormant position. Dad tried to oil the hinges to make them less noisy to no avail, and he finally gave up years ago.

Let me tell you about my home. It used to be the country manor, belonging to a rather grand family, who resided in London for most of the year. I don't mean that it's like a castle with a moat and a drawbridge, but more of a mansion. It was built in the late nineteenth century and has since been added to so many times that it's difficult to describe the style of it with any certainty.

The white house is set in landscaped gardens at the back and side, which were once much larger before portions were sold off. What is left are a mixture of gothic portals and columns on either side of the front entrance and exit. A large stone porch runs the entire length of the back of the house, with narrower ones at the sides, forming a sort of veranda on the ground floor. To the front, as you enter the iron gates, there is what can only be described as a circular parking area. The house is situated to the left and three large garages take up a lot of space to the right.

ACCESS ALL AREAS

When I parked the car outside my parents' house, Dad came straight out to help me with my suitcases. Mum was crying, and patting my shoulder and hugging me, as if someone had died. She shoved me in front of her into the house, leaving Dad alone to bring my stuff in, and sat me down in the kitchen. Then she started rummaging around, making tea, and hardly looking at me.

"I'm all right, Mum. Stop fussing," I told her in a jovial tone.

I accepted the tea cup Mum handed me, and both she and Dad joined me at the table. She placed a large, homemade fruitcake in front of me and a bowl containing clotted cream, and another of homemade strawberry jam. Mum loves to cook and I love to eat, so that worked out fine. I'm not a big girl, luckily enough. I can eat for England, but it never seems to make any difference to my weight. I'm lucky like that. I am twenty-six years old and moving back in with my parents, so I deserve to at least be lucky about the rate my body burns calories, right?

Grandma Blue says everyone is good at something; you just need to find out what it is. I am a failure at everything except burning calories.

"Where is Grandma Blue?" I asked when I'd eaten one large slice of fruitcake and was starting on my second.

"She's gone shopping with her cronies," Dad replied, and I saw my mother's eyelid twitch a little.

Mum always gets a little twitch in her left eye when she is stressed out about something. She moved over to the cupboard, where I knew she kept a bottle of wine, "for medicinal purposes". The only thing that relieved stress with my mother was ironing and the red wine in the cupboard. We have a weekly lady from the village who comes over to clean the house, who has offered to do the ironing on many occasions, but it is off-limits, as Mum's stress relief.

Suddenly, I heard the gate hinges squeak and a familiar, blue-haired, skinny old lady made her way down the path towards the front of the house. Our home used to be the local vicarage at one point until the Church of England decided the six-bedroom mansion was far too big for the priest and too costly to keep, so they put it on the market. My dad bought it, and the vicar took up residency in the tiny flat above the garage.

I think this flat was previously used by the grander former owners as living accommodation for their chauffeur. The C. of E. bought it, I'm told, because of its close vicinity to the local church. The vicar's living arrangements was one of the conditions of sale, apparently.

Mr Heritage, the live-in vicar, is a really nice man, never nagging us about our lack of interest in God or His church and very fond of a tipple with my father at the local pub. Dad used to have his GP surgery in two rooms on the first floor, so the patients could get medical and spiritual guidance from the same place; sometimes even at the same time, as the vicar was in and out of our house like he still lived there.

ACCESS ALL AREAS

As the years passed and the vicar was pensioned off, the new one was given a flat on the local housing estate and Mr Heritage remained with us. He is approximately the same age as Grandma Blue, but they don't have much in common. They get on okay, but it sometimes feels like they just tolerate each other's quirky personalities, instead of being friends.

Grandma Blue walked the distance from the gate to the front door in a strange, wiggly way. It looked like she was race-walking. You know, those competitions where they walk really fast and aren't allowed to run, and they jiggle their hips to go faster. Well, Grandma Blue's hips were wiggling and her arms were waving. She isn't a very big girl either, and has excess skin here and there, which was flapping around. I thought she resembled a colourful bird, trying to take flight with those bingo wings on her underarms.

Mum, Dad and I watched in shock as she wobbled towards the main entrance to our house, puffing and panting like a donkey with asthma. "What in God's name is she up to now?" my father mumbled under his breath.

"Hello, Charlie," she greeted me as she entered the kitchen.

My grandma was like a breath of fresh air, taking up much more space in our kitchen with her personality than her frail body suggested. Dad quickly excused himself, saying he had to go and drive his taxi, and left the room. However, I watched him cross the garden and make his way towards Mr Heritage's flat above the garage.

"So you have left your husband, and the glamorous life of booze and debauchery in London to move back home, and do what exactly?" Grandma Blue asked.

She is a very straightforward sort of person, always airing her views, even though they aren't always appreciated.

"I left him because he was a lying bastard and had sex with prostitutes, Grandma Blue. I didn't have much debauchery in London, as it was. I was in Sussex most of the time. I managed to have a lot of booze though, if that makes up for it?" I answered with my mouth still half-full of fruitcake.

"Couldn't you have just looked the other way?" asked Grandma Blue. "Women used to do that all the time in my day. The husband would be off out to the pub, seeing his fancy woman, and the wife would be dedicated and at home, making dinner and darning his socks. There was a saying, 'when you've made your bed you have to lie in it', but that doesn't seem to apply to kids these days. You are all a bunch of failures at suffering in silence," she added seriously, helping herself to a large piece of cake.

"Look at my new trainers. Aren't they the coolest you have ever seen?" my grandma continued as she lifted one foot off the floor to show me a pair of neon blue and yellow trainers. I noticed she was also wearing a pair of nylon Pop Socks, which lay ruffled around her pale, skinny ankles.

"I've taken up jogging," she stated matter-of-factly, and I could see my mother's eye starting to twitch again. "I've got my eye on a really sexy pair of lycra training pants and a top from Debenhams. It's black with neon-blue flames on it. Fits me as snugly as a condom," Grandma joked with a toothless smile.

My mother got up from where she was sitting, walked straight to the cupboard and poured herself a large glass of red wine. She took a big mouthful before she offered us some, which we both declined.

"You have to keep fit at my age, Charlie," Grandma Blue continued. "You have to make sure your body stays firm. Men like firm bodies, so there's no excuse in letting yourself go, especially now you are single again. You won't ever get yourself another man if you don't keep fit."

"Are you sure it's wise to jog, Grandma? You haven't jogged before and you might stretch a muscle or hurt yourself?" I answered diplomatically, being careful not to mention her advanced age as it was a touchy subject.

"Don't worry about me, Charlie. I'm easing myself into it. We are doing power walking this week and going for a jog in the park next weekend. Did you see my power-walking moves as I came up the garden path? It's all in the hip movement. It's not a wiggle. I know it looks like a wiggle, but it's a full rotation of the pelvis, which has all sorts of hidden benefits. It helps against incontinence. Not that I have any leaks, you know. But if I had it would help. I've got my eye on this really fit chap

41

who jogs in the park. He's going to be my toy boy. I've never had one of those, so I'm looking forward to that experience.

I noticed Mum raise her eyebrows at Grandma Blue's mention of a toy boy and take another sip of her red wine. I seriously doubt Blue knows what a toy boy is, never mind what she would do if she ever came across one. Come to think of it, wouldn't a toy boy for her still be a really old guy?

Are there any rules as to when you are classed as having a toy boy and when you are actually seen to be cradle robbing? When does it go from cradle robbing to something really unmentionable? Is it determined by how old the guy is, or how big the age difference is? Could Grandma Blue get locked up as a paedophile if she dated someone, say, fifty years younger than herself, even though that would make him closer to thirty? I made a mental note to Google it when I had the time.

"You should come jogging with me," Grandma Blue continued, waking me from my thoughts. "I could set you up with someone in no time. You need to get yourself out there dating again. It's like riding a horse. When you fall off, you just need to get yourself into the saddle again. I'll help you. I know lots of single horses... I mean men," she added far too enthusiastically.

As I declined my grandmother's offer of matchmaking with a giggle, I noticed her staring at my hair, and she touched the side of my head softly.

"I've always loved your hair, Charlie. I don't know where you get it from. I'm blonde when I'm not blue. Your mother is chestnut and your dad is dark brown, but you seem to have come in a light brown and it's so thick. No one in our family has hair that thick," she said, looking at mum sternly, as if she'd conceived me with an unknown man.

"I've had it coloured, Grandma. They can do anything these days," I answered cheerfully. "James wanted me to go really dark, but this colour is where I drew the line."

"Well, I bet it cost a fortune and you weren't bent over the bath like me, getting a neck strain. I lash on the colour and hope for the best," Grandma Blue told me.

She was right. I'd done a lot of beauty treatments over the last two years, just to have somewhere to go and something to do. How sad is that? I've never been that into make-up and styling. I would normally just splash on some mascara and put my hair in a ponytail, but that was before James got his clutches on me. He has a lot to answer for.

Full up of cake and tea, I excused myself, saying that I wanted to take my stuff into my old room. Dad had carried all my cases up, so I set about hanging up my lovely clothes in the closet. At least some good had come out of being married to the lying bastard. I had never wanted for anything and still had no less than six different credit cards in my wallet—the bills paid for by James' accountant.

Hearing music blasting downstairs from Grandma Blue's ghetto blaster, I imagined her break dancing, which made me smile. I placed my laptop on the old writing desk by the window. This was the room I had lived in all my life, only moving out when I went to university. After just two years of married life, I felt like such a failure to have to come back.

When James made his suggestion of changing our relationship into an open one, it had dawned on me that I couldn't stay with him. It was the straw that broke the camel's back. I had put up with his mood swings and his manipulating, and his sometimes damn-right egoistical behaviour for far too long. Finding out that James had been lying to me for the entire time I had known him was the little push I had needed to take my life back.

I sat down on the bed as my eyes filled with tears. I cried silently as the room below mine, where Grandma lived, fell silent, and I fell asleep on top of the covers.

Chapter 2
Melody Jones

Living back at home felt unreal. James had not encouraged me to visit my parents very often. I had missed them a lot when I lived in Sussex, and Mum and I had spoken on the phone every day.

Newbury, where I am now, is more of a village than a town. Several villages have grown together over time, and I don't know where one ends and the other begins. Most of my old friends have moved to the larger cities, and as I wandered around the streets I saw very few people that I actually knew. However, everyone seemed very friendly; several people even called out to me by name and said 'Hi' as I passed. I found their behaviour a little odd, but didn't reflect on it any further.

I've started to get into a daily routine of taking a morning run followed by a shower and breakfast. Then I spend the day either reading or hanging out with my mother in the kitchen where she's either tackling the north face of the ironing or cooking. I make sure I'm in the kitchen early to get a look at the postman.

The first time I saw him was a few days after I arrived home. I was in the kitchen with Mum and Grandma Blue when I heard the gate squeak as it was opened by an unusually fit looking, muscular guy in a postman's uniform. We all gazed at him, mesmerized, as he walked towards our front door.

He has got to be the best-looking postman I've ever
seen. We watched his tight bottom wander away
from us, and as he closed the gate after him, he
looked up and waved. I felt myself blush.

"Wow, I haven't seen him before," Grandma
Blue said in a throaty voice. "If I was ten years
younger I would definitely want some of that."

Her comment jerked me back to reality, and come
to think of it, I think that was the exact moment I
contracted nymphomania. It was the postman's fault.
I felt a desperate urge to touch his bottom! Oh my
God, I have to stop thinking about sex. Anyway, my
grandma's comment sent my mother off towards the
wine cupboard again since this guy was not much
older than me. Can you imagine Grandma Blue and
this fit, blonde Adonis? Now there's an image I will
have to stab my mind's eye with a fork to get rid of.

Grandma Blue comes and goes, and has a busy
social life. Her training clothes are becoming more
colourful as the days pass, in various loud neon
tones. James has not tried to call or contact me in
any way. I'm thankful for that, because I don't really
want to talk to him. I mean what would I say? "Hey,
how are you getting on with your three-in-a-bed sex
with the prostitute and her husband? Still enjoying
it? What sort of drugs are you on these days?"

I think it's better if I just don't talk to him. I
know I will have to get divorced at some point, but
right now I just want to let time and distance heal
my dented ego, because that's what it is. It isn't a
broken heart, because I don't really feel sad
anymore, so I've decided it's my ego that is dented.

ACCESS ALL AREAS

My plan was to get my head around things first for a few weeks and then decide what I wanted to do with my life. Perhaps now I will have enough motivation to write that bestselling novel. After all, I can't just hang around the house moping. I have to find out if there is anything else I'm good at, apart from burning calories, and then get to work doing it, if it makes me happy. There's no rush.

***

One sunny day, after I'd been at home for a little over a week, Grandma Blue knocked on my door in the early afternoon. She peeked inside and entered carefully, as if she wasn't sure whether it was safe to come in. I was lying on my bed with a book that I was trying to read. I'd found it on Grandma Blue's bookshelf, but I just couldn't concentrate long enough to grasp the plot. There was this sexy guy who liked to tie up his girlfriend. I really shouldn't read soft porn books, me being a nymphomaniac-light, and all. It wasn't helping.

"Charlie, can I ask you a very personal question?" asked Grandma Blue as she sat down on the chair by my desk.

I answered by raising my eyebrows. She knew what it meant—you can ask, but don't expect an answer if it's too personal.

"I might have done something to help you that you may or may not like," she said carefully, avoiding direct eye contact.

"What have you done?" I asked warily. "I'm not going on any blind dates, you know. I'm not that desperate. And you mustn't tell the postman I'm lusting after him."

"Hey, I'm lusting for the postman myself. No, it isn't that. Here, let me show you," she offered, turning towards my laptop.

Grandma opened the lid and I was surprised how fast her bony fingers typed. She logged on to her Facebook account and told me to take a look. I did so reluctantly. James had always claimed such sites were only for attention seekers. He told me 'we don't need to be part of that' when I asked him about it earlier. My friend from school had suddenly made contact and wanted to keep in touch online, but James was against it, not surprisingly.

Grandma Blue lifted the laptop off the table and carried it to my bed. She typed in James' name and I was surprised to see his smiling face on the screen. When she clicked on his profile, I could see his wall, which held numerous updates. I had no idea James even had a Facebook page.

"When did he get Facebook?" I asked, looking at the page, intrigued by it all. "He must have joined after I left."

Grandma Blue rolled down the screen and I could clearly see that his page had been active long before I left him. I was quite shocked, and it hit home once again how little I actually knew about the man I had married. My grandma then logged out and logged into a new page, and to my horror I could see it was mine. There was a photograph of me, taken at my engagement party, but without James. He had been edited out.

"I will kill James! That is an invasion of privacy. How dare he start a page in my name?" I was so angry that I was almost lost for words.

Grandma Blue flinched. "It wasn't James, Charlotte. It was me. The very first day you came home I wanted to cheer you up. So I thought if I started a page for you, and got in contact with all your old mates, then you would be happy," she said quietly.

I looked into my grandma's pale blue eyes, which matched her bright blue hair, and I could see that she only meant well. The anger I had felt just seeped away and I wanted to weep. She put a hand on my shoulder and gave me a hug, and we both started crying. I couldn't be angry with her.

Grandma Blue quickly taught me the layout and I saw that I had quite a lot of friends who I didn't actually know. They were mostly over eighty, so I'm guessing they were her mates. Recognising a few, I suddenly realised why certain people in the village had acted so familiar and greeted me so warmly—we were Facebook buddies! It explained a lot.

I was pleased to see my best friend, Camilla, had added me and sent a message. It was a short one, welcoming me into the digital world from the Stone Age life I'd been living until now. She asked if I would like to have dinner with her and a couple of friends at the Italian restaurant Zini's in the neighbouring town of Burton at 7pm that same night, since there was a rumour that I was visiting my parents. I found myself surprised and excited at the same time.

Camilla and I had been partners in crime for as long as I could remember. We were opposites; ying and yang. She was quiet and well-mannered while I was chatty and a bit cheeky from time to time, but it had worked. When we left school, Camilla married her school sweetheart and bore two children before she was twenty. She married a guy called Peter Warnes, who was a couple of years ahead of us in school. He and his brother, Robert, had been the most popular guys at school.

Robert was a year older than me and I had a major crush on him for a long time. Camilla kept trying to set me up with him when things were getting serious between her and Peter, but I felt too shy to actually talk to him, never mind double-date. I was sure I'd make an arse of myself by spilling something or biting my tongue, or choking on something.

Robert and I became friends of sorts as we became older, but it was an awkward and difficult friendship when there was so much pent-up sexual tension and attraction, and the timing was never right. We never seemed to be single at the same time.

The Warnes family owned the local shopping centre and numerous other businesses, and both brothers worked for their father's company. I clicked on Camilla's photos to see pictures of her and Peter, and their two children, now six and seven. They made such a lovely looking family that I flinched once again at my own dreadful situation.

"I wasn't going to tell you about this page until the weekend, when I got more friends for you," Grandma Blue told me, "but when I saw that invitation, I knew I had to tell you, because I think it would do you the world of good to meet Camilla and have a girly night out."

Grandma left me to explore my new page and Facebook friends, and I found that time just flew past. I actually quite liked this social-networking malarkey. As for Camilla's invitation, I fretted about what to wear, and whether to drive or get dad to take me. In the end I opted for a little black dress and black, studded platform shoes with killer heels I couldn't walk in. Tonight I would sit and pose, but not walk or I'd fall over. I decided to let dad drive, and after thanking Grandma for her help, I set off with him to Zini's wearing a smile on my face for the first time in days.

As I entered the restaurant I found it was rather busy. All the tables seemed to be taken. It was a modern-looking place with mirrors and marble tops—very posh. There were a group of men standing together at the bar, all with their hair slicked back and wearing snappy suits. I spotted a ponytail on one aging man who was so tanned and wrinkled that he looked radioactive. All the men turned to look at me as I entered, and first I thought I'd gone back in time to the yuppie era of the eighties, or was this a Del Boy Trotter Convention?

I glanced around the crowded room and spotted Camilla's dark hair straight away. She waved to me, and I made my way unsteadily on my heels to the table she shared with three other women. We greeted each other with hugs and kisses, and Camilla introduced me to the others.

Stacey O'Connor is the local estate agent, and I recognised her from before I moved away; a pretty brunette with the longest nails I have ever seen. She had painted them bright red today to go with her red dress, which was cut very low at the front. Stacey's boobs were pressed up into the outfit, giving her a deep cleavage and made her look like she was smuggling two bald guys into the restaurant. She had a matching bright, fire-engine red handbag and shoes, and looking at her was threatening to give me a migraine.

I found Stacey's presence odd, since neither Camilla nor I had ever liked her. I hadn't liked the woman much before, because she, like James, had a social superiority complex and they both seemed to feel they were better than other people, whom they deemed below them. Stacey could be bitchy and I imagined her gloating over my new 'single' status on Facebook. That was Grandma Blue's doing, not mine. She said it sent the right message to James that I was well and truly finished with him, and to any other single men who might be rummaging around, looking for single girls on Facebook.

My old friend, Lauren Owen, was elegantly dressed in a white trouser suit, and her blonde hair was bobbed in a symmetrical haircut that looked

fresh and very pretty. She had been a familiar figure
in Camilla and mine's social circle when we were
younger. The last person at the table was someone
I'd never seen before. Blonde and pretty with
shoulder-length hair, she eyed me steadily as I
greeted her.

"This is Charlie," Camilla announced as I held
out my hand. "This is Melody Jones, Charlie. You
haven't met before. Melody runs a music magazine
and lives in Manchester. She's here to cover
Birkshaw Music Festival, which, as you know, is
organised and funded by the Warnes Group, and I'm
so pleased she has taken the time to have dinner with
us."

"Hiya, how are you doing? You all right?" asked
Melody Jones in a bright Manchester accent as she
smiled at me. "It's about time I had a night off. I'm
run ragged normally."

I took a seat and the menus arrived. I looked at
the prices, thinking that Zini's food better be good at
those rates.

"Robert wanted me to be sure to say hi to you,
Charlotte. I think he mentioned something about
seeing you jogging. He said to tell you he'd be in
touch," Camilla said, and I blushed.

"Peter says hi to you all. He's at home looking
after the children, but he said tonight is on him, so
let's have a bottle of champagne to celebrate
Charlie's homecoming," she suggested cheerfully.

"So you run a magazine? What's it called?" I
asked Melody as we studied our menus.

"It's Melody, just my name really, but it's a music magazine, so it's apt," she answered. "It's a monthly and we do an online mag too. It's quite popular, and we have a cult following. I'm a photographer and started the magazine in 2008 to showcase my pictures, and it just grew from there. But it's a hell of a lot of work. I'm out almost every night and every weekend covering shows, but it's worth it when we sell well."

I listened politely. When the champagne arrived, I eagerly took a glass. I was feeling a little nervous for some reason and I thought Stacey's presence might be causing it. She hadn't really spoken to me directly as yet and I found it strange that Camilla had invited her in the first place. The champagne was quickly consumed and another bottle opened before the food arrived.

Conversation was easy and I found that I quite liked Melody. She seemed a very level-headed, straightforward person. I had always liked people who actually did something. There were so many 'talkers' with plans that never came to fruition, but Melody seemed to have a good head on her shoulders and was a no-nonsense kind of person. Her involvement in the music industry intrigued me as it was a world I understood absolutely nothing about. James had known a lot of the more successful bands as they used his financial skills to invest, but I'd rarely met any of them.

We were on our third bottle of champagne and everyone was a little tipsy when Stacey suddenly turned her attention towards me. I had been careful how much I drank. Being with James when he was entertaining clients had taught me to be careful of drinking in the company of people I didn't know, but I'd noticed that Stacey wasn't as wary, and she was slurring her speech after her second glass of champagne, which she drank rather fast.

I'd noticed her hand shake a little when she took her initial sip. At first I thought that perhaps she was a little nervous; now I could see that she probably had a problem with alcohol. She had excused herself after her first glass to go to the ladies, and I noticed she seemed just a little more unsteady on her feet when she arrived back at our table. I looked at Camilla with raised eyebrows at the time and she nodded knowingly, but didn't say anything.

"So, you left hubby then?" Stacey asked suddenly, butting into the conversation.

Camilla's mouth dropped open and suddenly shut again, and Lauren and Melody stopped talking mid-sentence.

"Yes, Stacey. James and I are separated," I answered diplomatically.

"I would have thought you a bit wiser than that, Charlotte," Stacey replied. "Couldn't you have stuck it out for the money and glamour? I certainly would have." She turned towards Melody and laughed at her own joke. No one else thought it funny.

"Charlotte was… I mean is married to James Matthews of financial-investment-to-the-stars fame," Stacey continued, almost spitting the words out. "You should get Charlotte to help you, Melody.

55

James has a lot of contacts in the music world.
Could do you some good and open a few doors."

Melody looked as if she had no idea what Stacey
was talking about. She shrugged her shoulders, but
wisely refrained from commenting.

"Yes, our Charlie has been in the world of the
rich and famous through her gorgeous husband. And
the silly girl has left him. Why did you leave him,
Charlie, or was it, in fact, the other way round and
he left you?" Stacey was laughing again. "That's it,
isn't it? He's left you. Well, I can't say I blame him.
You won't mind if I take over, would you darling?
All's fair in love and war, and all that," Stacey
added as she tried to get up from her chair, but
slipped back down again. "I must go to the
bathroom. Could we have another bottle of bubbly,
Camilla?" she slurred.

"I think it's about time we sent you home,"
Camilla answered quickly. She helped Stacey out of
her chair and herded her towards the door. The
woman didn't protest and willingly let Camilla push
her into a taxi, which had stopped outside.

"Thank God for that," Lauren exclaimed with a
giggle. "What the hell was that all about?"

"What did she mean about opening doors?"
Melody asked as I took a large sip of my
champagne.

"I have no idea, but I'm guessing she thinks I
know people who might be useful to you. I don't, by
the way," I answered.

Melody considered this for a while until Camilla
returned to the table without Stacey, thankfully.

56

"I am so sorry about that, Charlie. I had no idea Stacey was going to be here tonight. She just turned up and asked to join us. I know you don't like her much, but what could I say. I didn't want to be rude," Camilla said, sitting again.

"Actually, Stacey was right about one thing though. You could help Mel out," she continued. "Didn't James help with the opening of Bill Graham's London restaurant, Sticks and Stones, a few months ago?"

I nodded.

Bill Graham was an important client of James. He was the singer and songwriter of the band The Sticks, and the restaurant was originally owned by Tim Boyce, bass player to the other iconic group, Stone's Throw. Tim Boyce had been looking for an investor and Bill had a lot of money lying around, James had told me.

Bill Graham had recently made a big comeback and released a new album, and was going on a world tour at the age of seventy-two. I met him at the grand opening of Sticks and Stones a few months ago. He seemed a grounded individual with none of the 'rock star' about him and I'd instantly liked him. I didn't know who he was at the time, as he was at the height of his musical career before I was born.

His French girlfriend was a different matter entirely and not very friendly. The fifty-something, stick-thin ex-model called Yvette rarely spoke. She kept her arm linked to Bill the whole evening, like a boat with a mooring, and I got the feeling she was afraid of letting him go in case he drifted out to sea, never to be heard of again.

"Do you actually know Bill Graham?" Melody asked, surprised. "I have been trying to get an interview with him for years. After the death of his wife in the early eighties, he became a recluse, living in France and not answering any messages. He refuses to give interviews, and as far as anyone knew, he wasn't making any music either.

"His wife died of a drug overdose. There was a big scandal when she was found dead in bed with a young male model by the maid. They'd both taken a lethal amount of heroin, apparently. The newspapers wrote about them having a hedonistic lifestyle of drugs and sex orgies, and it was hinted that some of the girls and boys were very young.

"So, he's off the radar for over thirty years, and then suddenly he's back in the limelight again, as if nothing happened?" Melody continued. "Come to think of it, I saw a photo of you and your husband, James, in a magazine that was lucky enough to be invited to the opening of Sticks and Stones. I thought there was something familiar about you when you arrived."

"Yes, well, as Stacey told you, I've left James and he is the one who knows Bill, not me," I replied.

"If you could get me a contact for Bill Graham, I would be eternally grateful to you," Melody said, sounding hopeful, so I promised to see what I could do.

The rest of the evening was pleasant and Dad picked me up in his taxi after midnight when I was feeling a little worse for wear. Camilla, Lauren, Melody and I agreed to keep in touch, and Camilla said she would phone me the following day to arrange for me to visit her, Peter and the children. I happily let Dad drive me home.

As I entered my bedroom I happened to nudge the laptop on my table and it suddenly sprung to life. The screen lit up on the Facebook page that I had forgotten to close. To my surprise, I found I had friend requests from both Melody and Lauren, and another from Robert Warnes. I added them all quickly, my heart missing a beat when I looked at his image on the screen. I went to bed with a broad smile on my face and feeling more content than I had felt in a long time. Perhaps this single life wasn't going to be so bad after all.

Chapter 3
Rich, the Supplier

I woke up the next morning to the sound of church bells ringing and the smell of flowers from the garden floating in on a breeze through my bedroom window. I had a slight headache from all the champagne, but otherwise I felt good. It was as if a great weight had been lifted from my shoulders and I was free.

My eyes caught sight of the computer on my desk, and I rushed over to check that I hadn't dreamed it and I actually had been contacted by Robert Warnes. I clicked on his page and looked at his face on the screen. He was one of the best-looking men I had ever seen; tall and muscular with sand-coloured hair, and a big, bright smile with pearly white, perfect teeth. I guess he looked a bit like David Beckham, the footballer, but without the tattoos.

There were not many photos of Robert on his page, but I found one I liked where he was waving to the camera from what looked like a rowing boat. The person who had taken the photo was obviously very close to him. I could see the warmth in his eyes as he looked into the camera lens and I felt a stab of jealousy. Pull yourself together, Charlotte! He's probably married with six kids anyway. I didn't know the first thing about his life now.

ACCESS ALL AREAS

I checked out James' page and found that he hadn't changed his relationship status. Presumably, he didn't want people to see he had failed at anything as simple as marriage. I was just about to close the computer when I had a brainwave. Clicking on James' friends list, I found Bill Graham easily enough. I wasn't sure whether it was a fan page or really him, but I guessed the latter, because James was not a fan of anyone and would never be seen to be.

I sent a friend request, but was promptly told that Bill Graham had over five thousand friends and was not allowed to add any more, but I was now following him, whatever that meant. I made a mental note to ask Grandma Blue about that as soon as I could. I saw there was an option to message, so I sent a short one explaining who I was, and asked him whether *Melody Magazine* could get an interview with him at his convenience. I wasn't hopeful, but at least I could tell Mel that I'd made the effort.

Sunday breakfast was always a big deal in our house. We all religiously eat together, no matter what state we find ourselves in. Mum makes a big fuss if we are late and puts on a spread that the local restaurant would envy.

My sister, Agnes, arrived with my two nephews and her husband, John. The two of them have been together ever since the first time they met at infant school. Agnes is eight years older than me and everything about her is the opposite.

I was "a surprise", is how my mum describes finding she was pregnant with me. Although Agnes and I look alike with our long hair and slim builds, whereas I love to dress up, she dresses down. She always chooses things for comfort, preferring cotton jumpsuits and flat heels to my designer clothes and heels, but we get on all right.

John is really boring in my view, and all they both ever want to talk about is Michael and John Jr, nappies, potty training and nannies, or the lack of them since Agnes will never consider letting anyone look after her children. Needless to say, my sister has never worked.

Sunday breakfast at the Hart household is really a brunch, because we have to wait for Mr Heritage to return from morning service at the church. Even though he is no longer vicar, he always attends and comes back full of gossip about the parishioners, which he shares with Grandma Blue.

She, in turn, would never darken God's door and says they will have to carry her in feet first, which I think Mr Heritage is planning on doing when that day comes. Grandma Blue goes to funerals all the time, but never to the church service, which she says bores her to tears, preferring the social togetherness of a wake. We are not a God-fearing family, as you can tell. It felt good to be back in the familiar life I'd led before that fateful day I met James.

Mr Heritage entered our kitchen by the back door and heartily greeted everyone.

"Oh look, it's God's Gestapo!" Grandma Blue exclaimed cheerfully to Mr Heritage, who refrained from commenting as usual.

I think he feels she is some test of patience sent to him by God. Mr Heritage took his ample body to the table in the kitchen, where Mum had started to serve up the various dishes, and helped her to carry them into the dining room.

Agnes looked pale and unwell, and John kept fussing around her like she was a priceless antique he was afraid to break. John Jr and Michael were in the garden kicking a football around, and screaming with joy when one of them scored a goal. Dad took his place at the head of the table, and the two boys were called inside and sent into the downstairs bathroom to wash their hands before eating.

It felt so nice to hang out with my family and I was surprised when the doorbell rang, because we never have unexpected guests for Sunday breakfast. Grandma Blue blushed and jumped up to open the door. She came back followed by a strange-looking man bearing a huge bunch of flowers. His suit was worn and a bit grubby, and he looked about seventy years old, with an oddly shaped head and bad teeth.

"This is Rich Brewer. He's having breakfast with us today," Grandma Blue proclaimed to the family loudly.

I quickly helped to set another place at the table while Rich gave Mum the flowers and sat down with us. Nobody said anything to begin with. There was an awkward silence, like someone had farted and no one wanted to be seen to have noticed. I just assumed this was one of Grandma's boyfriends.

"So how do you know my Grandma Blue, Rich? Did you meet whilst jogging?" I asked and received a sharp kick in the shin from her sneaker-clad foot.

"Ha ha, this is my granddaughter, Charlie. She's a joker. Rich is a business acquaintance of mine. He supplies me with stuff. Charlie is entering into the world of sex, drugs, and rock and roll as a music journalist," Grandma Blue added proudly.

"No, I'm not," I answered, surprised.

"Yes, you are. You got a message from Bill someone, saying you could have an interview with him. Then you got a message from a magazine saying congratulations and that they will be sending their photographer, Raven, to assist you. You have got to check your messages, Charlie. I have an app that lets me know as soon as I get something, haven't I, Rich?" asked Grandma Blue and the man nodded.

They smiled at one another, like they were sharing a secret joke. No one was talking now and they all stared at me in shock. How did this happen?

"Sounds like you need to change your password, Auntie Charlie," said John Jr, knowingly. "It also said you looked like a pretty bit of strumpet and would you go out with a man called Simon, who is a friend of Blue. But we deleted him for you. I've added you by the way, but don't start commenting on my posts like Blue did or I'll block you."

I was shocked. Not only had Grandma been looking at my private messages on Facebook, but she had shown them to my nephew who was eleven! Did the whole family have Facebook? Were they all tuned into my private life?

"So, what were you all doing on my Facebook page?" I asked, embarrassed, and feeling scared that I'd been roped into something I didn't want to do for Melody.

"Well, someone has to help you, Blue said. I was called in to fix apps and get you Scrabble. Blue says it's the best place for picking up men," John Jr answered.

Mother got up and went to the kitchen to get some more bread, but I knew she would be pouring herself a huge glass of red wine to stop that twitching eyelid. Agnes and John didn't comment, as if it was the most natural thing in the world for their eleven-year-old son to be talking about picking up men in this way. I was shocked, but decided not to say anything since I didn't want to get Agnes started on her theories about free parenting and other such issues, which I found dreadfully boring.

"I'm sure the Lord will send you a man if it's your destiny to marry again, Charlotte," Mr Heritage said rather pompously. "You should just talk to Jesus about your worries and your prayers will be answered."

"Why should she talk to Jesus?" Rich Brewer asked. "What I'm saying is why Jesus? Is that the way it works in your business?"

Mr Heritage looked confused and blushed slightly. "We all need God at some point in our lives, Mr Brewer," he answered curtly.

"No, we don't," Grandma Blue retorted. "I've got no need for Jesus or God. I'm perfectly fine on my own, thank you very much. Send me the gravy, please."

Mr Heritage passed the gravy via John Jr and Grandma Blue poured a considerable amount on to her plate.

"What I mean," Rich tried again, "is why Jesus? Do you tell Jesus all your problems, and then he advocates on your behalf to God? Why can't you talk to the boss straight away and cut out the middle man?"

Mr Heritage's face became even more flushed at Rich's reference to Jesus as 'the middle man', and he concentrated on what was on his plate before he answered. "The Holy Trinity is one and all: the Father, the Son and the Holy Spirit," he said seriously.

"So you get a three for one," Grandma Blue told Rich, who nodded, and strangely nothing more was said on the matter.

We avoid talking about religion in our house, because the only person who is remotely interested is Mr Heritage, and he can talk about God until the cows come home, which is a fate worse than death to be caught up in.

After breakfast, when Agnes, John and the children had left, I excused myself to go up to my room. My mother was in the kitchen loading the dishwasher, assisted by Mr Heritage, and Grandma Blue and Rich had disappeared somewhere together, under the pretence of going for a walk. Dad had fallen asleep in his favourite chair in the living room, with the TV sports on at full volume.

Sitting down at my desk, I logged on to my Facebook page and read my messages. I had, indeed, gotten a message from Bill Graham saying he did remember me, and that I could interview him on Tuesday afternoon at the Sticks and Stones restaurant before they opened for business.

There was also a message from Melody saying, "Nice one. Brill to hear about interview. Bill contacted and wants you to do it, which I have agreed to. Raven will meet you there to do pics. Let me know how you get on, and make sure you are prepared. I'll send you some questions to ask later. I've got to dash as I'm picking my mother up to take her shopping, Mel, x."

Oh yikes, what had I got myself into? I didn't know the first thing about music or Bill Graham and The Sticks. I spent the rest of Sunday afternoon on Google, reading up. I was working hard and starting to think it would be a lot of fun to interview this person when I looked out the window to see Grandma Blue walking towards the shed at the bottom of the garden.

It was strange, because I've never known her to have any interest in gardening or sheds in general. A couple of minutes later, I noticed Rich walking towards it as well. He looked around carefully before I saw Grandma Blue's skinny arm pop out of the shed door and quickly pull him inside. Perhaps there was more than gardening going on in there today, I thought to myself.

Then, to my utter horror, I saw Mr Heritage making his way towards the same place and I panicked. I leapt up quickly and made a run for the door. I had to stop him from walking in on God knows what Grandma Blue and Rich were doing in that shed. Though I must admit, it looked like she was seeing a lot more action than I was. The woman had obviously caught my nymphomania, or it ran in the family and I'd got it from her.

I hurried past Mum who was smiling whilst kneading a large mound of dough and had a large glass of wine beside her, and I jogged out of the back door. Unable to see Mr Heritage any more, I started to hope he had passed the shed and gone for a walk towards the church via the field at the bottom of our garden.

Did I mention that our home has a large garden and a smaller place at the front where we park our cars in a sort of circular area? The house sits at the end of a driveway leading up from the entrance gates. Around the back is my father's pride and joy—a sizable, landscaped lawn, spreading all the way around the building and leading towards his shed at the bottom of the garden, where he keeps his tools. When he retired we thought he would spend more time gardening, but he seems to prefer a local company to come and take care of the heavier work and rarely goes into his shed, preferring to oversee changes instead of actually making them himself.

As I approached the little hut, I could hear voices laughing and someone saying, "Hyysshh, someone will hear us," and then Grandma Blue had a fit of the giggles, and was joined by not only one, but two male voices, laughing hysterically.

Intrigued, I sneaked closer, hoping I wouldn't catch Grandma Blue and Rich in the middle of something. Now that was an image I would have difficulty getting rid of, jeez. I moved nearer and was just planning to peek through the dirty window when I stepped on a rake that was lying on the ground. I know it sounds like a joke, but it can happen. Well, it happened to me anyway.

I was concentrating so hard on creeping closer, unseen, and stretching towards the window that I stepped on the end of that rake lying on the lawn. It flew up and gave me a hard whack on the side of the head. I cried out in pain. It isn't funny; it could have broken my nose or knocked my front teeth out. The door to the shed was suddenly jerked open and I was pulled inside. It was promptly closed behind me and three voices hissed, "Shush!" at the same time, followed by another fit of giggles.

I looked around to see Grandma Blue, Rich and Mr Heritage sitting together. On the table was an ashtray and in it lay a burning spliff of what I gathered to be marijuana. The small shed smelled sweet and sickly.

"What on earth do you three think you are doing?" I asked in shock and they all broke into yet another fit of giggles.

"If Dad finds out you are smoking that stuff, he will have a hissy fit. You know how he feels about smoking. And you, Mr Heritage, a vicar!"

Okay, so I sounded like an old maid, and as soon as I heard myself, I, too, had to laugh a little, or was it the fumes in the tiny shed getting to me? Here were these three seventy or eighty-year-olds hiding at the bottom of the garden smoking dope. My family is really weird. Whose grandma smokes dope, I ask you?

"Calm down, Charlie. This is our secret. I told you, Rich is my supplier. It's only a bit of dope. Promise you won't tell anyone," Grandma Blue said in a slurry voice.

"I only do this to help with my arthritis," Mr Heritage argued. "It has medicinal benefits. It is proven!"

"It's illegal!" I answered, as if he didn't know that already. "I will keep your secrets if you keep off my Facebook. I'm warning you, if you log on again, I'll tell Dad," I answered.

Then I made my way back towards the house with a smile on my face. I always knew my family were far from normal, but now I had proof. I walked around to the front door to avoid having to explain to my mother why I had been running out of the house and why I suddenly had a big red mark on my forehead.

To reach the front door, I had to walk down a narrow pathway and through a portal made of roses that Dad had recently ordered to be put up, but to my annoyance it had grown out of control, narrowing access to the garden. I swear its prickles were out to get me as I tried to walk through it without injury. I suddenly noticed a large car had stopped outside our front gate. What was strange was the fact that no one got out of it.

As our house is positioned at the end of a lane, only our visitors bother to drive down it now that Dad isn't practicing medicine any more. I waited for a little while before making my way towards the car. Perhaps someone was lost and needed directions. As I opened the gate with the squeaky hinges the driver opened his window—oh my God, it was Robert Warnes!

"Hi, Charlotte, I heard you were back from Camilla. How are you?" he asked, flashing his brilliant white smile at me.

"Hi, yes, I'm back. Not sure for how long; just getting my head together. So, what have you been up to for the last decade?" I asked, trying to sound funny rather than self-conscious and awkward, which is what I was.

He laughed at my joke. "I was just passing, and thought I'd pop over and see how you were," he said.

I didn't know what to say to that. I'd worshipped Robert at school, but we had never actually been close. I tossed my hair, trying to look cool, and a whiff of marijuana met my nostrils. Oh no, please don't let him smell my hair.

"Well, you've seen me, I'm fine, so I'll just go over there," I said stupidly, moving away from the car, so he couldn't smell me.

He seemed amused at my reaction and laughed. "You've been in the shed with Blue, haven't you?" he questioned, knowingly.

"What? Yes, but how do you know about that?" I asked, blushing. "I just caught them giggling over a smoke."

"Everybody knows about that. My grandmother told me. They're friends. After your grandfather died, they seemed to join forces to make the region unsafe for any available men. You do know they've started jogging?" Robert added, amused.

"I know, it's hilarious," I answered.

"Anyway, I'm on my way over to Peter and Camilla's for Sunday dinner. I'm sure they wouldn't mind if you came. In fact I think they'd be very pleased. I mean, if you haven't got anything better to do."

Robert kept staring at a point on my forehead, making me self-conscious. I placed my hand there and was treated to a sharp stab of pain from the bruise the rake had caused.

"Ah, no, I'm sorry, I can't. I've just had a huge breakfast with the family and I have to research an interview I'm doing in London," I replied, feeling a little flustered. "But, perhaps we could visit them together another day, when I get back?" I added, not wanting Robert to think I didn't wish to see him, because I desired that very much.

"How about I send you a message on Facebook since we are friends on there? We could have lunch one day and catch up?" he suggested.

"Yes, we can do that. That would be nice. I look forward to it," I answered as he started his engine and slowly drove away from me.

72

ACCESS ALL AREAS

Life was certainly taking a turn for the better.
One day I'd been in a dead-end marriage, feeling
unhappy and bored, and the next I was embarking on
a new career and perhaps dating again. I wasn't sure
what Robert meant about lunch though. Perhaps it
would just be two friends getting together for a
catch-up, but it felt like a potential date. I felt quite
giddy when I walked back into the house, but then
again it could have been due to certain drugs in the
shed.

Chapter 4
Raven

I drove to London early on Tuesday morning, not
wanting to get stuck in the morning rush-hour
traffic, and parked my car outside Sticks and Stones,
just off Kensington High Street. The restaurant
looked quite drab and boring from the outside. If
you were expecting some rock-and-roll inspired
place à la Hard Rock Café or Planet Hollywood, you
would be disappointed. It's just a burger joint.

The Formica tables and red plastic chairs in
booths were trying to spell American Diner, right
down to the checked curtains and the waiters' crisp
white aprons.

I sat there in my car, reading through the
questions I'd prepared for Bill Graham and the ones
Mel had sent me, feeling prepared. I'd bought a
digital Dictaphone, which I hadn't learned to use
yet, but planned on doing so while I waited for this
Raven guy. But, reading the instruction manual, it
was complicated; I just couldn't understand it.

Apparently, I could program it to only record
when someone said something and fade out any
background noise, but I couldn't even work out how
to turn it on. I was fiddling with it when I saw this
really scary looking punk standing outside the
restaurant. She was not very tall and her head was
shaven at the sides, but what she had on top was

long and jet black with a few bright, neon pink stripes in it.

The woman was wearing Doc Marten boots and thick black tights, which I'd previously only seen on a Salvation Army member singing on the street outside my hairdressers in London. Over those she wore a short, dungaree mini skirt that looked like it had been ripped at the bottom, and a black T-shirt with the words 'FUCK OFF!' written in bold, pink letters under a picture of a fisted hand with the middle finger erect—flipping the bird. Her left arm was covered in tattoos, all the way from her wrist to the top of her shoulder.

I felt uneasy, and just as I was wondering whether to perhaps lock the car door, she lifted what looked like a heavy black bag from the pavement where she was standing and moved towards the car. The woman looked at me and as she got closer, I noticed her tattoo didn't stop at her shoulder, but went up her neck and stopped just behind her ear.

She seemed scary and menacing, and I didn't like having her so close to the car. I mean, what if she decided to scratch my beloved Range Rover? Or worse, what if she opened the door and nicked my new, shiny Dictaphone. I'd heard that's what punk rockers did. They steal stuff and sell it on to buy heroin or glue to sniff.

I'd also read that they lived in squats and spat on people. What if she not only took my Dictaphone, but also spat on me? Now I was beginning to feel so scared that I jumped when the front door of my car was suddenly opened and the punk-rocker girl looked inside and said, "Hi, you must be Charlie. I'm Raven. Mel sent me." She sounded so sweet and girly that I was lost for words.

"Erm, yes," was all I managed to reply.

Suddenly, the back door of the Range Rover was tugged open and Raven threw her bag on to the back seat. She then jumped in the front beside me and held out her right hand for me to shake. I now noticed that she had a ring in her nose and I couldn't take my eyes off it. It was a thick one, like you'd expect to see on a very aggressive Aberdeen Angus bull. It made her look really scary close up and was in stark contrast to her voice. I felt all the more confused.

"Hi, I'm the photographer. What time are we going in?" she asked matter-of-factly while I did a mental slap to the forehead for judging a book by its cover.

Raven was younger than me, perhaps in her early twenties, and she was certainly a colourful person. She spoke in a deep cockney accent and her sentences were speckled with swearing, but I just found it colourful and inoffensive. Raven opened her bag by leaning over me, stretching into the back seat to retrieve one of her impressive looking cameras. My Dictaphone wasn't looking so shiny any more.

"I tubed it, and my bag is so fucking heavy that I wish I'd gotten my boyfriend to take me on his bike," she said as she fiddled with the camera, took the cap off and snapped a couple of photos of me.

"Hey, stop that, I look a mess," I lied, knowing I'd spent ages getting ready that morning.

ACCESS ALL AREAS

I had wanted to look nice, and not wannabe rock chic or something, as I knew I couldn't pull that look off, but I did want to be taken seriously as a journalist. I could call myself that now, right? I'd evolved from being a writer who didn't write to being a journalist who, as fate would have it, hadn't actually written anything either.

The door to Sticks and Stones opened widely, and a waiter wearing a chequered apron carried a bucket outside and started to wash the windows. We left the car and made our way towards the restaurant. I felt a little giddy as we entered. It wasn't that I was easily impressed by fame, but I was nervous about screwing up the interview as Mel wouldn't be pleased and I really wanted her to like me.

As we entered there was no sign of Bill Graham, but two waiters were cleaning the table tops, and laying out place mats and cutlery. It was all very clean and neat, and they looked up in surprise. The guy cleaning the windows had stopped and lit up a sneaky fag outside. As I watched, he put the cigarette out on the pavement and trod on it with his black shoe before lifting it up and throwing it as far away from the restaurant entrance as he could, in the general direction of my car.

I was just about to shout at him to stop when Raven nudged me in the side, getting my attention to the fact that Bill Graham had entered the room, together with a large, muscular man dressed in black. Bill was tall and thin with dark hair, which he wore long enough to cover the top of his shirt collar. It was messed up, as if he'd just gotten out of bed, but I suspected he had to work to get it like that. The bags under his eyes were heavy and he looked tired.

The other man was younger, probably a little older than me, and wore a black suit jacket over black jeans. I could see how his muscles rippled, straining the fabric in the jacket to bursting point. His eyes were a bright blue, fringed by dark lashes, and I think he was probably one of the best-looking men I had seen in a long time.

He waited a little behind Bill and I instinctively presumed he was a bodyguard. It was his air of awareness and the way in which he carried himself that led me to believe he was there to take care of the older man. It wasn't unusual for stars as huge as Bill to have a guard, but it felt strange that he'd brought him to a meeting at his own restaurant. I didn't remember seeing the guy at the opening a few months earlier.

"Hi, Charlotte, how lovely to see you again," Bill said as he came towards me and planted a kiss on each of my cheeks. I air-kissed back, since I was wearing Victoria's Secret pink lip gloss, which wouldn't go well with his black hair and stubble. Bill then held out his hand and greeted Raven. He didn't introduce the guard, who just seemed to hover close by.

"Hi, I'm surprised you remember me, Mr Graham," I replied as he led us over to one of the tables that had not been set for lunch.

"Of course I remember you, and call me Bill. James did me a great favour in finding this investment opportunity for me. I am not only the

part owner of this fantastic establishment, but my
partnership with Tim Boyce has borne more fruit
and we are in the process of putting a band together.
We have everything in place and that, young lady, is
all thanks to your husband who brought us together,
and for that I will always be in his debt. How is
James by the way? I don't see him much now that all
the paperwork is done."

I didn't know what to say. I was weighing it over
in my mind whether to tell him that my marriage
had, indeed, recently ended or to lie and say that
James was fine when the dreadful Yvette entered the
restaurant from somewhere behind the bar. Raven
hadn't sat down with me and Bill, and was
rummaging around in her huge black bag, placing
some impressive looking lenses on to an equally
dazzling camera. Aren't punk rockers supposed to
be poor?

Yvette had been speaking French very quickly to
one of the waiters, who walked after her into the bar
carrying a crate of beer bottles. It sounded like they
were arguing, but not being fluent in the language
they could well have been talking about last night's
football match on TV from all I could make out of it.

Yvette stopped talking and looked at me in
surprise, and then she gave Raven a look that said
she perceived her as the skid mark of society. Raven
didn't notice as she was snapping away with her
camera at Bill and me. I sneaked another peek at the
good-looking guard, while everyone's attention was
on Yvette, and I could see he was wearing one of
those earpieces, behind one ear. I saw his gaze meet

Yvette's, and I am definitely sure she looked back with the same utter contempt she used for everyone, except Bill. By the look on the guard's face, the feeling was mutual.

"Shall we just get stuck in?" I asked and Bill nodded.

Raven was snapping pictures of the interior of the restaurant haphazardly and as she got closer to the bar, Yvette turned her back to her, making it impossible to take a photograph of her face. The guy who had been washing the windows entered the restaurant again, carrying his bucket and laughing, as it had started to rain heavily outside.

Raven turned back to me, and waited while I rummaged through my papers and fiddled with the Dictaphone, unable to work out whether it was on or not. Raven looked at it, flicked a switch and placed it on the table in front of Bill.

"Shouldn't that go in the middle, between us?" I asked.

"No, you want to record his answers. You've already written down all your questions," she answered, sounding exasperated, and I felt a little silly. I saw a glimpse of humour in the bodyguard's eye and then it was gone.

"Right," I began, looking at Bill. "You spent your youth as practically a hoodlum in the fifties and sixties in East London. You got caught by the police for breaking and entering into a chemist..."

I glanced up to see all eyes on me. Raven looked at me, horrified, unable to believe I'd just brought up Bill Graham's criminal past and thrown it in his face. The waiters stopped what they were doing and stared at us in shock. I noticed that even Yvette turned to see what would happen and how this would go down. The bodyguard had that same naughty glint in his eyes again and he suppressed a smile, the cheeky sod.

"Was there a time when you thought to yourself 'fuck it, I'm not doing this anymore', and started to form the idea of getting a band together instead?" I asked, carrying on as if I hadn't noticed the shocked expressions on everyone's faces.

Bill smiled at me steadily and answered straight away: "Yes, there was, there definitely was. I come from a poor background. We didn't have money for music lessons or instruments. All my friends were tea leafs, and we'd steal stuff and get nicked all the time. Then, when I got done for the chemist thing, I decided I'd had enough. I got together with my mate, Wally, and we decided we needed some instruments to learn to play and form a band, instead of all this dead-end crap, which would end with us getting banged up."

"So we did a few more thefts, since we didn't have any money for instruments, and then we taught ourselves how to play them by watching others on the telly and things like that. So, that was my first band. It was just me and Wally, and a couple of mates, but that was how it started," Bill explained enthusiastically.

The interview lasted over an hour, at which point I had to ask Raven to turn off the Dictaphone, and it ended with her and Bill going outside to get some shots of him standing in front of the entrance to the restaurant, as the rain had stopped briefly. Raven shook Bill's hand and I air-kissed him again, and suddenly he was gone.

Raven started to pack her equipment into her bag again, removing a very large lens from the camera in the process. I was just going to ask her whether I could drop her off anywhere when she bent over to close her bag and a small guy in a hoodie came running towards us. He pushed Raven so hard that she landed head-first on the pavement in front of me, and then he quickly grabbed the biggest lens from her open bag and made a run for it. It all happened very quickly. I remember her screaming out in pain as she fell and I called out in shock.

Before I knew it, my instincts kicked in and I was chasing after the hoodie guy. The recent rain had made the pavement wet and slippery. The guy ran towards a grassy area and I ran after him, not making much headway as I was wearing heels and he had sneakers. From behind me I heard the bodyguard cry out, just before I slipped on the wet ground, tumbling forward. My falling body tripped the man and we tumbled together. I landed squarely, sprawled right on top of him, my knees either side of his hips and my face just inches from smashing into his head.

The hoodie guy hesitated for a second, not believing his luck. I looked up, straight at him. The hood of his jumper was pulled tightly over his head, but I got a brief, yet clear view of his dark brown eyes and extremely bushy eyebrows. He gazed back at me in amusement and then suddenly placed the camera lens down on the pavement. Turning, he ran off even faster and was soon out of sight.

I was so embarrassed. As I started to get up off the guard, I realised that he was laughing. "Are you okay?" he asked in an American accent.

"Yes, I am so sorry. I slipped," I answered as I tried to stand up in the mud, noticing that the whole front of my white T-shirt was now wet and stained.

"No kidding! Hi, I'm Brody," he said and smiled. "Next time I get to be on top!"

I blushed. After picking up the lens, I walked breathlessly back to where Raven was standing with Bill, Yvette and one of the waiters. I handed her the lens and she looked it over.

"Fucking moron," Raven said as she dabbed the bleeding graze on her nose with a napkin that Yvette had given her.

"You are not safe anywhere these days," I replied lamely. "I'll drive you home. Come on."

Bill looked shocked, but Yvette's expression was blank. I found it strange, but presumed she was either not easily fazed or had used too much Botox. During the whole time we were standing outside, she never said a word to us; just handed a napkin to Raven before going straight back into the restaurant.

Bill offered to pay for the lens, but Raven said it was fine, and we once again said our goodbyes. We got into my car whilst Bill and Brody watched us from where they were standing in front of the entrance to Sticks and Stones. They were deep in conversation and smiling, and looking intently at the front of my T-shirt. I glanced down to find that the water from the grass had made the material practically see-through, and I blushed again before I started driving towards Maida Vale in North London where Raven lived.

"That was really strange," she remarked as I started negotiating my way through Kensington.

"If you mean my T-shirt going see-through, I agree. So embarrassing; I'm practically topless. It cost a fortune too," I answered.

"No, I meant the attempted theft, if that's what it was?" Raven said thoughtfully.

I cast a glance at her and gave a look that implied I obviously didn't understand what she was talking about.

"Why go to the trouble of trying to steal my largest lens and then leave it?" she asked. "There wasn't a chance in hell that you would catch him."

"I don't know. Brody looked like he was going to get him if I hadn't gotten in the way. Anyway, perhaps he didn't really want a lens, but a more expensive camera, and then decided it wasn't worth the hassle."

"No, that lens is very expensive. Also, did you not see that he could easily have made his escape, because you and that bodyguard were rolling around in the grass by that time? So why leave it when he had gone to the trouble of stealing it in the first place? Perhaps nicking the lens wasn't the goal of the exercise," Raven concluded. "Perhaps it was a warning."

"Warning for what? Not to take photographs in central London? He had a hoodie on, for God's sake, Raven. I've read about people like that. They steal for a living," I answered and then felt silly as Raven raised one jet-black eyebrow at me, as if knowing how I had felt about her on first sight.

Feeling guilty, I shrugged. "Okay, so what do you think he was warning us about?" I asked whilst trying to manoeuvre the Range Rover around a London cabby and into a quiet street.

"I don't know yet, but I'm sure I'll find out one day," Raven answered.

"I know Bill Graham is a big rock star, but didn't you find it strange that he turned up at his own restaurant with a bodyguard?" I said, keenly getting into this conspiracy theory thing. "He's American and called Brody."

"I overheard Bill call him his driver, but the way Brody reacted when the guy knocked me over was awesome. He was like this superhero. God, he's hot," she observed, and we both laughed.

We drove together in silence for a few minutes until Raven guided me to the place where she lived. It was a small, brick house on a street with other small, brick houses that looked exactly the same. At the end of the road was a large pub called The Warrington. As I parked the car, a strange-looking guy came out of the front door of the house and walked towards the kerb. He was covered in tattoos and had several painful-looking piercings in his face. Tall and muscular, he wore a matching black singlet and jeans, and the same type of Doc Martens that Raven had.

Her face virtually lit up when she saw him. "Come on, Charlie, come into the squat with me and meet the guys. I can lend you a T-shirt, so you don't have to drive home practically topless. This is Nigel, by the way," Raven said as she hauled her heavy bag from the back seat, jumped out of the car and gave the guy a big, wet kiss on the lips.

"Wow, what happened to your face?" Nigel asked, looking concerned. His voice was not what I'd expected. He spoke with the same posh West End accent as some of James' friends. "Why is she dirty?" he asked Raven, indicating my T-shirt. "Nice bra," he added, smiling, and I blushed again, which made them both laugh.

I didn't really want to meet these people. I'd never met any punks before and I wasn't sure what to make of them. However, I couldn't refuse as it would have been rude, so after briefly protesting, I got out of the car and went to greet Nigel.

He smiled at me as he very politely took my hand and in a very posh, upper-class voice said, "How do you do? Pleased to meet you. Would you like to come inside and have something to eat with us? Jason has been cooking."

I walked behind them down the garden path and into their home. I'd never been in a squat before and I don't know what I was expecting, but certainly not what I saw when they opened the door and motioned me to enter. The house was very tidy. There were no anarchy symbols sprayed on the walls or broken furniture, and there was a smell coming from the kitchen that made my mouth water.

A tall, gangly teenager peered out from the kitchen wearing a white apron. The first thing that struck me was his hair. It was probably shoulder length, but he'd put it into a tight ponytail at the top of his head.

"This is Jason," Raven said in explanation. "We found him one night, homeless at King's Cross train station. We said he could stay the night since he had nowhere to go. That was over two years ago. Jason's an excellent cook, so we let him stay. He's a right little Hitler in the kitchen though."

"Hi," Jason said and smiled. He couldn't be more than fourteen years old in my opinion.

"We've had a tough time of it lately. The social has been around here, wanting to take Jason into care. He ran away from home, because his father was violent and his mother didn't care about him," Raven explained. "He's been so happy since he moved in here with us and it would kill me if he had to go into care. Who would want to adopt a fourteen-year-old boy?

"Nigel and I have been looking after Jason. He was into drugs when we first met. Only light stuff, like glue sniffing and a bit of pot, but now he is the total opposite and very careful of what he puts into his body."

Jason appeared again at the door to the kitchen, taking a keen interest in my T-shirt. His mouth turned up at the corners as if suppressing a smile. "If you are eating, you all need to wash. You know the rules: no dirt in my kitchen! And that applies especially to you," Jason said, pointing to my dirty top and white, skinny jeans.

Nigel took a bottle of spring water out of the fridge and placed it on the side.

"Get that filthy thing off my counter, Nigel. You know that bottle has been all over the place before we bought it. It's filthy and you are contaminating my counter," Jason said angrily.

Nigel picked up the bottle quickly as Jason proceeded to spray Dettol all over the counter and then he polished it vigorously with a paper towel.

"See what she means?" Nigel commented, laughing. "He's passionate about his kitchen and his cooking. I reckon he's going to be a fantastic chef one day, mark my words."

If this was a squat and these people were squatters, they were the weirdest ones I'd ever heard of. Raven appeared and handed me a black T-shirt with the words 'Shut the Fuck Up' on the front in bright red lettering. I put it on, and found it to be very soft and much more comfortable than my own top. I noticed that my white skinny jeans had dark green and brown patches on the knees, and the start of a hole, but I wasn't bothered. I'd get Mum to fix that when I got home.

We sat down to eat stew and rice, which was flavoured with the most heavenly mixture of spices that I had ever tasted. There seemed to be a lot of vegetables and something with a meaty texture, but I couldn't work out what it was. It was good though, and I was starving.

ACCESS ALL AREAS

"So, you are squatting here?" I asked, making polite conversation. By the look on Nigel's face, I could see he felt uncomfortable and blushed.

"Yep," Raven answered proudly. "We took over this house a few years ago. It had been empty for over a year, so we moved in. We don't know who owns it, but we've made it our home and we try to keep it nice. Just because we squat doesn't mean we have to ruin things. The owner should be thanking us that we keep it so nice. It's in much better condition now than when we moved in."

Raven was eating her meal, but sounded more passionate about what she was saying than what she was consuming. Her dark eyebrows darted up and down.

"I hope I don't sound rude, but wouldn't it have been easier to buy a place that you could perhaps sell on later with a profit, instead of squatting?" I asked carefully. "What will you do if the owners find you here and want you to move?"

Raven seemed eager to answer my question as Nigel and Jason exchanged quick glances. I suddenly realised I had probably waved the proverbial red rag at a bull.

"Squatting is a statement or a response to the political system that's causing it. During our latest recession foreclosures on houses have been increasing. Need-based squatting has arrived hand-in-hand with politically motivated squatting. Needless to say, we are politically motivated. With the system that's in place today, people are being almost forced to rely on the welfare state and hand-outs from this crap government to survive."

Raven held her fork near her face, but it never seemed to actually make it into her mouth. She sounded angry, but I sensed she was just passionate about her squatters' rights and the political system.

"Then they cut back the amount of welfare people receive whilst increasing the amount of spending on useless wars in other countries. Do not get me started on this, Charlie. I am passionate about this country and the need for change," Raven stated, and no one dared to interrupt. I noticed that Nigel looked almost embarrassed. "Rant over," she added and we all laughed a little nervously.

I made a note to myself: don't mention politics, squatting or anything about wars abroad when Raven is around. "This is a great stew, Jason. What meat is in it?" I asked, trying to change the subject. "I can't make up my mind if it's lamb or ham."

"We are vegan, so you won't find any meat in anything that's served in this house. We don't believe in the needless and cruel slaughtering of animals to feed us when we can get the same nutritious food from vegetables and herbs. We don't drink alcohol either," Jason replied enthusiastically.

"Why? Don't you believe in cruelty to grapes?" I joked, but no one seemed to get it, so I shut up. Note to self: add meat to my list of the non-mentionables whilst in Raven's company.

After the meal, I excused myself by saying I had a long drive back home. I really liked these three people. They were not what I had expected and I made a mental note not to be so judgemental in future. Raven walked with me to the gate outside and we stopped for a little while.

"I'll keep in touch on Facebook and get the photos off to you as soon as I've edited them," she said matter-of-factly.

"Shouldn't you be sending them to Melody?" I asked.

"No, you're writing the article, so therefore you get the photos and, together with Mel, you should choose which ones are used. It's your name on the article, after all," Raven replied. She paused and smiled at me, knowingly. "You haven't done this before, have you?"

"No, but I'm sure everything will be fine," I answered reluctantly.

Actually, I was beginning to feel nervous about my ability to pull off this article. I also felt like I'd fallen into some parallel universe where everyone I came into contact with turned out to be something else: Raven the vegan punk rocker; Jason the squat-living cook and Nigel the squat-living, upper-class punk rocker. It was all wrong. And then there was the hoodie who stole the lens, only to leave it on the pavement for us. I was getting a headache and felt an urgent need to get back to the safety of my parents' house.

I parked my car outside our home just as Mr Heritage came walking out of the door and into the front garden. He looked at my attire with a disapproving expression, so I lifted one eyebrow in a gesture that said, 'What? You can smoke weed, but I can't say shut the fuck up with a T-shirt?'

He got the message without either of us saying a word and quickly made his way to his flat above the garage.

Chapter 5
Roundhouse, Camden

The next morning I was brutally woken by my mobile phone buzzing relentlessly—I had a message. I think someone should invent a snooze button for messages. Perhaps there was one, but I hadn't learned all the finesses of my smart phone. Not only do I have a technical phobia, but I'm completely computer illiterate too. I shouldn't be let out really.

I'd had a vivid dream that I was making love with the postman. Or rather, he'd removed his pants and was asking me how much I wanted him when his face suddenly changed and it was Brody, the American bodyguard. He was naked and sweaty, and panting in my ear, and the sound got louder and louder, and that's when I realised it wasn't panting, but the phone buzzing. Why couldn't the flaming thing buzz after I'd ravished him? Jeez.

I made a mental note to get myself laid as soon as possible, because this celibate situation was not agreeing with me one bit. It was making me grumpy.

The smell of coffee and bacon being fried in the kitchen made its way up to my room, and I felt a dull tug in the pit of my stomach—hunger. Mum always made a big fried breakfast for Dad if he was working. On his days off he was lucky if she bothered to toast him a couple of slices of bread.

I grabbed my phone and saw I had a message from Melody to phone her PDQ, ASAP or sooner even. Yawning, I grabbed my dressing gown and made my way down to the kitchen. Mel would have to wait because my stomach came first. I'd barely had a few mouthfuls of coffee when the phone rang again. I was waiting for the Adonis postman and didn't really want to talk, but when I saw it was Melody, I knew I had to take it.

"Hi, I was just going to phone you," I lied.

"Do you know what time it is? Have you got the interview transcripted yet? We're off glamping tonight, so I need to edit it and finish it before I go. The printer is nagging me for the next edition. Oh, and by the way, do you fancy doing a gig review for us?" she asked quickly.

What on earth were glamping and a gig review? "What?" I said, yawning as I motioned to Mum to give me some more bacon and scrambled egg. Then I waved to my father, who was on his way out to his taxi, munching on a piece of toast.

"Bill Graham emailed asking after you, and he hoped Raven wasn't hurt. He wants to know whether you would be interested in covering his gig at The Roundhouse in Camden on Friday night. Why would he think Raven was hurt?" she questioned slowly and clearly, as if talking to someone with a bad grasp of the English language.

"It's a long story. Never mind. She's okay though. We had an accident, but nothing serious. We got mugged by a hoodie who stole Raven's lens," I said absentmindedly as Mum poured me more coffee and passed me some toast and jam. "So, a gig review involves going to a gig, right, and that's a concert, right? What on earth is glamping?" I asked as the garden gate was opened by my gorgeous postman.

Mum and I stopped what we were doing, and gazed out of the kitchen window in amazement as the young man walked towards our house. He was tanned and his shirt sleeves were rolled up, showing off his muscular arms as he gripped a stack of letters, his blonde hair flopping around in the summer breeze.

"What?! Mugged by a hoodie? What happened?" Mel blurted out, her voiced full of shock and concern. "What's a hoodie?"

"It's a guy wearing a hood. You know; the criminal type of person. He tried to steal Raven's expensive lens and I ran after him, but then he decided to drop it, which was strange since I was wearing six-inch Louboutins and had no chance of catching him, especially since I managed to roll over Bill's bodyguard. But, anyway, tell me what a gig review means," I said as I watched the postman in the garden and felt my mouth go dry.

"Oh, right, bodyguard?" Mel gasped. "Okay! Yeah, you go to the gig and then you write about it. I'll send you a list of things to think about before you go. You'll have to stay over, and Sticks' management have arranged for you and Raven to stay at the same hotel as the band. You are a lucky lady.

"I wouldn't mind doing the photos myself, because they are using Will Hero as support. I love him. I met him a few years ago, and he gives me goosebumps. Glamping is just glamorous camping. We have all the mod cons; Jacuzzi, telly and internet," Mel continued as I watched Adonis put something into the letterbox and smile with his perfect white teeth, before turning his back towards me—with a wave, of course—and swaggering out of the gate.

Phew, it feels hot today. Do you think I'm in early menopause or is it one of the side-effects or symptoms of nymphomania? I will have to Google it later, because surely there must be some sort of treatment for this?

Leaving the kitchen, I made my way up to my room to get started on the article. I hadn't considered that I would actually have to do some real work. The realisation hit me that I hadn't thought this journalism malarkey through, but there was no way I could back out now. I was pretty sure James would hear about me asking Bill for an interview, and if one was never published with my name on it in a magazine, he would most certainly hear about that too. He would love it if I failed.

It was important to me for James to see that I could actually make a life for myself without him, and be good at something. Now all that was left to do was the actual writing. My first hurdle would be working out how to use the Dictaphone.

Before I started writing, I checked Facebook, hoping there would be a message from Robert, but there wasn't one. I'd gotten an email from *Melody*

Magazine already, containing all the details of how to write a good gig review, the time and place of the concert at the Roundhouse in Camden, and an invitation to attend the 3 p.m. soundcheck.

The email also stated that it was not usual for the band management, or magazine, to pay for accommodation, but there had been a last-minute cancellation and the cost of the room would not be refunded. So, Mr Graham had suggested it be given to *Melody Magazine's* representatives in exchange for a good spread in the publication, thus elevating it from a gig review to a main feature.

They promised us a double room, so if Raven wanted to stay instead of making her way back to Maida Vale late at night, she could, if I didn't mind sharing. We would just have to agree about the details of all that between us.

Melody was clearly a person who was on top of things. I was beginning to get excited about this new career I seemed to have slid into, without knowing exactly how, at the same time as the weight of expectation was starting to set in. I had never written anything remotely like this before. To be honest, I hadn't written anything before.

Hearing Grandma Blue shuffle along in the hall outside my room, I called out to her, "Hey, can you help me work this contraption?"

It only took her a couple of minutes to get it working. She sat beside me, turning it off and on, so that I could type up the interview answers in my article. Piece by piece, question by question, we got it all down on the computer. For the introduction, I added a little piece about the band that I had Googled, along with some of the information Melody had sent me from a press release for the latest Sticks album, but changing the wording to make it my own. There followed my questions and Bill's answers.

Four hours later, and filled with anxiety, I emailed *Melody magazine* my article/interview and an assortment of photographs that Raven had sent me. Fifteen minutes later, I got a message back, saying, "Brill, it looks good, but I've only read a little bit on my phone. It needs some editing, so I'll get back to you later. Nice one, and welcome to the *Melody Magazine* freelance team."

I can't say I've ever felt this proud since winning the Children's Progress Prize at Infant School, and I was ready to burst! I couldn't wait to see my article published and my name on it. Thinking that I'd have to order some copies at the local newsagent, I realised that I had no idea whether *Melody Magazine* was sold anywhere close by.

I planned to order ten copies and have them framed. I'd give one to Agnes and John for Christmas, and Grandma Blue would have to have one. I was so proud that I didn't really consider the fact that perhaps not all my relatives would want my article on their wall.

***

On the day of the Roundhouse gig, I was up at the crack of dawn. I had planned to sleep late, but the excitement of my trip to London kept me awake. I'd packed a huge suitcase, just to have a good choice of clothes with me.

First, I drove to Maida Vale to pick up Raven. Nigel was waiting with her at the gate to their house, and she was not acting as lovey-dovey towards him as she had been before. Throwing her overnight bag and camera bag into the back seat, she jumped into the passenger seat and told me, "Drive!"

Nigel was looking downcast and staring at the back of my car as I drove away.

"What was all that about?" I asked as I made my way through the narrow streets towards central London.

"Fucking Nigel's been acting really weird around me this week. Something's going on and he won't tell me what it is," Raven replied sourly. "He says it's nothing, but I know there is something wrong, because he's not sleeping well and his phone keeps getting messages, which he keeps deleting quickly."

I made no comment since I didn't want to upset her any more than she already was, but it certainly sounded like there was something going on that Nigel didn't want her to know about.

We soon arrived at the Roundhouse in Camden. The large, round, brick building was originally built in 1847 as a railway roundhouse, but had been used as a performing arts venue since 1964. It was restored several times, most recently in 1998.

I had never been inside before, but Raven seemed to know her way around. The front of the venue was closed, so she led me around to the back where a huge band bus was parked, bearing The Sticks' logo in large, bright red letters on either side. It was the biggest bus I had ever seen. Three men were hanging around, smoking and chatting. The door of the vehicle was open, but I couldn't see inside, as the windows were too high up and blacked out.

"I covered Patti Smith's gig here in 2010. It was my first job for a small music magazine and I can't tell you how nervous I was," Raven said.

There was a glass entrance to the building, but it was locked. Beside the door was a window and inside we could see a man sitting behind a desk, ignoring us. When Raven tapped on the window, he slowly made his way over to open it a tiny crack. I think he was afraid we would try to force our way in.

"Photographers have the worst working conditions. We only get to be in the mosh pit for the first three songs and photos have to be taken without a flash. Some bands have a black backdrop and poor lighting, so it's almost impossible to get a good shot," Raven told me as the window was opened a little wider by the bored-looking man.

Looking at him, she announced, "Raven Baker and Charlotte Hart; we are guest-listed for tonight and the soundcheck. We need a photo pass and a press pass."

I stood beside Raven, trying to look like I knew what I was doing while the man rummaged around for his list and ticked us off. She stuck her right hand through the window, and I watched as the man expertly tied a bright red band around her arm with three gold-encrusted letter A's on it.

100

Raven nudged me, and I did the same. The man made sure the armband around my wrist was just tight enough so as not to be removable without actually cutting it off, but not too tight as to be uncomfortable.

The man pressed a button, and the door opened and we both entered. We were now in the backstage area. How cool was this? I tried not to grin too broadly, for fear of looking an idiot. I'd never been backstage for anything in my whole entire life.

Raven glanced at her wristband in surprise. "Fucking hell, Charlie, Triple A passes! I've never had one before. Triple fucking A! Nice one," she exclaimed, but I had no idea what she was talking about. She looked at my moronic expression and laughed. "It stands for Access All Areas. That means we can go anywhere we want."

"Yeah, so I knew that," I lied.

"Let me explain. Triple A means we have access to everything. Sometimes I'm not even allowed to stay after my three songs are done. Some bands are really greedy and turf the photographers out straight after their shoot. They want to see all the photos before we publish and reserve the rights to use them for their own publicity without having to pay to use the copyright. This is so great!

"You should do a behind-the-scenes gig review for *Melody Magazine*," Raven went on as we found our way down various dark corridors and past numerous locked doors until we heard ear-splitting feedback from what sounded like a very large amplifier. We followed the noise and entered a huge, circular space with an enormous stage at one end.

I looked around the stage to see several people working and one guy duct-taping some electrical cable to the floor. Two girls sat towards the front of the stage on chairs looking bored, but there was no sign of Bill Graham.

Raven and I walked out on to the stage, and a couple of the guys looked at us in surprise, but they didn't say anything. I did not know what to do. There was nowhere to sit and the girls simply went on with their chatter, ignoring us. Raven decided to walk over to a man assembling a drum kit on a podium at the back to ask for help when I heard my name.

"Charlie?" a man called out to me again as I turned. Tall and slender, and covered in tattoos, he wore loose-fitting jeans ripped at both knees over his skinny legs and a T-shirt that was probably white at one time, but had turned grey with wear.

The man's face was deeply lined with age and his shoulder-length dark hair seemed to be thinning on top. He held out a skinny hand, riddled with protuberant veins, which I automatically shook. It was warm and soft to touch, which was not what I'd expected.

I looked into his pale blue eyes, which furrowed at the corners as he smiled, and instantly liked him. "Hi, welcome. I'm Tiger," he said. "I play bass. Bill is running late, so he just texted me to look out for you."

Tiger led me over to the girls sitting on the stage after introducing himself to Raven. As I got closer, I could see they were not as young as I first thought. One of them was blonde and skinny, wearing too much make-up and looking tired. She was probably in her late fifties or early sixties, but had a youthful-looking body dressed in tight, skinny jeans and a black T-shirt bearing a bright red The Sticks logo.

The other woman was a little younger, perhaps in her forties, and dressed in a similar way, but her T-shirt said 'I prefer the drummer' in yellow lettering on a black background. Her shiny, auburn hair was the first thing I noticed about her; her bright red talon nails was the second.

"This is my missus, Tracy." Tiger indicated to the blonde. I smiled and nodded, and we shook hands. "The other gorgeous babe is Keith's lady, Marianne," he explained.

From researching The Sticks ahead of my interview with Bill, I knew that Tiger Edwards was the bass player and a founding member. Keith Raymond had joined in the early eighties, after the original drummer, Wally, died of heart disease. Keith had not been with The Sticks for many months by 1983, when Bill's wife died under unfortunate circumstances and they disbanded.

The third member was Ronnie Waller, the guitarist, who was new to the band, but certainly no newbie to the music industry, having played in a number of well-known groups before joining The Sticks this year.

"We have had to delay the soundcheck because the roadie morons fucked up and didn't get here in time to set up," Tiger continued. "How about I take you all up to the dressing room and we have something to drink?"

Tiger seemed like a cheerful, nice guy, in stark contrast to his ageing rock-star exterior. He put his arm around Tracy as we walked with him back into the catacombs of the backstage area, which I found endearing. They acted like a couple of smitten teenagers, although I knew they'd been together for half a century.

Tiger opened a door using a card and code, and we all trooped into a room that held two large comfortable looking leather sofas and a table, and a small kitchen area. Raven and I had not been given a key card, so Access All Areas obviously didn't mean that after all. As Tiger made a big show of putting the kettle on to make us some tea, Tracy sat down beside me and smiled while raising her eyebrows at her husband's jokes.

"A cup of tea is probably the only thing he can make. In all the years we've been together, I've never managed to domesticate him," she said.

"I can believe that. Do you always go on tour with him?" I asked.

"Yeah, we met at a concert before The Sticks became famous. They were just starting out in the early seventies, and playing small pubs and that, and we just clicked. We've never been away from each other since then," she replied in a northern accent that I couldn't quite place.

"So no kids then?" I asked, already knowing the answer to that one.

"No, unfortunately we don't have children. I would have liked to have some at one point, but it never seemed like the right time. Tiger has hepatitis, so it's tricky. Back in the day, when I was young enough to conceive, it was believed that people with hepatitis couldn't have children. Of course, that's not true, but the medication Tiger was on for a while was pretty heavy stuff, so we decided it was best to not have any," she explained, and I was surprised by her openness as I was, after all, 'The Press'.

Tiger placed mugs on the table in front of us. Each one had a teabag inside and a teaspoon sticking out at the top. He lifted the kettle that had just boiled and placed it on the table, together with a bowl of sugar, before sitting down beside Tracy.

"I'll be mummy, shall I?" he offered as he lifted the kettle and poured boiling water into each of our mugs in turn.

"I love a cup of tea. Best thing in the world. Where are the fucking biscuits?" he asked and then smiled at our attempts to get our teabags out of the cups, only to find there was nowhere to put them.

I suddenly noticed the criss-cross of scars on Tiger's arms. They looked like thousands of slits carved with a very sharp knife. He saw me looking and smiled. "War wounds," he said, placing both arms in front of him, palms up, so that I could see the scars more closely.

I'd never seen anything like it before. "Wow that looks painful. Were you in an accident?" I asked naively, and Raven supressed a giggle.

"No, they are self-inflicted," he replied. "I suppose you could call it an accident, because I was too out of my skull on heroin to know what I was doing. At the time, I found cutting myself comforting. When I look back, I can't believe all the stupid, pathetic choices I made. But then Tracy got me sorted out, and all that changed," he added.

"Tiger works with drug addicts and young people with problems. It's something we both wanted to do ever since he got clean," Tracy said. "There are a lot of kids out there making the same bad choices we both made, and it's good they can see there is hope and you can change."

The door to the room flung open and a man walked in briskly, slamming it shut behind him. He was small, but portly built with a beer gut under his suit and white shirt. The guy looked like a banker, except that his hair was a very unnatural-looking dark black. He was talking into a small telephone and carrying a brown leather bag.

"Tell them it will be fine. Everything is ready, Darren. Don't worry. Can you get someone from the record company to send a guy over with some green stuff? I need it straight away. I don't care if they are busy; I'm busy too. Send an envelope with the green stuff. Shut the fuck up, Daz, and bring it yourself if you have to." The man hung up the phone, placed his leather bag on the sofa and sat down. He didn't look at me or Raven, nor did he make any attempt to talk to us.

"Fucking hell, Tiger, Darren is doing my head in today!" he said loudly. "You'd think he'd never been on tour before. I asked him to get Bill's guy, Brody, to do something and he almost fucking shat himself. He's scared shitless of those fucking guys, the weak piece of shite. Make me a cup of tea, Marianne, I'm knackered."

Straight away, she jumped to her feet and started fussing, grabbing a mug and spoon.

"I'm scared of those guys too. That Brody is a big man, Malc—used to be a US Navy SEAL. I would keep out of his way and not piss him off, if I were you. Where is Bill, by the way?" Tiger asked as we all sat in silence. The mere mention of Brody's name made me blush.

"Sorting out those fucking roadies! They all got pissed after the Dublin gig last night and didn't leave in time this morning. The hotel management aren't pleased and are threatening legal action. I've told Digger that I hold him responsible. If we're sued, they can fucking well foot the bill themselves. Ah, ta, love," he said as Marianne placed a mug of piping hot tea in front of him.

I watched fascinated as she spooned three spoonful's of sugar into his drink and stirred it, before removing the spoon and placing it in the sink. It was obviously not the first time Marianne had made him a cup of tea.

"This is Malcolm, our manager, in case you were wondering," Tiger said in my direction.

I had gathered it was the infamous Malcolm when he arrived, but he didn't look much like the old photos I'd seen of him. He, in turn, looked in my direction and nodded, not offering his hand in greeting, nor any encouraging words of welcome. Charming, I thought.

Malcolm's phone rang again and he glanced at it, but didn't answer, just as the door to the room was once again opened, this time by a small, shabby looking roadie. His eyes were bloodshot and he looked tired. I guessed this was one of the culprits from the previous night's fun and games in Dublin.

"They are ready for you!" he announced and disappeared back down the hall in the general direction of the stage.

Tiger got up, as did Raven. I noticed her take two earplugs out of her pocket and place one in each ear before she expertly tugged her heavy camera bag on to her shoulder and followed Tiger out of the room.

I didn't have earplugs, nor did I know what to do at a soundcheck, so I simply remained in the room with Malcolm and the girls, hoping I could have another look around later. Secretly, I hoped to bump into Brody accidently on purpose. Malcolm looked at his phone, as if reading something very interesting, and drank his tea in silence, ignoring the rest of us.

I looked at Tracy, who smiled reassuringly. "What did you and Tiger do during the years that The Sticks were disbanded? I asked her.

"Well, for the first few months we stayed in England. Tiger had some problems back then, which

108

we had to sort out. Then we went to Crete for a year to get our heads together. After that we went to France and stayed with Bill for a while. It was nice in France, but Tiger was missing his chocolate finger biscuits and proper tea, so we came back to the UK. He played in different bands, but always hoped Bill would get the old line-up back together. And here we are," she answered brightly.

"Thank you for being so frank and open. I won't add any of this to my article since this is a private conversation," I said in an attempt to become closer to Tracy.

I liked her and Tiger, and I wanted them to like me. I knew there had been a lot of controversy in the early eighties when the band split up. There had been a lot of gossip at the time and lots of theories in the tabloids, but nothing seemed to come of any investigation into what happened or why Bill Graham simply left England, not to return for many years.

"Thank you, but the fact that both me and Tiger have been into some heavy drugs is well documented, so it isn't a secret at all. You can write anything I tell you. If I didn't feel comfortable talking about it, I wouldn't say anything. Tiger got himself into trouble with heroin mainly, back in the early eighties. He was off his head most of the time and it was getting to be a problem."

Tracy took a sip of her tea before placing her mug carefully on the table.

"I did a little, too, but nothing close to as much as Tiger was putting into his body. Bill threatened to fire him if he didn't pull himself together, but then the band split up because of the death of his wife, Delphine. I wouldn't mention her if I were you—touchy subject," Tracy continued. "Isn't that right, Malc?"

Malcolm was still busily reading something on his phone and barely looked up, but he nodded. While I'm not proud to admit it, I had taken an instant dislike to him. The guy seemed distracted, arrogant and very rude, barely acknowledging my presence. When he had looked directly at me for a second or so, as he entered the room, it was as if I was a bad smell or something.

The door was once again opened and a man entered carrying a briefcase similar to Malcolm's plus a white envelope. He was ordinary looking, probably about sixty, with short brown hair and a round face with big ears, like a human version of Dumbo. The man looked around in surprise at my presence, but didn't greet me either. What was these people's problem with me?

"Ah finally, Darren," Malcolm said happily. "Is that for me?" he asked, indicating the envelope.

Darren nodded and handed it to Malcolm, who eagerly opened it and smelled inside. He expertly rolled himself a cigarette using the contents of the envelope and lit up the spliff without further ado. Soon the air smelled sickly, and I sat there staring at him, wondering whether perhaps this wasn't the best environment for Tracy, given what she had just told me. She, in turn, didn't react.

"So Malc, are you up for some fun tonight?"
Darren asked as he sat down beside him in the sofa
opposite us.

"What did you have in mind?" Malcolm
answered with a sly smile on his face.

"Well, I've got some cool stuff lined up for the
after-party, and I'm thinking we could enjoy some
Triple A action!" Darren suggested and they both
started to laugh. I didn't get the joke.

"Yeah I might be up for it, but it better be better
than the last time. Where did you dig up those
dogs?" Malcolm asked, laughing.

"You are just making excuses, because you are
too old to get it up anymore!" Darren retorted and
they both laughed.

Tracy and Marianne shifted nervously beside me
on the sofa, so I got up from where I was sitting and
started to make my way towards the exit.

"Right, it's been lovely meeting you all. I'm
going to go and find Raven. I need to check in at the
hotel too, so see you later at the gig," I said
cheerfully as I opened the door and left.

The fresh air in the hall outside was a relief after
the stuffiness inside the room, caused not only by
the marijuana, but also the atmosphere. I followed
the sound of music down the corridor until I found
the main stage again.

Raven was running around between the band
members, taking photos from a dozen different
angles as the band played one rock song after
another. She was not used to being allowed this
much access, and I noticed Bill was enjoying it and

acting for the camera, but the guitar player, Ronnie, seemed to like jumping around on stage and Raven kept getting in his way.

Brody was standing with his back to the stage, gazing in my direction. Hmm, that man was fit. He was wearing a black T-shirt and jeans, which seemed to be his standard gear. I had just decided to wander over and apologise for landing on him after the hoodie incident when I saw Raven move too close to Ronnie at the same time as he went forward.

She stepped backwards and her foot caught one of the electric cables that had been duct-taped to the floor. I saw her facial expression change from happy to utter horror as she tried to regain her balance. Raven moved back further, not realising there was nothing to step back on. She was right on the corner of the stage and fell, as if in slow motion.

I jumped forward to try to catch her. What the hell was I thinking? She would have flattened me! Brody obviously had the same instinct and he leapt forward. Needless to say, we all fell together in a heap on the floor in front of the stage, with Raven still clutching her camera for dear life. Brody somehow managed to land on the bottom with us girls on top of him.

Raven had screamed as she fell and Bill, who had tried to grab her arm, and Ronnie, who had stepped back, both came running to the edge of the stage and were now looking down on us.

"I'm alright! I'm alright!" Raven said loudly.

I quickly got up from where I was sitting straddled across Brody's body, whereas Raven was lying across his legs clutching her camera. He sat up and I could see that he was laughing at me.

"What?" I asked. "It was an accident."

"That's the second time you've thrown me to the ground and sat on me this week," Brody said, laughing. "If you are that interested in close bodily contact, just ask me instead. I promise I won't charge you my usual rates."

I blushed. What the hell did he think I was doing? "Yeah, very funny, but I'm not that desperate," I said angrily, as I got up and tried to dust myself off. My elbow had landed squarely in his stomach and it hurt. It had defiantly not landed on anything soft.

I glanced up at the stage where all four band members where chuckling hysterically. Bill Graham was laughing so hard that it looked like he couldn't breathe and Tiger was doubled up over his bass. Tracy and Marianne entered the stage as Raven and I started for the door. Just as we were leaving, I heard the two women and the rest of them howl with laughter. How did I keep getting myself into these situations? Flaming embarrassing!

Raven and I decided to head over to the hotel, and get checked in and cleaned up. Outside the Roundhouse, a group of about seven young girls were standing by the band bus. They could not have been very old, fifteen or seventeen perhaps at the most, with short skirts and too much make-up. They giggled and chatted to one another, and a couple of them were smoking cigarettes. I watched them with interest. It looked like they were fans waiting at the backstage entrance, hoping to catch a glimpse of their idols.

The door to the bus was still open and suddenly a very young girl came out, followed by the hung-over roadie I'd seen before. I think his name was Digger. He had a broad smile on his face and was scratching his crouch, like he wanted it to be very clear what he'd just done with this young girl in the bus. The other roadies, who were standing around smoking, hardly reacted. The girl adjusted her short skirt, and joined her friends to cheers and laughter.

I suddenly got it. These were not fans at all; they were young groupies—girls who follow bands and sleep with as many as they can, even a roadie or two, if they could get them into the gig and after-party. I gazed at them in fascination as Raven nudged me to open the car door; she was struggling with her heavy photo bag.

"Those girls are a bit young to be hanging around here," I remarked as I got into the driver's side of my Range Rover.

Raven jumped into the passenger seat and put her belt on. "Yeah, well, some of them can be even younger than that," she replied. "They know exactly what they are doing, no matter how young they are. I see girls like them at the gigs all the time. It's like a sport with them—who's fucked the biggest stars!"

"I wonder if their parents know what they're up to," I pondered.

"I doubt that very much," Raven answered. "I am usually just at the gigs for the photos, but I regularly see young girls just like them, with Triple A passes, going backstage as soon as the gigs are over."

"What does Triple A stand for again?"

"Access All Areas. Why?"

"It was just something someone said, and I found it strange," I replied. "This guy came up to the room backstage with Malcolm's drugs. He was called Darren."

"Darren is his assistant. They are both quite famous in the music-managing business. Malcolm has managed a lot of very famous bands and Darren does all his footwork. They have a reputation for being ruthless, but every band that signs with them are treated like royalty, and there isn't anything they can't get you," Raven explained. "That's the talk on the street anyway. When I say 'anything', I mean absolutely anything."

"Well, Darren asked Malcolm if he was up for some fun at the after-party tonight and said he could get him some Triple A action. I'm guessing that means a few of those young groupies will be in attendance," I said.

"Well, we haven't been invited to the after-party, and I'm not sure I'm in the mood to be honest. This thing with Nigel is really worrying me. He looks so guilty. The other day I caught him checking the post twice, and when he finally got it, I'm sure he hid something from me. I think he might be seeing someone else," Raven said. A tear slipped out of her eye and ran down her cheek, which she quickly wiped away. Pulling herself together, she cleared her throat.

I felt so sorry for her; it was heart-wrenching to see her suffer, but I couldn't help, because I didn't know Nigel. "I can only suggest you confront him," I suggested. "But I've just separated from my husband, so I'm not the right person to give relationship advice."

My cell phone rang and I put it on speakerphone. "Charlie here," I said loudly, as I continued to drive towards our hotel, located a few miles away in central West End London.

"Hello, it's Mel. How are you getting on? Have you been to the soundcheck yet?" she asked.

"Yeah, we just left. We're off to the hotel to get cleaned up," I answered.

"Why do you need to get cleaned up? What have you done?" she asked warily.

"Nothing, we're okay; no harm done. Raven fell off the stage," I explained.

"We are okay, because Charlie and I landed on Bill's bodyguard again, and the camera is fine too, thanks for asking," Raven shot in.

"What? Why does he have a bodyguard?" Mel asked.

"That's what we've been wondering. We don't actually know that he is a bodyguard for sure. Raven says he's Bill's driver, but he is huge and muscular, and has one of those earpieces like I saw on that film with Whitney Huston and Kevin Costner," I continued.

"And he's drop dead gorgeous and Charlie keeps throwing herself at him," Raven added with a laugh.

"Shut up, I don't. It was an accident," I insisted, not seeing the funny side at all.

"Well, you girls try to behave. Have you met William Hero yet?" Mel asked, and I could detect an edge of amusement in her voice.

"No, not yet," we both answered in unison.

"Well, remember to say hello from me. Tell him *Melody Magazine* is keen to interview him. Say I want a big feature, and that I'll do it myself. We can do a photo shoot—the full package," Mel said. "Actually semi-nude would be good, unless he wants to go the full monty. No, wait, don't ask him that or you might scare him away. Just say photo shoot and feature. I don't think I could trust myself with him nude," she added eagerly.

Raven and I looked at one another, raising our eyebrows in a knowing gesture, laughing. "We will. Bye!" I said and hung up the phone.

"Ooooh, somebody has a hankering for a hero," Raven said and we both giggled.

Chapter 6
See Me Through Until the End

The Palace Hotel, just off Bayswater Road on the north side of Hyde Park, had originally been five large Victorian townhouses and it was not what I expected.

The interior reception area was elegant, boasting high ceilings with chandeliers and large, comfortable looking rooms, previously home to the aristocracy. I could just imagine a lord or lady relaxing in front of the huge fireplace whilst the servants served high tea.

The guest rooms, however, were a different matter altogether. Our room, on the second floor, which was supposed to be a twin and turned out to be a double, was tiny. The bed was rock hard, and the bed linen thin and worn. The door to the en-suite bathroom could only be opened three-quarters of the way before it knocked into the end of the bed, which dominated the room. The windows gave us a view of Hyde Park, but they couldn't be opened completely. I managed a tiny crack to let some air in.

Glancing in the bathroom, I saw the tiles needed repairing in places, and the bathtub was worn and yellowing. There was a plastic shower curtain that had probably once been white, but was now yellowed with age and wear, and at the bottom I could see some sort of brown stain. I made a mental note to keep well away from it. The room smelled of cleaner and furniture polish, and there was an underlying tinge in my nostrils of something more sinister, which I couldn't quite put my finger on.

Oh yeah, what a luxury hotel this was… not. I was surprised that a band with the money and reputation of The Sticks would ever consider staying in such a shabby establishment, but I was sure there was a reason for it.

Raven threw her overnight bag onto the room's only chair and let me have the luggage rack for my suitcase. "Look at the size of that! How long are you planning on staying here for?" she teased me.

A little later, when Raven and I, in turn, had used the shower and freshened up, I saw the band bus pull up outside the hotel. It was expertly parked on the street below. The driver, who happened to be the hung-over looking guy from earlier called Digger, made his way from the hotel towards Oxford Street. It was strange to think that such a little guy could drive that huge bus so well; in fact, he had parallel-parked it. I was impressed.

I was just pondering whether to drive to Camden for the concert or get a cab when the phone on the dressing-room table rang shrilly, making Raven and I jump. "Yes?" I answered, wondering who knew we were at the hotel and why anyone would want to call us.

"Charlie, is that you? It's Bill," he said. "I just wanted to let you know that we are having something to eat in a bit downstairs, and you and Raven are welcome to join us. I've arranged for us all to go to the concert in the bus afterwards, so you don't have to worry about parking in Camden. It can be a bit tricky when there's a concert on, I'm told, and tonight's sold out."

"Erm, yes, I'm starving. We'll be down straight away, thanks," I answered in surprise.

"Your ex-husband must have made a very deep impression on Bill Graham or I'd say he's got a thing for you," Raven teased me. "Well, if he can get past Brody," she added, and I threw a pillow at her.

I got dressed in skinny jeans and a Christian Dior T-shirt, elaborately embroidered with the image of a butterfly on the front, designed by John Galliano. Sitting down, I was just putting my feet into a pair of black platform, crystal-encrusted, six-inch-heel ankle boots when Raven emerged from the bathroom having changed into plain black T-shirt and black jeans.

"Oh, my God, is that what you are wearing?!" she exclaimed loudly.

"Yeah, what's wrong with it?" I asked.

"You haven't been to many gigs, have you?" she sighed. "Those shoes are going to hurt tonight. You need to dress down and wear flats, or you're going to regret it."

"I'm willing to suffer to look good," I argued, as I tossed my hair and applied a little more lip gloss.

"Here, take this," Raven said, throwing her black leather biker jacket towards me.

Normally, I would never be seen dead in such an item, and I was just about to refuse when I saw the determined look on her face. The leather jacket felt really soft to the touch, so I put it on and I had to

120

admit that it looked pretty cool teamed with the
jeans, and it hid the huge Dior logo on my T-shirt.
Reaching for my suitcase, I pulled out a small, black
handbag that bore Chanel's 'CC' symbol in white on
the side. Raven's eyes hit the ceiling in protest, but I
had to have somewhere to put my Dictaphone, right?

"I can't dress up for the gig as much as I'd like to.
It's a photographer's code to be very inconspicuous
whilst in the pit. We all just wear black to blend into
the background, so as not to distract the audience
from what they have really come to see—the band
on stage—and not to distract the band from doing
their jobs well. So, all black it is for me tonight,"
Raven confided.

I could see the logic in what she said, but
considering her jet-black hair with pink stripes, she
was anything but inconspicuous.

We went down to the reception desk, where we
were told that although the hotel did not have a
restaurant, the band and entourage had taken one of
the larger ballrooms and food was on the way. We
made our way up the stairs to the first-floor ballroom
and were met by one of the roadies at the door. He
checked our Triple A passes on our wrists before
letting us past.

The room we entered was elegant with the same
sort of Victorian design as the reception area. It was
predominantly baby blue in colour with a large
fireplace at one end, and comfortable sofas and
chairs scattered around. Towards one wall was a
long table set up with glasses and plates, but no
food. A waiter offered us a glass of rosé wine, which

I eagerly accepted. Raven declined and asked for a soft drink, which was immediately provided. I felt a little awkward as everyone was already there and sitting in groups talking.

"Hey, Charlie, come over here," Bill called out over the noise of the others' chatter. He was sitting in a rather elegant blue chair with Tracy and Tiger, who were sitting on a sofa, and Brody, who occupied the other chair.

Raven and I walked over to them. I was grateful of the carpet as my heels had a tendency to slip on wooden flooring. My feet were starting to ache already. Tiger and Tracy made room for me on the sofa, and Raven perched on the armrest beside me. Everyone seemed to be wearing jeans and T-shirts, very casual, except Brody, who was dressed in his signature black jeans and black T-shirt, but now teamed with a dark suit jacket.

Brody looked very elegant compared to the other two men. His face was tanned, like he'd been on a recent vacation, and that made his teeth look, if possible, even whiter. His dark hair was cut short and it looked like he would have curls if he let it grow, as it was not straight and seemed to slightly lift at the ends.

"Good to see you again," Bill said politely. "Sorry, I didn't have time for much of a chat at the soundcheck. How are you both by the way?" He smiled in amusement.

"Yes, we are fine. No bruises, thankfully, since Brody broke both our falls," I answered, feeling embarrassed.

Bill smiled again. "How is your room?" he asked. "Not much of a hotel this, but we always stay here when we have London gigs. The staff are very good at keeping people out."

"Yeah, keeping people out and their mouths shut," Tiger added. "Malcolm books it because it's one of the few hotels that let him smoke in the room. I don't mean cigarettes, if you get my drift. They look through their fingers at a lot of things here. Personally, I prefer somewhere a bit fancier, but I can't complain."

At that moment the door opened to reveal no fewer than two pizza-delivery guys, each carrying five large boxes and a few smaller ones in bags strapped to their backs. The hotel staff started to rip the lids off the boxes and place them on the tables by the wall, creating a buffet of takeaway food that smelled delicious. Everyone got up at once and filled their plates with an assortment of pizzas. There was also something that looked like noodles and fried rice with shrimps, smelling strongly of garlic, along with a smaller box of sushi, and some oriental dishes I had never seen before.

Tiger and Tracy grabbed some chopsticks and loaded their plates expertly with sushi. Raven and I opted for the pizzas, and I found myself standing in front of Brody in the queue.

"You are looking very pretty today," he remarked as we waited our turn.

"Thank you. You are looking very dapper yourself. Hey, I'm really sorry for flattening you earlier… again," I said, looking into his bright blue eyes for a moment before I had to glance away.

Oh, jeez, what was I doing now? Taking a big sip of the wine I held in my hand, I felt the glass shake a little as I put it to my lips. I would definitely have to stop drinking as I had a very low tolerance and wine normally sent me to sleep.

"I'm keeping you at a safe distance in future," Brody replied, laughing. "You seem to have it in for me for some reason."

"It was an accident," I answered, but I was laughing too.

"You're not good for my image, Charlie," he said, smiling. "It's very entertaining, but I'm supposed to have this tough guy image, which seems to get quashed every time you sit on me."

"So, what is your role on this tour?" I asked, feeling hopeful of a straight answer.

"What makes you think I have a role?" he asked.

I was at the head of the pizza queue now, and annoyingly enough, I didn't get to question him further. It was a strange answer. There was definitely something going on between Bill and Brody, and I was determined to find out what.

After we had eaten and consumed more drinks all round, we left for the Roundhouse. My first impression of the band bus being large didn't begin to describe it; it was enormous. The vehicle had two storeys, with a steep staircase leading up to a very comfortable top deck with a TV screen at the front.

We drove the distance to the venue and parked at the back of it. The area had been sectioned off now, with barriers that closed again as soon as the bus passed through. There were several guards manning the barrier and thirty or so fans hanging out, looking for a glimpse of their idols. They howled as the bus passed them and rushed forward, only to be stopped by the guards.

The bus was parked in such a way to enable everyone to get out and enter the venue without being seen from the barriers. We heard a few fans scream Bill's name as we all trouped in through the back entrance to the Roundhouse; me on my tottering heels. Brody kept close to Bill and he seemed to be very alert. If he wasn't a bodyguard my name was Fanny Cradock!

I soon found myself back in that same room backstage with all the people who had been there earlier, and now there was the support band fronted by Will Hero too. The door was open and people had spilled out into the hall, talking in small groups. Inside, the table was covered in beer and wine bottles, so I helped myself to a glass of white, and sat with Tracy and Tiger to chat.

Tracy was drinking red wine and enjoying herself, but I thought everyone seemed to be a little on edge and the atmosphere was tense. Malcolm was smoking pot continuously, and handing it around from time to time. He looked so high that his eyes were just little black slits in his skull.

"He's going to be well out of it if he keeps that up," Tracy whispered into my ear and I nodded in agreement.

William Hero and his band were standing around in the hall waiting for the first support band to finish before it was their turn. I'd seen him on TV before, but I was more interested in him now since I suspected Melody had a crush on him. The man was of medium height with short, light blonde hair. He was also very charismatic, but quiet and he seemed a little shy, although his leather trousers that revealed more than I felt comfortable seeing belied this fact.

Will's tight, slightly ripped top revealed a muscular build and I could see several females in the room looking at him with interest. He seemed to be unaware of the impact he was having on them, preferring the company of the other band members who were all male. They left the room to do their warm-up before I had a chance to give Will Hero Mel's message. If she was really interested in the guy, she would have to take her place in the queue.

There was another unknown group performing before him, whom I had not met since they were already on stage when we arrived. It was all very exciting and I suddenly realised my wine glass was empty. Tracy offered me red wine, which I declined, so we found a bottle of ice-cold white in the small fridge.

"I can't drink red wine. It puts me to sleep. Also, my tongue and teeth get so stained from the red colour that I end up looking like Dracula's sister," I said and she burst into laughter.

"God, you are funny, Charlie," she replied, but I wasn't trying to be; it was all true.

Tracy topped up her glass and I realised she was starting to slur her speech a little. I made a note to slow down or I'd be of no use to anyone. Meanwhile, Malcolm was getting totally off his head and suddenly wanted to talk to us.

"Are you taking notes, Charlie?" he asked me.

"No, should I be?" I answered, not understanding the question.

Malcolm looked at me unsteadily. "I can get a set list to you tomorrow, so just kick back and enjoy yourself," he said in a very slow voice, his tongue not really cooperating, but still managing to pronounce all the words correctly.

I nodded and smiled, and made a mental note to find out what a set list was from somebody quickly, so I didn't come across as completely incompetent.

"The record company sends us support bands for free. It's in our contract that we have to use their bands, so I always have fun choosing one that's the opposite of what we are. That way, I know the fans that have paid to see The Sticks will absolutely hate them. It's fun in an otherwise tedious tour," he said, and I realised just how much I disliked this man.

"We have an American R&B band as first warm-up. They are called Sleuths; bloody pathetic name. We got Will Hero for this gig, but tomorrow we're off to the Manchester 02 and using another death metal band. They are all shite and the crowds quickly become hugely unimpressed, and the bottles start flying. It's so much fun," Malcolm continued.

We heard a roar from the crowd downstairs as Will Hero and his band left the stage. Bill, Tiger and the rest got ready to enter it. Tracy topped up my glass once again, and I caught Brody looking at me sternly before he left with the band members, who were making their way towards the stage. Following behind, Tracy, Marianne and I stayed close together. We were all a bit tipsy now. Raven had left earlier to get photos of all the evening's acts.

There was a sensational rumble from the audience as Keith took his place behind his drums, followed by Tiger, who entered the stage wearing his bass. Ronnie, ever the energetic showman, ran on stage and plugged in his guitar, and the audience went wild as he started to play the opening riff of 'Leggy Blonde Bombshell' just as Bill entered the stage. I thought the fans couldn't get any wilder, but I was wrong.

Suddenly they were on, and then they were off. It was all very exhilarating and I had a great time. The band ran back for an encore of four of their most popular songs, the last of which contained the lyrics, "If I die and have to leave you, see me through until the end." It was a ballad and it gave me goosebumps as I watched from the side of the stage. I could see Brody standing on the opposite side with another big guy dressed in black, watching the audience intently and glancing in my direction from time to time.

The band rushed back to the dressing room and I noticed they were in a completely different mood than before they played. Now they were more relaxed and upbeat. A few of the young girls I'd seen outside earlier made their way into the room and helped themselves to drinks.

One girl sat on Malcolm's knee, as there were not any more chairs available. I watched as he fondled her breasts and spoke softly into her ear. She laughed and seemed to be enjoying herself. It was all very strange to me. What could a teenage girl possibly see in a guy who was old enough to be her grandfather? It was a mystery and I found it quite disturbing.

Tracy was a bit drunk and Tiger had his arm around her, joking that he would have to keep her on her feet. She laughed at everything he said and was a happy drunk. Raven had appeared backstage as soon as the concert was over.

"Raven," I whispered in her ear. "What's a set list?" I was a little tipsy though, and ended up pronouncing it 'shetlisht'.

"It's a list of all the songs played at a gig in the order they were performed. I've already got one for you from the head roadie, Digger. Now there's a character. He's tiny and like a little rat, but he knows what he's doing," Raven answered. "The other roadies are scared of him. He smiled at me a while ago and his teeth looked like they've been thrown into his mouth. The guy looked at me like I was dinner and he was ready to pounce. I'm telling you, he is seriously screwed up. Scares me a bit."

I had seen Malcolm conferring with Digger several times that night. The roadie seemed to magically appear whenever he was needed, and like a wizard he conjured up what anyone required. He was active throughout the rigging of the stage and drove the bus, bossed the other roadies around, and

even took his place at the mixing desk when the
bands went on stage to ensure the sound was perfect.
None of the other roadies dared say anything to him,
although I did hear one or two comments behind his
back—something along the lines of him being an
arrogant oink.

It was soon time to get into the bus and go back
to the hotel. We had been in the dressing room for
about an hour since the concert had finished. People
came and went, and I was beginning to feel a little
lightheaded from the excitement and all the wine I
had consumed. We made a rush for the bus outside,
and a few waiting fans screamed as the engine
started and we made our way back to the West End.

Sitting beside Raven, I began to feel really tired.
The bus was quite full now, as we'd taken Will
Hero's band and the other support with us, plus an
array of young girls.

As we piled out of the vehicle and back up to the
ballroom, Raven told me she felt shattered and
needed to go to bed. It was very late, but I wanted to
thank Bill for letting me be a part of this and say
goodnight, so I went to look for him in the crowded
ballroom, but I couldn't see him anywhere. The
party was really taking off, with music playing
loudly, and some of the young girls had coupled up
with various guys here and there. Tracy and Tiger
had gone straight to their room, not wanting to party.
She'd had a little too much red wine, after all, and
was feeling tired.

I noticed that more fast food had arrived whilst
we had been away. There was more pizza, but now

there were also mini-burgers and fries, and a huge
carton filled with donuts glazed with icing of varied
colours. I had just picked up a pink one in a napkin
and gone to sit down on one of the comfortable baby
blue sofas when I saw Brody entered the room. He
had removed his jacket and his black T-shirt was
threatening to rip around his muscular arms. For a
moment he stood in the doorway as if looking for
someone, and seeing me, he made his way over.

Brody sat down as I took a huge bite of my donut,
only to find it was filled with vanilla cream, which
oozed out of my mouth at the sides. He smiled and
simply dabbed his finger in the cream on my lips
and placed it into his mouth. "Mmm, that is good,
but you do know that's just empty calories and not
good for you?" he said.

"I'm too tired and too drunk to care," I answered.
"I shouldn't have had all that wine. I'm beginning to
regret it. So you're American, but where are you
from?"

"California originally, but I have lived in a lot of
places," Brody answered.

"Do you want to taste?" I asked, putting the donut
to his mouth. He bit off a large portion, laughing
when the vanilla cream oozed out again.

"You are very secretive," I said, as I ate another
piece of the donut before popping the last bit into his
mouth. "But I'm beyond asking any decent
questions, so I think I'll just have to give up finding
out why you are here and go to bed."

Brody nodded in amusement as I got up to leave.
My feet were absolutely killing me. I watched

Malcolm and Darren take one particularly drunk young girl with them up the stairs; I assumed to their rooms. If I'd seen something like that at another time, I might have protested, but after what I'd witnessed earlier, I decided that the girl probably knew exactly what she was doing, so I left them to it.

I walked slowly behind them up the stairs. The young girl stopped at intervals, kissing one and then the other before laughing as Malcolm lifted her short skirt and put his hand in her knickers at the back. I didn't want them to see me behind them on the stairs, so I sat down on the soft carpet on a step and removed my ankle boots just as Brody was climbing the stairs towards me.

"Can I help you?" he asked in amusement.

"Yes, please, I'm a bit tired and my feet are hurting," I said, sounding drunk and feeling silly.

Brody glanced up at Malcolm and Darren, and shook his head. "That's okay, I'll help you," he said.

Taking my hand, he walked me up the stairs to the second floor. I had no idea what time it was, but I'm guessing very late. We stopped outside the door of my room and Brody let go of my hand. "So good night, Charlotte, sleep well," he said quietly and his face was close to mine.

"Thank you for helping me, Brody," I replied, not really wanting him to leave.

He moved closer to me and I could smell his aftershave; he smelled clean, and before I knew it his lips were on mine, very lightly and very briefly, and then he was gone. I turned towards the door, my heart pounding as I fiddled with the key card. I put it into the door, and as I was a little drunk and unsteady on my feet, I managed to snap it. Half the key was lodged in the door and the other half still in my hand, and I really needed the toilet.

"Fuck!" I said to myself. I knocked, but Raven didn't wake up.

"Do you always get yourself in trouble?" I heard Brody ask me. He was once again standing behind me.

"I seem to, and I really have to use the bathroom," I said, and then I felt embarrassed because it wasn't something I would normally tell a guy I hardly knew.

Brody glanced at the broken piece of card in my hand and had a quick look at the door, only to find there was no way of removing the plastic that was lodged in the hole.

"Come with me. You can use my bathroom, and I'll go down to reception and get someone to help you get into your room," Brody offered, and I willingly followed him when he took my hand and led me to a door a little further down the hall. Opening it, he indicated for me to go inside. "I'll be right back," he told me and was gone.

Brody's room was much nicer than ours. It had a queen-size bed and a large wardrobe. I went into the bathroom, and when I finished I examined all the stuff he had placed around the sink. There was an aftershave that I smelled and it was really nice, and he had a shower gel in the same range. Walking back into the bedroom, I sat down on the bed, thinking how I'd just rest a little until Brody came back and helped me get back into my room.

I woke up to that same nice scent of aftershave, not understanding where I was to begin with. I was in bed with my clothes on, and my face was lying against something soft and hairy. I opened one eye and couldn't see anything as it was dark, so I tried to sit up, but someone had their arms tightly wrapped around me. I desperately tried to work out where I was and remember what had happened last. Pulling the duvet down a little, I felt the other person stir.

"Where am I?" I asked quietly.

"You were locked out of your room," Brody said, and I suddenly remembered.

"Reception said they can't get someone to fix the door until tomorrow. When I got back up here, you were fast asleep," he continued, pulling me back towards his naked chest.

"Oh God," I gasped, "did we...?"

"Absolutely not," Brody answered. "You are going to have to try a lot harder if you want to get me into bed. I don't put out on the first date."

I got the joke and giggled, nuzzling into his warm chest, as I realised there was nothing I could do about my situation. I could neither rouse Raven nor get into my room. Brody had his arms around me and he kissed the top of my head, and we both fell asleep again tightly wrapped together. It didn't seem weird to be there with him, just nice and cosy, and I felt safe.

I was abruptly reawoken by a bloodcurdling scream, like I had never heard before. It was a wail

that continued on and on, and sounded like it was
coming from further down the hall on the same floor
as us. Brody sat up sharply, suddenly wide awake,
and jumped out of bed as I turned the light on. He
was wearing boxer shorts and nothing else.

Quickly, Brody threw on a T-shirt and some
combat pants that were lying by the dresser, and
opened the door to the hall. I got up and followed
him outside, barefoot. The screaming was much
louder and we both ran towards the sound. It faded,
so we stopped and listened for a couple of seconds
before it started again. The yells were coming from
inside one of the hotel rooms.

Brody banged on the door loudly and lifted his
telephone to his ear to call someone. Still, there was
no response from the room. Other guests had
wandered out into the corridor, wondering what on
earth was going on. Brody took two steps back from
the door, and he was ready to kick it off its hinges
when a sharp voice was heard above the sound of
the screaming and crying: "Don't do that!"

A man came running down the hall carrying a key
card in his hand, and I recognised him as the night
watchman from reception. He hurried over to us and
placed the key card in the door, which clicked open.
Turning, he called out, "Go back to bed,
people—nothing to see here." Then he looked at me
and Brody, and said, "Not you two. Help me."

As the door opened we carefully entered the room
to find a small lamp lighting the bed, on top of
which Tracy was crying hysterically while holding
Tiger's body. She was rocking back and forth, like

she was cradling a baby. Tiger was as white as a sheet. The colour had drained from his skin and I couldn't even see his lips anymore; everything was the same parched grey colour. He was lying, fully clothed, on top of the duvet.

My heart was beating fast as I made my way over to the bed. Brody was feeling Tiger's arm for a pulse while the other man dialled 999. I looked into Brody's eyes and he very briefly shook his head. I glanced at the hand he was holding and noticed that Tiger wasn't wearing his Triple A pass on his wrist, but had been holding it in his hand. It had slipped onto the white duvet cover when Brody checked for a pulse.

I watched in shock as Tracy grieved. It was heart-wrenching to see her hug the dead body of the man she had loved for half a century. Tears streamed down her face and she was chanting, "No, no, no, dear God, please don't take him from me. Please wake up, wake up!"

I started to cry silently. Brody hugged me and held me. The ambulance turned up after a few minutes. I don't know how long we stood there. The medics came into the room and checked Tiger's pulse. Shaking their heads, they headed out again.

"Hey, where are you going?" I shouted at them. "Aren't you going to do anything to help him, for God's sake? Help him, please!" I urged.

"It's too late. He's been dead for a while. I'm sorry. The police have been alerted and they will send someone to pick up the body when they have seen the room."

I couldn't believe it. Tiger, the lovely Tiger, was dead. Tracy was beginning to calm down now and gently held her husband, stroking his face and telling him it was okay. Brody and I stayed with her while the night watchman went down to reception to meet the police when they arrived. On the way out he whispered to Brody not to touch anything, which made him frown. We had already tried to console Tracy and touched almost everything there was to touch in the room.

A few minutes later, two tall, well-built, plain clothes detectives arrived, together with a uniformed female constable. They took our names and contact information, and asked a few general questions. They said it was just in case they needed to contact us later, since they did not yet know the cause of death, but it didn't look suspicious as far as they could tell.

The police had a quick look around the room and then the coroner arrived to take Tiger's body away to the morgue, but Tracy refused to let go of him. They tried to reason with her, but she wasn't listening. Brody had his arm around me and it felt good to snuggle my face into the warmth of his T-shirt and block out the reality of what was happening.

"I'm sorry, but we have to take him now," the two guys from the morgue told Tracy over and over again, after they had taken pictures of the room and of Tiger, thereby giving her a little more time.

"No, I can't leave him. I don't want him to be alone," she answered in anguish through her tears.

Brody and I tried to console her, but there was nothing we could do. Suddenly, Tracy started singing ever so softly the last ballad that The Sticks had played that night: "If I die and have to leave you, see me through until the end…" And that was exactly what she was doing.

Chapter 7
Hornsey Coroner's Court

What happened after Tiger died is a blur. I made my way back to my room and finally managed to wake Raven after knocking loudly for a few minutes. She had been wearing her earplugs because of the disturbance from the after-party, and she became very upset when I told her the bad news.

I had not slept more than a couple of hours that night, so the drive home was a nightmare. When I arrived back, I slept for fourteen hours non-stop. It felt surreal to be back in my old room, as if nothing had happened. I had a lot of unanswered questions and endless thoughts spinning in my head, giving me a headache.

Tiger had died suddenly at the age of seventy-two. He had not appeared to be ill or complained about anything, as far as I knew, but I suppose you can suddenly die at that age. Perhaps his heart stopped. Well, obviously it did, but what made it stop? And why did Bill Graham need a bodyguard? There was no doubt in my mind that was what Brody was. Why else would he follow Bill around like he did?

***

It was a little over a week since Tiger's death, and I was having coffee with Mum and Blue in the kitchen when my grandma made me aware of a small article in the local newspaper. The headline

read, 'Drug addict overdosed. Police investigate
death of Sticks' bassist.' It was well documented
that Tiger had been a druggie, but that was many
years ago. He couldn't have overdosed; it was
impossible. The article went on:

The Hornsey North London Coroner's Office has
demanded an autopsy and investigation into the
death of former bass player with The Sticks, Alfred
'Tiger' Edwards.
Edwards was found dead by his wife, Tracy
Edwards, after The Sticks' sold-out concert at the
Roundhouse, Camden last week. The police have
issued a statement saying the cause of death was an
overdose of morphine and alcohol, and they are
treating the death as suspicious. The inquest into
Edwards' death will be held at Hornsey Coroner's
Court on Monday, the 5th of August.

I was speechless and totally shocked at what I
read. Passing the newspaper back to Grandma Blue,
I went up to my room to think.

I did not have a contact for Tracy, and I had no
idea whether the investigation would be a closed-
door case, meaning that only people invited to attend
the inquest would be allowed in, but I decided I
should be there. I'd sent Bill a message on Facebook
earlier in the week since I did not have his phone
number, but I hadn't received a reply. As far as I
could tell there had been hundreds of condolence
messages on Bill's wall, but none that he had posted.

A short statement had appeared in the national press from Malcolm, saying the current Sticks tour was cancelled, and asking that the press leave the other band members in peace to grieve for their friend, but nothing as yet about an overdose.

I refused to believe it. It made me angry that people were saying this about Tiger, who didn't even touch a drop of alcohol at the gig. Tracy was the one who had been drinking, and rather a lot of red wine, but not him.

***

I drove down to Hornsey on the day of the inquest and parked close to the red brick building that housed the coroner's court and the morgue. There was a crowd of people outside and a guard on the door checking IDs, so I guessed it was a closed-door case and that I wouldn't be allowed in. I watched as Bill Graham arrived to massive press attention, together with Brody. I felt my heart beat a little faster when I saw the broad back of the bodyguard. He turned and glanced around before entering the building as I ducked down in the driver's seat of my car, hoping he had not spotted me.

Soon, Tracy arrived and the press went crazy, shouting questions at her and taking photos. She looked pale and tired, and a lot older than she had appeared to be a week ago. Tracy turned and looked straight at me with a blank expression before entering the court.

I sat in the car for hours, waiting for them to finish, feeling unsure of what I would do, or what I

141

was doing there in the first place. I must have fallen asleep, because I jumped when someone banged on the window of my car and opened the door. It was Brody.

"What are you doing here?" he asked as he sat down in the passenger seat. "Are you okay?"

"I wanted to go to the inquest, but I can't. I don't know what to do," I answered sheepishly. "Have they come to a conclusion?" I asked, looking closely at his face. He looked strained and tired.

"They are not finished yet. There have been a lot of unanswered questions and they've called Tracy back in to explain herself for the second time tomorrow," Brody replied.

"Why?"

"Well, because the doctor who did the autopsy, Dr David Johnson, told the court that Tiger had died from an overdose of alcohol and morphine, but no equipment for administering drugs was found in the room," Brody explained, "and there was no alcohol either. First they thought Tiger had taken an overdose whilst drunk. Perhaps he got his dosage wrong? The doctor said he would have been unconscious within a few minutes of taking the drug."

I studied Brody's face as he talked and felt a longing in the pit of my stomach to touch it, but I couldn't. The intimate feeling I'd had when I slept in his bed had gone and he would probably think me weird.

"So it was assumed it was death by misadventure," he continued, "right up until the

142

point when the police witness said none of the drug
equipment you'd normally expect to find when an
addict overdosed was in the room and there was no
alcohol. Everything in the mini-bar was intact. Tracy
doesn't believe it. She says they went to bed and
she's adamant that Tiger would never drink or take
any drug. Tracy said they went to bed after she'd
had a bit too much wine. She fell asleep and when
she woke up, just before 5 a.m., he wasn't breathing.
So they have called her back."

"Why are you there?" I asked, looking him
straight in the eyes. I wanted to see if he was going
to lie to me.

"I can't tell you that," he answered softly.

"Okay, I will make a wild guess and say that Bill,
or perhaps Malcolm, hired you to be his bodyguard.
Now Bill is a big pop star, but he would only need
help during the concerts if it was just for his general
protection. You seem to be around him all the time,
even when I did the interview with him at his own
restaurant, so that leads me to believe that he needs
protection from something or someone. But I'm
wracking my brain trying to work out who, or why,"
I said.

Brody did not look at me, but just sat there
staring straight ahead. "I would like to tell you
everything, but I am not at liberty to talk about any
of this. It isn't that I don't trust you, but I can't," he
answered sadly.

"Okay," I replied whilst I took a piece of paper
out of my handbag and I wrote my mobile phone

number on it. "Can you please give this to Tracy and say I need to talk to her?"

Brody took the slip of paper I handed to him and placed it in his pocket. Slowly, he opened the car door and got out. "Have a safe drive back to Sussex," he told me, and I flinched.

Of course, if he had asked Bill about me, he would have been told about my husband who had helped him to invest, or he might have overheard Bill and me talking while I interviewed him.

"I don't live in Sussex any more. It didn't work out, so I'm back with my parents. I left several weeks ago," I explained as he closed the door.

I waved to him and started my drive back home. My head was spinning. Would Brody have acted differently towards me if he didn't think I was married? Then I started thinking about Tracy and I knew I had to try to help her. There was something wrong with this whole situation, but I could not put my finger on what it was. I was sure it was staring me in the face, but I just couldn't see it. I didn't get it at all. Reaching for my cell phone, I put it on speaker and dialled.

"Blue!" Grandma answered briskly, and I could hear her panting, so I guessed she was either jogging or doing more of her power walking.

"Hi, Grandma Blue, it's Charlie. I need a favour. Is there any chance you could invite Rich over for a chat as soon as possible?" I asked.

"Why, you're not getting a habit are you?" Grandma wheezed as she spoke; it was definitely more jogging breathing than power walking. She sounded like a donkey with asthma again.

"No, definitely not, but I need to ask him some stuff. Pick his brain about his field of expertise," I explained.

"Okay, I'm sure he'll help you if we feed him. Men need an incentive and food is as good as any," she answered and we hung up.

A few minutes later my phone rang again and it was Tracy. "Hello, Charlie, Brody said you wanted me to call," she said in a strained voice.

"Yes, hi, I hope you are feeling better. I am so sorry about Tiger. How are you coping?" I asked.

"I'm taking things one day at a time. I don't believe Tiger took any drugs. He wouldn't, but the doctor has no reason to lie. I just got so angry about it all, because it isn't making any sense," Tracy answered. "Why would he get drunk and take heroin after all the years he'd been clean? I can't sleep. I have all these thoughts going around in my mind, trying to make sense of it all. Where would Tiger have got heroin from? He was with me all the time."

"I have the same feelings as you do, Tracy," I admitted. "Something is wrong about this, and I'd like to try and help you find out what. Perhaps a fresh pair of eyes will make things a little clearer. I'm on my way back home, but I can come down to London again in a couple of days. Perhaps we can meet and try to make some sense of this?" I asked, hopefully.

"Yes, Charlie, I would like that very much. I can let you have a copy of the autopsy report if you like," Tracy responded. "I'll email it and you can see if you can make any sense of it, because I can't."

I accepted, gave her my email address and we hung up.

At around 4 p.m., I got back home to find Dad asleep in his favourite chair, pretending to watch TV. I put my head around the door as I was taking my shoes off to see Mum and Blue in the kitchen making dinner. Grandma was wearing Raven's top with the words 'Shut the Fuck Up!' sprawled across her tiny chest. The smell of dinner had hit me as soon as I opened the front door of the house, making me feel starving hungry. I suddenly realised that I hadn't eaten all day. No wonder I was feeling lightheaded.

"Hey, Charlie, I've borrowed this T-shirt from you—I didn't know you had cool clothes," Grandma Blue shouted to me over the noise of clattering pans. "I think I might change styles now and get myself one of those Mahicans. I think it would suit me, so I'm going to go puck for a while."

"That's not my T-shirt. I borrowed it from a friend and I'm sure she'll want it back soon. And it's called a Mohican. A Mahican is a Native American Indian tribe and it's called punk, not puck," I answered, laughing at her mistakes.

"Oh right. Then I might have a go at this punk stuff," said Blue. "I'm starting to feel all badass and dangerous. Jogging isn't really doing it for me anymore. Doris Warnes has stopped, saying she can't be bothered, so it's just me and Jean. She's so fat she's holding me back; she can't run as fast as me and she's cramping my style."

Dinner was not quite ready, so I went to my room to check my messages. It had been almost two weeks since Robert Warnes had driven past our house and vaguely asked me out to lunch, and yet I had not heard from him, so I was beginning to think he didn't want to see me. Now I could see a short message on Facebook from him, asking me if I was available for lunch on Wednesday, along with his mobile number.

I could not muster up any excitement over the prospect of seeing Robert at all. As I couldn't think what to write back, I left it, thinking I would answer later. I checked my email and, true to her word, Tracy had sent me the autopsy report. I had a quick skim through and realised I would need help, because I couldn't make any sense of it at all.

I printed out the report and took it downstairs with me. Rich, Grandma's dealer, had arrived. He was probably wondering why he was so popular with us as to be invited back for dinner on a Monday night. The man was wearing the same worn-out suit as last time with a little gravy stain on the front, but he didn't seem to notice.

Mum had done herself proud as usual and we gathered around the table in the dining-room, where she had placed a large meat and stout pie, served with an assortment of vegetables from our garden. We all tucked in eagerly.

"Dad, I need help with some medical stuff. Someone I know has died, but I can't understand what he died of. Can you help?" I asked and he nodded as his mouth was full of pie.

I handed him the printout over the table. "The autopsy report says he had a blood alcohol level of 199 milligrams per decilitre. How much is that really?" I asked.

Dad nodded again, knowingly. "That is a lot, Charlie. Between 80 and 199 milligrams per decilitre of blood is regarded as binge drinking. You know, when someone knocks back their drinks quickly and becomes really drunk very fast," Dad answered.

"But exactly how drunk would a person with that sort of alcohol level be? Would another person notice?" I questioned. "What I mean is could a person with that sort of alcohol level in his blood be able to hide the fact?"

"No, definitely not," Dad said. "He would be suffering from ataxia, which means he wouldn't have much muscle coordination. A level of 199 milligrams means you're on the verge of throwing up and passing out."

"Totally pissed then is what you are trying to say," Grandma Blue suggested, and she and Rich smiled at one another as my mother rolled her eyes.

"Who is this person you are talking about? Is it the guy in the newspaper, that Tiger fellow?" Grandma asked.

"Yes, the thing is Tiger was a heroin addict, but that was over thirty years ago. His wife swears he was clean and serene. He didn't drink or do drugs, and hadn't done so for thirty years, so that's why it

148

is strange that the report says he was drunk and had overdosed on morphine. Isn't that a strong painkiller they use in hospital?" I asked my father again.

He was just about to answer when Rich answered instead. "What does it say he took on there?"

"It says morphine: 0.8 milligrams per litre blood," Dad answered.

"They mean heroin. It's known as diamorphine in medical terms. Heroin is one of the most powerful known painkillers around, and much more powerful than morphine. I don't know much about doses, but that sounds like a lot," Rich said, and my father raised his eyebrows.

"Rich has this field of expertise, Dad. He has an interest in drugs and how they affect people. It's a hobby, right, Rich?" I lied, and Rich nodded.

Dad continued, "Well, I know for a fact that 0.8 milligrams of morphine per litre blood is very high; in fact 0.5 is considered fatal, so it looks like this friend of yours might not only have overdosed, but done it on purpose. If he was an addict earlier, he would not have taken that much, because he'd know it's lethal. This doesn't sound like a case of him getting the dosage wrong, because he's been away from it for a long time. It sounds like suicide to me," Dad concluded.

"There is something very wrong about this. I don't believe Tiger would take drugs. He had been strong for so long," I answered thoughtfully.

"It can happen, Charlie," said Rich. "Actually, I've seen it a number of times where someone has a little relapse and takes too much, because they don't realise the fact they've been clean for a while makes them less tolerant of the drug. But in this case I have to agree with your father. No addict would take that amount of heroin if he wasn't intentionally trying to kill himself."

"So there is no way it could have been an accident?" I asked him. "Perhaps the heroin was stronger than usual?"

"Heroin in its pure form is a white powder. The usual stuff that's sold on the street will be anything from dark brown to grey. Any addict who sees heroin that's pure white will be alerted to the fact that it isn't diluted, but pure. Of course, Tiger might have been too drunk to think about the colour, but it's doubtful," Rich explained.

"How do people take heroin?" I asked. "I tend to think of it being injected, but can it be taken any other way, say eaten or smoked, perhaps? I'm wondering whether he could have been given heroin without knowing it."

"No, heroin is rarely smoked. It's an expensive drug and the effect would go up in smoke, so to speak. It can be smoked by heating the heroin in some foil and breathing in the fumes, I suppose. It doesn't dissolve easily, so usually it has to be dissolved in a spoon with water and heated up. Some people filter it through cotton or even cigarette filters before they inject it," Rich answered.

"So, let's say Tiger relapsed and for some reason drank a lot of alcohol, and then, being totally blind drunk, he decides to put a deadly amount of heroin into his arm. How long would it take from the drug entering his body until he was unconscious?" I asked.

"It depends on where he injected it: intravenously or intra-muscularly," Dad replied, and once again he studied the autopsy report on the table beside his plate. "It says it was intravenously injected, so the effect would have been rapid, because the drug enters the bloodstream and reaches the brain quickly. With that amount of heroin he would have been unconscious within a couple of minutes. Actually, he would have been dead within a couple of minutes in my opinion. Heroin slows down the system and the heart rate," he added.

I thought for a second. "Okay, so let's say, for the sake of argument, that Tiger fooled us all and was secretly planning on taking his own life. He would've had to get the drugs somehow, and hide both them and the alcohol from his wife. She says he never left her side all day, but I suppose someone else could have supplied him with the drug."

"So, here's this guy who is totally in love with his wife for fifty years, and off drugs and alcohol for thirty of them. Then he is asked back to the band he played with thirty years ago, which he loved, and they have a new album out and are going on tour, and he suddenly fools everyone and decides to kill himself. Can you see why it doesn't make sense?" I asked.

After pausing for a second, I continued, "Tiger was seemingly happy and upbeat, but let's say he managed to fool everybody that he was okay, bought the alcohol and drugs, and took his own life. Two things are worrying me about all this. The first thing is how could someone so totally off their head drunk manage to prepare the drug and inject himself? And, secondly, after having injected such a huge amount of heroin into his body, how could Tiger have got rid of the equipment before he became unconscious? I was one of the first people to walk into that room after Tracy found Tiger dead, and there was no drug equipment or alcohol that I could see."

"And Brody, Bill's bodyguard, told me today that the police have witnessed to there not being anything in the room that you would expect to find if an addict overdosed, and no evidence of there ever having been alcohol there," I concluded.

Mum suddenly joined the conversation, and I could see that she was starting to find it interesting. "It looks like perhaps he had some help injecting the drug and then someone hid the equipment," she suggested. "Could it have been his wife?"

Grandma Blue nodded. "I've read about that sort of thing happening. The wife helps the man die because he has some illness or something."

Dad looked at the autopsy report again and told us, "Well, there is no mention of any potentially fatal diseases."

"Tracy was totally devoted to Tiger, in my opinion, as he was to her," I pointed out. "She said she woke up to find him dead. He was in bed with her, and she was so distressed that there is no way, I believe, that she could have assisted him in a suicide or hidden any drugs. What I did think strange was the fact that she had gotten undressed and gone to bed, but Tiger was still dressed in his jeans and T-shirt and was lying on top of the duvet."

"That's strange," Dad commented. "He had traces of cannabis and diazepam in his blood."

"What's diazepam?" I asked him. "I never saw Tiger with cannabis."

"Diazepam is a benzodiazepine type of sedative," he explained. "It's used to treat a lot of different problems, but mainly anxiety associated with depression, panic disorders, seizures and muscle spasms. Valium and Xanax are probably the best known. As a doctor, I would never prescribe diazepam to anyone who had a drug problem, because of their addictive nature." He looked more closely at the autopsy report and scratched his nose.

"Well, that depends what information the doctor had about the patient," Rich suggested. "Certain people can be very clever and devious when it comes to their addictions. A person I've known for a few years is now a full-blown heroin addict, but even his closest family don't know about it. He is a successful banker in the city and was first using cocaine, but he moved on to heroin three years ago. Not even his wife and mistress know.

"What you have to realise is that it's not okay to be a heroin addict. It is frowned upon, even in the music industry, where drug use is rife, so the people who find themselves addicted keep it a secret. They find different ways of hiding it. There are certain places I know where people can go and jack up and be themselves, but mostly they are terrified of being found out."

"You've got us interested now, Charlotte," Mum said with a smile.

I had to agree that it had been a long time since the family had engaged in this much conversation around the dinner table. I quite liked it.

"Tracy told the police that Tiger didn't leave the room once they got there," I told everyone. "She said she'd had too much wine, and was feeling a little drunk and very tired, so they went straight up to their room as soon as we got back to the hotel after the concert. It was around midnight, I think. The band went on stage at 10 p.m. and the concert didn't last more than an hour or seventy-five minutes. Then we waited a little while backstage, because they didn't want to risk the fans getting in the way of the bus. We were back at the hotel sometime between midnight and 1 a.m. And we heard Tracy scream at about 5 a.m.," I added.

Mum who had been tidying up, appeared from the kitchen with a large apple crumble and a jug of custard, followed by Grandma Blue carrying some dessert plates. I was totally full up, but I could never turn down my mother's apple crumble, so I was glad for my calorie burning skills. Going by the size of Rich's belly, I would say he wasn't as lucky as me.

"I didn't see Tiger smoke any cannabis either," I carried on, after tasting some of the small amount of pie and custard I had put on my plate. "The manager, Malcolm, did though. A lot! He was asking for 'green stuff' from his assistant, and as soon as he got it, he had a spliff in his hand

154

continuously all night. I really didn't like him.
Anyway, I never saw Tiger with a spliff."

"Well, you wouldn't necessarily have seen him
smoking the cannabis because that is something he
could very well have eaten," Rich replied over his
huge helping of dessert. "Nobody has ever made a
better apple crumble than this, Mrs Hart. It is the
best I have ever tasted."

Grandma Blue actually giggled. "It's an old
recipe from my mother," she revealed.

I had tried her apple crumble in the past and it
tasted nothing like this one. Perhaps Mum had
perfected the recipe. "Could someone have given
Tiger something containing cannabis without him
noticing?" I asked Rich.

"Oh yes, absolutely. A hippy friend of mine
makes hash brownies; very tasty, but very potent,"
he replied. He then blushed a little when Dad raised
an eyebrow and Grandma Blue kicked him under the
table.

"This is getting stranger and stranger," I
observed. "I know what a person who has taken
cannabis looks like, because I watched Malcolm.
There was no sign of Tiger being the least bit high at
the concert; he was fine. So, he has cannabis and a
sedative, and then gets blind drunk before killing
himself with heroin, but manages to get rid of the
drug equipment, and any alcohol or empty bottles
before he dies. The police have searched that room,
and other areas on that floor and the one above, and
there was nothing."

"Are you suggesting someone other than Tiger killed Tiger?" Grandma Blue asked me.

I shrugged. "I don't know. It does look like he wasn't alone though."

"Perhaps the cannabis and diazepam was Tiger's way of numbing himself to the fact that he was going to kill himself. Then he had to drink a lot to get the courage to do the heroin," Dad suggested.

"Okay, but that doesn't explain who hid the drug equipment because somebody must have. It can't have been Tiger himself," said Mum, glancing at me. "You said Tracy was too distraught to have been able to clean up something like that. Besides, what would be the point? If he'd overdosed, the doctors would find it out in the autopsy and it would be seen as death by misadventure. So it wouldn't be in his wife's interest to remove the equipment, if she did indeed help him to inject or even kill him. That just leaves one alternative: someone else was with him when he took the heroin."

"That someone removed the drug equipment and alcohol for some reason, and they would have to have had access to his room. This person seems to have gone to a lot of trouble, and it looks like they might have either assisted his suicide or even killed him," she added, and everyone in the room went silent.

Chapter 8
Tracy

Early on Wednesday morning, I drove down to London, having been invited to attend the last closing statements of the inquiry into Tiger's death by the coroner's office at the request of Tracy, for moral and emotional support.

Tracy and I had agreed on me being there with her, and that we would go somewhere for a chat afterwards. I was anxious to hear what the verdict would be and whether they had made more sense of it than I had so far. I entered the building, having pressed myself through a crowd of press photographers and journalists, though not causing much interest.

Bill Graham's black sedan limousine stopped briefly by the pavement behind me, and the press surged forward to get photos of him leaving the car, closely followed by Brody, as the driver sped away from the kerb.

Inside, the court turned out to be a rather small room with a few rows of wooden pews with red leather seats, an elevated witness box and a place where the coroner sat. After giving Tracy a hug, I sat down next to her and we waited for the coroner to arrive. Bill took the pew behind us and gave us both a warm hug, as did Brody. They were sombrely dressed in dark suits.

The room was not as crowded as I had expected. There were representatives from the police, as I recognised the two officers who had been at the hotel. Neither of the other two Sticks members nor any of the roadies were present. In fact there were very few people present at all, and I realised that I knew very little about Tiger and his family. The coroner, Dr Francis Crompton, arrived and took his place at the elevated seat at the front. Tracy grabbed my hand.

"At the inquest into the death of Alfred Edwards, the following conclusions have been made: it must follow from the medical evidence that this man had a fix of heroin. The absence of any evidence to indicate when this was taken, and the absence of any evidence such as a syringe or other material for drug abuse, leaves some enormous unanswered questions." Dr Crompton said solemnly.

"Initially, this was perfectly straightforward. A man who had been a heroin abuser while under stress took a fix that proved to be fatal. There is, however, no evidence at all to support a finding that his death was due to misadventure. The gaps in the evidence leave me to record the only possible finding in this matter, which is an open verdict."

"Let me explain to you what this means. An open verdict in this inquest is when the evidence is insufficient to deliver one of the specific verdicts: natural causes, unlawful killing, suicide, accidental death or death due to industrial disease. However, if new evidence becomes available at any time, the inquest can be reopened. All of the above-mentioned

verdicts have to be established to the test within
the balance of probabilities, except for suicide and
unlawful killing, which have to be proven beyond a
reasonable doubt." He added.

"It has been stated that there was no evidence in
the hotel room of any equipment to administer
drugs, such as syringes or other material you would
expect to find if a person overdosed and became
unconscious within minutes of administering the
drug. It has also been stated that there was no
evidence of alcohol in the room either. So, even if
this court concluded that there was a reasonable
doubt as to what happened on the night that Mr
Edwards passed away, there is no evidence to prove
it. Therefore, an open verdict is the only option left
to us, so that this case can be reopened should new
evidence or newer technology lead to the need for
further inspection into what happened that night."

Tracy and I made our way out of the court,
together with Bill and Brody. We stood outside in
the hall for a while, trying to take it all in. If I had
expected closure into what happened to Tiger, I was
obviously not going to get it through forensic
evidence or police investigation.

Thinking back to when the police had questioned
us briefly at the Palace Hotel that night, I
remembered how they did ask if I had seen Tiger
take any drugs or whether he had been drinking
heavily. I felt they were just going through the
motions of investigating the death of a pop star.
They seemed to assume he was both a junkie and an
alcoholic because of the line of business he was in,

and because it was a well-documented fact that he had been an addict earlier. I had learned a lesson lately of not judging a book by its cover, and I was pleased the coroner didn't write off his death as quickly.

As the two police officers entered the hall, I strode over to them and introduced myself, in case they did not recognise me from the hotel. The older man, perhaps in his mid-fifties, smiled at me and shook my hand warmly.

"What will happen with this case now? Will there be any further investigation into what happened?" I asked as I greeted the other police officer, who was younger, perhaps in his early thirties.

"This case is a non-starter, I'm afraid," the older officer replied. "I think there is more to this than meets the eye, but since certain people are sticking to their story there is nothing we can do until we get new evidence or a lead."

Both officers were looking in Tracy's direction, as if she was a suspect.

"I doubt very much that Tracy had anything to do with what happened to Tiger, so what you are saying is that you are going to do nothing?" I asked heatedly.

The older officer took a card out of his wallet and handed it to me. "Well, if you find out anything or something turns up that you think might help then feel free to give us a call because, like the coroner says, there is no evidence of anything. Without that we are stuck."

I glanced at the card, which read Detective Inspector Jack Baldwin.

"I'm a huge Sticks fan. I can't believe I'm standing here a few yards from Bill Graham," he said, surprisingly. "I'd like nothing more than to put away whoever helped Tiger to shoot up or tampered with the evidence by removing the equipment. But there is nothing I can do, and no way forward in this investigation. Doing anything now would be like pissing in my pants to keep warm—totally useless. So, little lady, should you hear anything, give us a shout." With that the detective inspector left, closely followed by his assistant. I placed the card into my handbag for safe keeping.

It was time for Bill to leave too. He hugged Tracy and wished her well, and they spoke about the funeral, which was to be held at the weekend. It had been delayed due to the morgue not releasing Tiger's body until they had finished the inquest. I stood with Brody as they talked and made plans.

"How are you doing?" he asked me.

"Yeah, I'm okay," I answered. "My father is a doctor, and I got him and a drug-dealer friend to explain the autopsy report to me."

Brody raised an eyebrow.

"Don't ask!" I said, smiling. "Anyway, I think that verdict was the only correct one to make. There is something fishy about all this, and I think I'm going to see if I can find out more about it."

"I think it was correct too, but I don't think it's wise for you to go messing around with people in the drug world. There are some very dangerous people out there and there is big money at stake. They don't like it when people start asking questions," he warned in a serious voice while looking at me with concern.

Brody obviously thought that Rich was one of those drug barons whose cage I'd rattled. His concern was heart-warming. As Bill started to end his conversation with Tracy, Brody turned towards me and said softly, "I kept your mobile number. Can I call you?"

I blushed. "Of course," I replied, instantly blushing again, and he leaned in and kissed me squarely on the mouth. It was just a fleeting kiss, but it was so warm and soft that it made my face turn even redder, if that was at all possible.

Bill looked very surprised by Brody's action, but he didn't comment. We said our goodbyes, and as Tracy and I made our way towards my car, I suddenly realised that I hadn't told Bill about my separation from James yet. He probably thought me a right slag, flirting with his bodyguard like that. I would have to tell him as soon as possible.

I drove Tracy into central London and parked in Kensington, outside a gastro pub aptly named HMV (his master's voice). It was quiet inside as it was early, just before mid-day. We took a table by the window, overlooking a quiet road just off Kensington High Street. We ordered lunch from the menu and made small talk whilst we waited for our food to be served.

"So you and Brody seem to like each other,"
Tracy remarked. "He's a very nice man, but I don't
think he is being honest about who, or what, he is."

"Yeah, I really like him, but I don't know him.
He won't tell me if he was hired as Bill's bodyguard
or anything much about himself. It's all very
secretive," I answered.

Tracy didn't reply as our food and drinks arrived,
but when the waiter was far enough away from the
table so as not to overhear us, she leaned in and told
me, "Well, I can tell you all about that. He might not
be able to talk about it, but no one has asked me to
keep it a secret, so I have no problem talking about it
with you, as long as you promise to keep it to
yourself. This is one of those times when we are off
the record. Agreed?"

I had already forgotten my job as a journalist.
Although I'd written my gig review for Melody,
which was short and to the point, she had sent it
back to me to add more details twice, thinking it a
little thin. She also wanted me to write about finding
Tiger, but I refused. She added her own footnote to
the article wishing her condolences to his wife and
family, which I though was nice, but I realised I had
neither the instinct nor drive to be a good journalist.

"Brody is on Malcolm's payroll. Bill has refused
to set foot in England since 1983, when his wife
died. As far as I know, he was threatened, and he
must have taken it pretty seriously to leave like that.
I'm guessing the threats have been ongoing, because
why else would he need protection now, so many
years later? There are actually three bodyguards who

work around the clock, all hired by Malcolm and all ex-US Navy SEALs. Tiger told me he'd heard Malcolm and Darren talking about them. Darren was scared of them, mostly of Brody, as far as I've gathered," Tracy explained.

"Why is Darren scared of Brody?" I asked. "Brody is such a sweet and caring person."

I remembered Malcolm saying that Darren was scared of Brody earlier at the soundcheck. It felt like years ago that we had been at the Roundhouse; so much had happened.

"What I got from Tiger was that Darren had tried to boss the bodyguards around and he tried to send one of them off to pick up some gear from him. That didn't sit well with the guys and Brody told him, in no uncertain terms, how he felt about being asked to do things like that. Also I think he read the riot act to him about his arrogance and mistaking the bodyguards for being his personal servants. It didn't sit well with Darren. I'm not sure exactly what Brody threatened to do to Darren should he keep up this behaviour, but Tiger said it did the trick, because Darren avoided Brody after that," Tracy explained with a smile.

I was pleased to hear that Brody wouldn't let anyone treat him or his team like lackies and actually had the guts to stand up for himself, instead of going to Bill or Malcolm about it. So that was another thing I liked about him.

"So what happened back then to make Bill open to threats?" I asked.

"I don't know what you've heard, but it's a complicated story. Bill was married to a French ex-model called Delphine. They had barely been married a couple of years when he found out she was using all sorts of drugs, supplied by her best friend, a woman called Simone Labyre. I know about this because she also supplied me and Tiger at the time. She was a pretty lady and butter wouldn't melt, but inside she was a ruthless drug baroness," Tracy said.

"I guess Bill was devastated when Delphine died?"

"No, I'm sure he was upset, but the word back then was that Bill wanted to get a divorce. He'd just had a top ten hit and a new album out, and Delphine was becoming a liability—a shackle around his ankle, if you will. Bill was trying to create a wholesome image and didn't want to be associated with anything in the line of drugs. That's why he fired Tiger the night Delphine died," Tracy added.

"Wow, he fired him? I'm guessing it was because of the drugs?" I asked.

"Yes, and quite rightly so," Tracy replied. "Tiger was going on stage high and playing off key. He was embarrassing himself and the rest of the band. They wanted to take their fame and fortune as far as they possibly could, and Tiger was ruining it for them. He knew he had to choose between heroin and music. You either come off it or you die. Bill had said he could come back if he got himself cleaned up. It was the driving force behind Tiger's recovery; that he would one day once again take his rightful place on stage with Bill and The Sticks, besides almost dying from an overdose shortly after. Can you see why it doesn't make sense that when it all finally happened, he fell off the wagon and topped himself?" Tracy asked.

I nodded. "Yes, I see what you mean. Are you sure he didn't take anything at all that night?" I questioned, choosing my words carefully.

"If I am honest, I have my doubts about a couple of things now," Tracy admitted. "I know he was clean and sober right up to the point that we entered our hotel room. He was so geared up to be playing with Bill again, and I thought he seemed a little tired too. Like he was thoughtful, instead of his old chatty self, but I was too tired to pay much attention to it."

"We'd taken a couple more bits of sushi up to the room with us for a snack and a couple of those donuts and some brownies, but I didn't eat any more fish. I couldn't stay awake. It actually felt like I passed out. I usually get tired when drinking red wine, but that night I was extremely so. I fell asleep on the bed after eating half a donut. Can you remember, when you found me in the room, did you see any food?"

"No, there was nothing there. I can't remember there being any brownies downstairs either. The police asked Brody and me whether we had seen any drugs or drink, and I remember it well. There was nothing. I would have remembered it," I answered. "Could Tiger have decided to go out after you fell asleep? Perhaps he was afraid the sushi would smell and wanted to throw it away. Is it possible he left when you were sleeping?"

"On that dreadful morning Tiger died when I woke up, before I knew it was a drug and alcohol overdose, I would have said there was no chance. But now, with hindsight, I think that's what happened. I felt unwell when I woke up—groggy and sick. I put it down to the fact that I'd just had a huge shock. I'd lost my husband and best friend, and the drink from the previous night made me a little hung over. They took me to hospital after they had taken Tiger's body away, but they didn't take any blood samples from me. I was admitted for rest and they let me go home the next day."

"Oh my God, do you think you were drugged?" I gasped, as if the thought hadn't crossed my mind before when really I had been thinking along those lines for a couple of days since talking to Dad and Rich.

"I will never know," she answered.

"Let's go back to 1983. I haven't heard much about Delphine and how she died. I think I read there was some sort of scandal?" I queried.

"Yes, Delphine was found in bed with a young Australian model by the maid. They had both overdosed on heroin," Tracy recalled. "It wasn't a big deal or unusual in the industry to have little flings. There were groupies all over, both male and female. It would hurt Bill's career up to a point, but it was hardly going to turn his fans against him. That's why his reaction to the whole thing was so strange, and out of character."

"They had a hearing into the deaths, much the same as Tiger's, and came to the conclusion that it was death by misadventure, but, strangely enough, they found no drug equipment back then either. There was a big argument over whether the maid had removed it, but she said she didn't touch anything. So the case was left open, like this one," she added.

Tracy had gotten me interested now. What were the chances that those deaths and Tigers were somehow connected?

"That's a strange coincidence, don't you think? We should try to find this Simone, the dealer, and see what she's been up to for the last thirty years, and find out whether she might have been in London on the night of the concert," I suggested, feeling very much the detective.

After paying our bill, Tracy and I walked out into the sunny afternoon. We agreed to stay in touch and keep each other in the loop regarding any developments. Then we hugged once more before I set off on the long drive back home. This was a journey I found myself taking rather a lot lately and it wouldn't be the last. I had Tiger's funeral to get through in a few days' time.

Chapter 9
The One That Got Away

I searched Google for hours, trying to find out more about what had happened back in 1983. I phoned one of the big London tabloid newspapers and spoke to a very nice lady in the archives department, who promised to look into it for me. She told me she would have to search the old editions that were in storage since their computer systems did not go back further than 1985. After leaving my mobile number and email address with her, I logged back on to the internet to search for information on Delphine and Simone. There was not much there.

I had already checked Bill Graham's listing on Wikipedia and read all I could find about the other band members. I had no real interest in Ronnie, the guitarist, since he only joined earlier this year, but I looked through what I could find anyway just to make sure I didn't miss anything, but nothing interesting turned up.

Still working away in my room, I was suddenly disturbed by my mobile. "Charlie here," I answered, still reading online.

"Why are you not answering my invitation to lunch? Have I offended you?" Robert Warnes asked.

As I had not given him my mobile number, I was guessing that he'd got it from Camilla since it was unlisted. James had insisted we have numbers that were only available to our friends.

"Hi Robert, I am sorry. No, of course you haven't. I've just been very busy lately," I answered, and my attention was no longer on the screen in front of me.

"Well, everyone has to eat, so will you let me take you to lunch?"

"What day did you have in mind? Like I said, I'm really up to my ears in work, and I have to go to London again soon," I answered, noticing that I sounded more disinterested than I actually was.

"How about now?" Robert suggested. "I'm parked out front and I reserved a table for two at Zini's on the off chance you'd agree."

I smiled at his eagerness to see me, although I was unsure how I felt about it now. I'd been very distracted lately to the point of feeling almost cured of my nymphomania. For days I hadn't even ogled the postman. I was too caught up in what had happened to Tiger. But I was feeling a little hungry.

Mum was shopping, Dad was driving his taxi and Grandma Blue was out with her friends, so there was the option between sandwiches in the kitchen on my own or a nice chat with a gorgeous guy at a lovely restaurant with nice food. I needed a break, come to think of it, but I felt awkward going out alone with Robert.

I realised that I had not seen him on my own since Camilla and Peter's wedding. Robert had been best man and I the matron of honour. We had shared a kiss that night in the garden after rather a lot of champagne. I still blush when I think about it, because if we hadn't been disturbed by Robert's

170

father, I don't know what would have happened. I know what I wanted to happen at the time, but, of course, the timing was wrong.

It was a kiss that represented years of stored-up passion and longing on my behalf, and it felt like it was mutual. Then we heard Robert's father lighting up a cigarette behind us and we jumped apart. I spent the rest of the party avoiding him, because I felt dreadfully embarrassed. It was all a bit silly really and nothing ever came of it. That was not because I didn't want it to, but because he never called me.

A few months later, I heard that Robert was seeing some foreign intern at Warner Group and that it was serious. So I got over it. It took some time and I felt heartache, but the last thing I wanted to do was go back to torturing myself over whether he would call me, if he perhaps thought I was a bit too keen, or whether our kiss had meant anything to him at all. I finally realised it probably hadn't and that he had simply moved on to the next person.

I looked out of the window and there he was in his black jaguar, parked outside our gate. He waved to me and I waved back, feeling a lot of those old feelings coming back, like a dull ache in my chest. If I was going to see Robert, I would have to play it very cool and not let myself get too carried away, or let him get too close to me. The last thing I wanted was to get hurt again, I thought, as I scrambled to find a dress and some decent shoes.

***

We got a table in the garden at the back of Zini's restaurant. The sun was shining and it was a fairly warm day, so I wore a pair of black Gucci sunglasses that covered most of my face and also gave me a false sense of security.

I was afraid that things would be very quiet and awkward, but as soon as I'd gotten into the car with Robert, I felt at ease and we spoke freely. We shared a past, friends and some family, after all. His grandmother, Doris, and Grandma Blue were best friends. It felt good to talk to him.

Robert wore a dark suit jacket over white jeans and one of those brightly coloured jumpers with a large polo horse as the logo. He looked tanned and sporty, and very handsome. I had quickly thrown on a nude-coloured dress plus heels and grabbed a matching handbag.

"So what's been happening in your life lately?" Robert asked finally after we had ordered. "Spill the beans! Why are you back at home with your mum and dad? Did you get sick of the big city and the luxury lifestyle?"

I laughed. "It wasn't very exciting. I left my husband because he was cheating on me. It's a long story and I won't bore you with the details. How have you been? I heard you married the intern you were seeing before I went to Uni," I said, trying to make light of the fact.

"Yeah, that's all a long time ago, and a lot of water has passed under the bridge since then," he replied, and I raised an eyebrow, not understanding what he meant.

Robert took a deep breath before explaining, "I did marry Alicia, hastily and briefly. I was on the rebound and I threw myself into a relationship when I was feeling low. So I married her, and we divorced very quickly, but she fell pregnant just before. She wasn't the mothering type, so I got my daughter, Lauren, and Alicia went back to her native Brazil, never to be heard of again," he added matter-of-factly.

I was surprised by the fact that he had been on the rebound, and I gathered it must have been another brief relationship after Camilla and Peter's wedding, since I hadn't heard anything about it. I had pestered Camilla for information at the time and felt rather obsessed, but she didn't mention there being anyone else. What Robert had just said made the kiss we'd shared even more meaningless to him, obviously. I pulled myself together and tried to forget it.

"That's a shame," I said. "At least something good came of it. You got a daughter."

Robert smiled broadly when he mentioned her. "Yes, you are right. She is absolutely gorgeous."

He then took out his phone and showed me a couple of photos of a pretty young girl aged about five years old. She had Robert's good looks and blue eyes, and her mother's dark hair. I was guessing this since Alicia came from Brazil—there I was, typecasting people again.

"I spoke to Melody Jones a couple of days ago," he said, changing the subject. "She does the music festival we support and she mentioned you had been writing for her magazine. That sounds really interesting and exciting."

Our food arrived, and I found myself telling Robert all about the interview and the concert, and Tiger's death. It all just poured out of me. I mentioned Brody as a suspected bodyguard, but I left out how attractive I thought he was and the intimate though brief kisses we had shared.

Robert listened and asked some questions from time to time. I found myself staring into his clear blue eyes and they felt so familiar to me… I blushed again.

Robert noticed and laughed. "What? Did I say something to embarrass you?" he asked, jokingly.

"No, of course not, don't be silly," I answered, feeling flustered. "I just realised I've been bending your ear for ages about this stuff and I'm sorry. I'm such a chatterbox."

"No, it's really interesting. Actually I'd like to help. As far as I've understood, you need to find out more about what happened at that party in 1983, and you need to talk to that drug dealer, Simone. When Lauren was just four months old, Alicia brought her over to my house, as she had done many times before, only this time when she left she didn't come back. When Alicia went back to Brazil, I was left holding the baby, literally. She and I had divorced already, and there was no chance of us getting back together. So, as I didn't want to risk her coming back later to claim custody of Lauren, I had to track her down to get the paperwork in order. I used a really good detective; a retired policeman called

Alex Proctor. He did a great job. We could talk to
him, fill him in on it all, and see what he comes up
with," Robert suggested.

After lunch, he paid the bill and drove me back to
my house, with us still talking excitedly about
finding Simone and how we could discover more
about that fateful party. When Robert parked the car,
I was almost sad that lunch was over. It amazed me
how quickly we had felt at ease with each other, and
all those old feelings had come rushing back to me.
Robert switched off the engine and turned towards
me.

"It has been such a lot of fun catching up with
you again, Charlie. There is something I have to ask
you," Robert said.

I instinctively thought he wanted to say
something about our kiss at the wedding. He
probably wanted to apologise for being drunk and
that was something I didn't want to hear, so I
quickly said, "No, don't please. Let's not talk about
that. It was an embarrassing mistake." Grabbing my
handbag from the floor of the car where I'd left it, I
turned to open the passenger door.

Robert placed his hand on my arm to stop me.
"What? I'm sorry you feel that way, but I was only
going to ask you if you knew anyone with black and
pink hair in a Mohican, because there's a punk in
your garden, and if you don't know her, I will come
with you and get her to move on," Robert said
seriously and I felt foolish again.

How did that happen? I accidentally managed to
tell him that our kiss meant nothing to me. How do I

175

get myself into these situations? It wasn't my fault, I decided.

Glancing in the direction Robert was pointing, I saw Raven sitting on the porch steps of my house. She had styled her hair into the biggest Mohican I'd ever seen and she looked to have been crying, because her face was blackened with runny mascara. On the ground beside her was her large, black photo bag and another on wheels, along with what resembled a guitar case. I gazed at her in shock.

"She's a friend of mine. Not dangerous at all, unless provoked," I said, trying to be funny.

Robert leaned in and placed a brief, warm kiss on my lips in much the same way as Brody had done. After saying he would be in touch, he was gone. I stood by the gate and watched the car speed off. My life had suddenly become very complicated.

Raven was upset and weeping, and could not tell me at first what all the fuss was about. So I took her into my mother's kitchen and let her cry while I made us both a cup of tea, and placed a large piece of cake in front of her. Taking a leaf out of my mothers book; when all else fails—eat! She soon calmed down enough to tell me what had happened, between snotty snivels.

What Raven told me was that she had given Nigel an ultimatum: to either tell her what was going on, and why he was acting so strangely, or she would leave him. Even Jason had noticed that things were not right between them. It had all come to a head in a huge fight, after which Nigel refused to talk to her, so Raven had packed her bag and gotten the train to stay with me for a few days.

I could not remember ever saying that she could stay with me. Actually, I was sure I hadn't told her where I lived, except that it was north of London, but here she was, and I couldn't turn her away.

I got Raven installed into our guestroom on the first floor, next to mine. She helped me put some sheets on the bed while I filled her in on everything that I'd just told Robert Warnes. My throat was dry from talking so much, but Raven wanted to know everything as it would distract her from her own worries.

Raven was wearing black nail varnish on her short nails, some of which had chipped off, and one of her black T-shirts with the middle finger turned up in a gesture that said fuck off without any need for words. Add her signature short, ripped denim skirt and black thick tights, teamed with black Doc Marten boots, and she looked extreme and menacing. The Mohican was large and stiff, and she had to be careful when walking under lamps and doors.

Raven's mobile kept ringing at intervals and she would glance at it, but not answer. Finally, she turned it off altogether and placed it in the drawer beside her bed. I was guessing it was Nigel, but I didn't want to upset her more by commenting.

Hearing noise from the kitchen, I decided to take Raven downstairs to introduce her. I didn't want anyone to bump into her accidently and think she had broken in to the house or something. As we

177

entered the kitchen, I was lost for words when I saw
my grandma with the exact same hairstyle as Raven,
albeit a much smaller version.

Grandma's blue hair stood on end in a perfect
half-circle on top of her head. The hair at the front
sides was thinning, but the rest made a perfect
Mohican. Raven stood in the doorway to the kitchen
with her mouth wide open. Grandma Blue had taken
to wearing the 'Shut the Fuck Up' T-shirt as often as
she could, and today she had teamed it with bright
blue and yellow training pants and matching
sneakers.

"Oh my God, who are you?" Grandma gasped
when she saw Raven.

I couldn't make up my mind which of them was
more shocked to see the other. Mum was putting her
groceries into the cupboards and didn't seem to
think it shocking at all. I noticed a large glass of red
wine on the kitchen table.

"Oh my God, that's my T-shirt!" Raven
answered, mimicking the expression and sounding
shocked. "I'm Raven."

"I'm Blue," Grandma said.

"Yes, you are," Raven replied, looking at her
hair."

"You are not only Raven, but there's some pink
there too," Grandma Blue observed, pointing. "I like
it. I might get myself some of those tattoos. I've
always wanted one," she added, indicating Raven's
arm.

"Since when have you wanted a tattoo?" I asked.

"Since always," Blue replied nonchalantly.

Mum's eye started twitching again. Grandma and Raven made their way into the living room, talking about the Sex Pistols' first and only album, *Never Mind the Bollocks, Here's the Sex Pistols*, which Blue had just picked up at HMV in the shopping centre.

"I'm easing myself into the music by starting with the Sex Pistols and then moving on to more badass stuff later," I heard her tell Raven. "I'm not too keen on them disrespecting the Queen though. I want a T-shirt with 'Never Mind the Bollocks' on the front too. I think that would be really cool."

"I have one. It's yellow. You can borrow it if you like," Raven answered. "You should listen to this Irish punk band called Outlaws. They are so cool and much more up to date than the Sex Pistols."

I excused myself and made my way back up to my room to check my messages, but there were none. I felt that my life was moving in leaps and bounds. One minute nothing was happening and the next it was flashing along so fast that my head was spinning.

Chapter 10
RIP Tiger

Raven and I dressed in black for Tiger's funeral. She wore black a lot anyway, so I just had to get her to lose the Mohican for the occasion. The only black clothes I own are evening wear, so I ended up choosing a cocktail dress from Escada Couture. It has long sleeves with white silk cuffs and gold-studded cufflinks. It was a relatively warm day, so I didn't wear a jacket.

I teamed the dress with my black-and-white Chanel handbag and gorgeous black Jimmy Choo shoes, with heels so high that I ran the risk of falling over. But then I wasn't going to be doing any walking at a funeral now, was I?

I drove us to the City of London Cemetery and Crematorium; a stunning Grade 1-listed building in the heart of East London. A tree-lined avenue led us to a beautiful stone archway and the parking area where there were many cars already. Somehow I managed to squeeze my Range Rover between a huge Bentley and a tiny electric car that only needed half the parking space.

The press were there in abundance, but they had to stay in the car park and were not allowed past the archway, which was gated and there was a guard there checking people off on a list. The press barely raised an eyebrow as we left the car to walk up the beautiful woodland lane towards the Five Chapels and Crematorium Catacombs. There were numerous headstones in the landscaped area that led to the chapel, and I noticed there was an option for woodland burials too. The whole place felt calm and serene, and I was pleased Tracy had chosen it as Tiger's final resting place. It felt apt somehow.

If I had expected only a few people to turn up, like there had been at the inquest, I was in for a surprise. The chapel was full to bursting point with family and friends. Raven and I kept to the back where we found a pew with a little space left.

I could see Tracy sitting on the front row with some people I had never seen before. Bill Graham and the rest of the band sat together with their wives and girlfriends. I noticed Bill's partner, Yvette, was latched on to him again, linking her arm through his as she usually did when out in public, looking afraid that he'd make a break for it should she let go.

Marianne and her boyfriend, Keith Raymond, The Sticks' drummer, sat together, and Darren and Malcolm were there too. Marianne was constantly dabbing her eyes with a white tissue, which reminded me to get mine out of my handbag.

The service was beautiful and the vicar did Tiger proud. Readings were done by Bill and Keith, who had both known Tiger since the early seventies. There was not a dry eye in the chapel as the organist played 'If I die and have to leave you, see me through until the end' as the six coffin bearers carried Tiger's coffin to his final resting place in the landscaped cemetery.

181

I cried and cried, quickly using up all of the tissues I had brought with me. During the service, I had noticed Brody standing at the back of the chapel, but he had gone into the cemetery before the coffin was carried out. He was wearing a dark suit and looked very handsome, yet he was not there in the capacity of Tiger's friend, but was alert and definitely working, as usual. I noticed he sometimes talked briefly into his little ear piece, obviously communicating with someone.

When the congregation left the chapel, following the coffin to the grave, I noticed two rather large men standing to one side of the burial ground in the shadow of an oak tree, observing the crowd. I had noticed them when I first arrived and now I found myself wondering what they were doing there. I didn't recognise them, but they had that 'thug' look about them. It was just a vibe I got.

When everything was over, the two menacing looking men made their way towards the funeral guests, who were standing around in small groups talking. They did not say anything, but seemed to be searching for someone. I saw Brody react to them immediately by positioning himself next to Bill, keeping the men in his line of sight and talking into his earpiece thingy, which he always seemed to have behind one ear.

I got the sense that something was very wrong and that something was going to happen, so I nudged Raven and she nodded. She had noticed them too. The guests were making their way back towards the lane, which led through the woodland to

182

the archway and car park, when the two burly men seemed to pounce on Malcolm. Although discrete, they almost forcibly pulled him aside from the other mourners.

People turned their heads in surprise and I caught sight of Malcolm's ashen face. Strangely, Darren did not rush to his aid as he was almost frogmarched by the two guys towards the car park. Raven and I were keen to see what would happen next, so, together with a crowd of people from the funeral, we hurried after them. My feet were killing me as usual, and I had difficulty keeping up, but no way was I going to miss out on what was going down with Malcolm.

There, to my surprise, were two police cars and another unmarked one. The two men conferred with the other uniformed officers who were waiting, and then they literally shoved Malcolm into the back of one of the police cars and drove off. You could have blown me over with a feather. I was so shocked that I was speechless. Raven mouthed 'Oh my God' to me without actually saying the words as we watched all of the police drive off. What on earth was that about? Did Malcolm have something to do with Tiger's death?

I did not see anyone from the band or their girlfriends in the car park, and neither did I notice Darren nor Brody, although I was sure they would have seen what happened to Malcolm. I then realised they had gone back to the chapel to avoid the paparazzi feeding frenzy. The press, who had been waiting outside the gates of the cemetery for the mourners to return, had almost thrown themselves at

183

the police cars as they drove out. Then they started taking photos of anyone else around who looked vaguely familiar.

Raven and I got back into my Range Rover, and I drove to Kensington, where there was going to be a small gathering of family and close friends at the home of one of Tiger's relatives. My mobile rang shrilly, making us both jump, and I put it on speaker.

"Hey, Charlie, it's Brody. Where are you?" he asked.

"I'm on my way to Kensington Gardens," I replied. "Where are you? Are you coming?"

"No, there has been a change of plan. We can't go to Kensington. The press have gone wild and we've been warned they are staking out the house. They have decided to cancel the wake."

"What on earth has happened? Did Malcolm have anything to do with Tiger's death?" I enquired.

"I don't know anything about that. What I can tell you is that Malcolm has been taken in for questioning by the Metropolitan Police Operation Yew Tree team. I still don't know exactly what it's about yet. I think it would be a good idea for you to go back home and I will phone you tonight. Is that okay?" he asked, and the last question was said with such warmth in his voice that Raven nudged me in the side while raising her eyebrows, which made me laugh.

"Yes, I'd like that. Bye," I answered and hung up.

Raven logged on to her mobile internet as we drove back up north and read out the breaking news from her phone: "A seventy-year-old man is being

184

questioned by the police about the alleged rape and abuse of underage girls in the seventies and eighties. Detective Superintendent David Black, leader of Operation Yew Tree, which was set up to investigate claims against the late Jimmy Savile, but who also works with the Serious Case Team of the Metropolitan Police Service's Child Abuse Investigations Command, said the man in question was not being charged with any offence at this moment. He is helping the police with their enquiries."

Raven paused and then exclaimed, "Bloody hell, Malcolm a pedo?! Well, I don't know why I'm so surprised. It looks like he's always been at it with the groupies."

"Yeah, but those groupies at the Roundhouse knew exactly what they were up to. I saw Malcolm and Darren take one of those young girls up to their room at the hotel and, if anything, she was the instigator," I answered and Raven nodded in agreement.

"Isn't it strange that they would come and take Malcolm like that at the funeral? It felt like they wanted to take him at a public event with lots of press coverage," she said.

"I thought exactly the same. They could have pulled him aside quietly at the wake or even later," I agreed. "They don't mention him by name in that article, but it's just a matter of time until the photos from the funeral car park surface, and people put two and two together. I wonder why they did it there."

"Well, one thing I've noticed with that lot is that they seem to arrest one celebrity after another at dawn raids," said Raven. "Do they expect seventy and eighty-year-old geezers to jump out of the window and make a run for it across the garden hedge? It looks to me like they want the publicity. I'm not saying they are wrong about those old geezers touching up young girls back then, but it just feels like a witch-hunt to me," Raven said and I had to agree.

When I parked outside my house, we got out, keen to stretch our legs. Heading inside, we noticed a lot of boxes sitting in the hall and Raven recognised the logo on them as being that of a large music store chain. We both practically jumped out of our own skins when we heard a loud noise coming from Grandma Blue's room. It sounded like feedback from an amplifier.

Rushing towards her door, I was about to knock when I realised the noise would drown it out, so I changed my mind. We opened the door and peeked in. Grandma Blue was wearing Raven's yellow T-shirt with the 'Never Mind the Bollocks' logo on the front.

I thought Doris Warnes, Robert's gran, dressed sombrely, as ladies of her advanced years should, but as she turned towards me I saw Grandma Blue had lent her the 'Shut the Fuck Up' number. Rich, the drug supplier, and another young guy I'd never seen before were assembling what looked like a drum set and an amplifier for an electric guitar. We watched in amazement as the young, rather camp guy, proceeded to hit each drum in turn.

"Right, Blue, the drums! Okay, pay attention everyone. The four major drums are the same as the four strings on that bass guitar. So, the drummer, who's that again?" the guy asked loudly.

"Me!" Rich answered from where he was sitting on Grandma's bed.

"Yeah, so the drummer has to work closely with the bass player. That you, Dorrie?" he asked Robert's grandmother. I had never heard anyone address her like that before.

"Oooh, you and me working closely is nice, Rich," Doris flirted and his cheeks went a lighter shade of scarlet.

"Who do you have on guitar?" the young guy asked.

"We don't have one of those yet," Grandma Blue answered.

"What's your role, Blue?" he questioned.

"I'm the front and vocals. We need someone charismatic, like me. But I can't manage guitar too, on account of my nails and being musically challenged," she answered, holding up her manicured nails to illustrate her point.

Suddenly, they all seemed to notice Raven and me standing in the door with our mouths wide open in shock, horror and mild amusement.

"Musically challenged is right, Blue. You can't sing," Doris said, laughing.

"That's why we are doing punk music, Doris. You only have to wail and swear, and spit at people.

I think I'm going to enjoy that bit," Grandma Blue answered matter-of-factly. "I haven't quite mastered it yet. I try for a blob and it just comes out like a spray. I shall have to practice more."

"What on earth is going on here?" I asked as I entered the crowded room with Raven behind me.

"We've started a band!" Grandma announced. "We are having a festival in three weeks and we needed bands to play, so we started one. Can you ask your mates to chip in and play for us? That band who lost their bass player—Doris can step in for one night only, can't you Doris?"

"I'd easily go on a whole tour with that Bill Graham. He's fit. Tell him I'm available for as long as they need me, after I've learned how to play that thing," Doris answered, pointing to the huge bass guitar perched on top of an amplifier in front of her.

"Bloody hell, steady on, Doris. Here she is, our newly appointed bassist, and already she's looking at another band and threatening to run off with someone younger," Rich said jokingly.

In all fairness, Doris was probably closer to Bill's age than his current girlfriend, Yvette. This band nonsense made me laugh, but if it gave them something to do and have fun with, I was all for it.

"Couldn't we get Jean to play guitar?" Doris suggested.

"Nah, she's too fat! There wouldn't be room for anyone else on stage. We have to be ruthless, as she doesn't really fit in with our style," Grandma said and Doris nodded in agreement. "She can be our manager and run our fan club though," Blue added.

Doris picked up the bass guitar from where it was sitting on the amplifier and put it on... the wrong way.

"No, no, no, Dorrie, darling, I've told you a million times that the strings are supposed to be pointing away from you," said the young guy from the music shop, sounding exasperated as he helped her to rearrange the instrument.

"My arms are too short to play this thing," Doris replied as once again she was holding the bass the wrong way.

"Charlotte, could you give me and Rich a lift home later, when we are finished with rehearsal?" Doris asked me and I nodded.

"I could possibly help," Raven offered meekly. Everyone turned to look at her, standing behind me. "I play the guitar and bass pretty decently, if I can say so myself," she said. Picking up the electric fender guitar from its rack, she played an impressive riff to jubilant cries from the rest of the room.

"You are hired," Grandma Blue told Raven, and they all got stuck in talking about songs and notes, and three cords.

It was all way over my head, so I made my way up to my room to check my messages. There was one from the private detective, Alex Proctor. It said Simone Labyre, followed by an address in Manchester; nothing else. I looked at my watch. It would only take a little over an hour to drive there. Despite feeling quite tired, I decided that I'd go and take a look at this drug dealer/ baroness.

I put on black jeans, a black T-shirt and sneakers. Okay, so the footwear was multi-coloured and Nike, but I made a mental note to get some black ones. I teamed this with a black baseball cap to hide my hair. My phone rang and I jumped. I would have to change the ringtone; it was making me nervous.

Thinking it was Brody, I picked up my mobile and said, "Hiya dude, how did you get on?"

"Hiya dude yourself," Robert Warnes answered to my utter embarrassment.

Why was it that every time I talked to this man, I ended up with my foot squarely lodged in my mouth?

"Sorry, I thought you were someone else," I answered.

"So I'm not the only guy calling you? I might have guessed. Seems to be the rule with you," he said, but his tone was light, so I guessed he was joking. "Did you get the address from Proctor the detective?" he continued. "I told you he was a fast worker."

"Yeah, I'm just going to take a look at her," I replied, and regretted it straight away.

"You are *what*?! That could be dangerous. She's a drug dealer! You should just tell the police and they can handle it," Robert said sternly.

"Don't worry. I'll do a drive-by and see if she's in. I don't have anything to tell the police yet. I'm sure they already know she was at the house on the night of the deaths in 1983. It could all be innocent. I'll take someone with me," I assured him.

"Yes, that someone will be me. I'm not letting you go there on your own. I'll pick you up in a few minutes," Robert said and I knew there was no point in arguing, but I had promised to drive his grandmother and Rich home.

"No, I have to drop some people off. Why don't I just meet you there?" I offered and he agreed, grudgingly.

Chapter 11
Simone

I peeked into Grandma Blue's room and everyone was getting ready to leave. The music shop guy had already gone and they looked at me in surprise when I entered clad in black (except for the sneakers. I know, just a minor detail).

"Where are you going dressed like that?" Blue asked.

"Nowhere," I lied.

"And this 'nowhere' that you are not going to, am I expected to come with you?" Raven enquired and I nodded. "Good, but I'm starving, so we have to stop for fish and chips on the way," she answered.

"I'm hungry too," Grandma Blue said and she started towards her coat. "What are you up to, Charlie?"

"I'm just going to look at a house in Manchester for an article I'm writing," I lied again. It was a white lie. Actually, I might just write an article on all this someday, just so as to not be lying all the time.

"Investigative journalism? I like it. We'll come with you," Rich insisted.

"No way," I answered. "Definitely not! Over my dead body!"

Five minutes later I was sitting in the Range Rover. Raven sat beside me, and the backseat was occupied by Grandma Blue, Doris and Rich. I had tried everything I could think of to get them to agree to go home, but they wouldn't hear of it. So we set off to see what Simone looked like.

I was secretly hoping the woman would talk to me, and I was starting to worry what Robert would think of me bringing his granny on our stakeout. We stopped at a fish and chip shop just down the road from Simone's place, and then I parked a few yards from her front gate on the opposite side of the road. The house was a small, brick semi-detached in a boring street in a boring area. If Simone was indeed a drug baroness, she had not done very well for herself, or was this humble exterior perhaps a really good cover?

We sat and watched the dark house while we ate. My car stank of grease and fish, but you can't get anything like this down south, and it was the first portion of fish and chips I'd had in two years, so we all got stuck in. Mine was dripping with vinegar and covered in ketchup. Suddenly there was a knock on the car window beside me, which made everybody jump. Doris let out a shrill scream.

"Shhh. We are supposed to be inconspicuous," I whispered and Grandma Blue started to giggle. "I need to pee!" she said, and now Doris started to laugh.

"We are sitting in a white Range Rover. We are about as inconspicuous as a tarantula on an ice cream," Doris remarked.

"Don't you mean Angel food cake?" asked Raven, her mouth full of hot chips.

"What's Angel food cake?" Rich asked.

"It's a Raymond Chandler quote," Raven answered. "She just got it a bit wrong."

I opened the window to reveal Robert. He took one look in the car and his jaw dropped in surprise. Well, I was not really surprised by his reaction, considering my car was full of old-age pensioners dressed in T-shirts bearing rude messages on the front.

"Why on earth have you brought our grandmothers with you?" he asked. "What have you done with your hair, Blue?"

"Don't ask," I answered. "Have you seen anyone in Simone's house?"

Robert stole a chip from the paper bag I was holding and was just about to answer when a small car pulled up outside Simone's house and parked on the street. A tall woman got out and walked inside, seemingly not noticing my car or Robert, who ducked down out of sight. My first reaction was relief, my second thought disbelief. I had parked a huge white Range Rover in a humble residential area, clearly filled with people, and this woman didn't bat an eyelid? If she was a drug baroness, she couldn't have been a very good one, I thought to myself.

"I really have to pee," Grandma Blue said again. "I've been like this all my life. As soon as I get excited, I need to pee. I couldn't play hide and seek as a child, since I'd need the loo every time I found a good hiding place and anyone got close."

The lights went on inside the ground floor of the small house and then upstairs. I opened the car door and got out. A dog barked loudly a few streets away. Apart from that all was quiet.

"Wait here," I told everyone except Robert.

"What are you going to do?" he asked me as I walked towards the house. "You are not going to contact her?"

"Yes," I answered, walking up the garden path followed by Robert, who was trying to talk me out of it.

"You can't just ring on her door bell!" he protested.

I rang it as Robert lifted his eyes to heaven in frustration and a minute later the door was opened by a dark-haired woman in her sixties. She had probably once been very pretty; her features symmetrical and pleasant. Her hair was greying in places, but overall she looked good for her age. "Yes?" she said.

"Simone Labyre?" I asked.

"Who wants to know?" she answered, looking at me closely and then at Robert.

"I'm Charlotte Hart and this is Robert Warnes. I'd like to talk to you about the death of Delphine Graham," I replied just as I heard a car door slam. The garden gate opened and Grandma Blue led Doris, Rich and Raven up the path towards us.

"I tried to stop her," Raven said.

"I told you I have to pee. At my age when you have to pee, you have to pee *now*!" Grandma insisted.

Simone gazed at the blue-haired old lady with a Mohican in surprise and then started to laugh. "Hello, Rich," she said and he nodded.

I couldn't believe that he actually knew her, but then why was I surprised? They were in the same line of business.

"Top of the stairs, to your right," Simone said to Grandma Blue, stepping aside. "You better all come in then," she added, leading us into a small living room on the ground floor. She sat down in a comfortable looking chair and the rest of us squeezed on to the sofa.

"How's business?" Simone asked Rich.

"Oh, I can't complain," he replied. Robert looked at him in surprise, but didn't say anything.

"Who are you and why do you want to know about Delphine?" Simone finally asked.

"Charlie's a journalist and wants to talk about The Sticks. She's just written a big article about them for *Melody Magazine*," Rich answered for me.

I quickly filled her in on Tiger's death and the similarities to Delphine's. She watched me, thoughtfully listening to what I had to say.

"I was really sorry to hear about Tiger's death. Anything I tell you is off the record. I don't want my name mentioned in any of this," she replied when I finished and I readily agreed.

"I can vouch for her. She's a good 'un," Rich said, and Simone nodded.

"When Tiger died there was just something wrong with the whole thing, so I'm basically just trying to find out what happened and if there is any connection to what happened back in 1983," I told her.

"Delphine was like a sister to me, but she had a huge habit. I was in the business of providing certain services at the time and she would use my expertise," Simone replied vaguely.

"I get the picture. You provided her with what she needed," I said and Simone blinked once. "What I don't understand is, firstly, how she came to do a little too much of the stuff you provided her with and, secondly, why Bill Graham ended up leaving the country straight afterwards?" I asked.

"The service I provided was grade A stuff and she'd had it many times before—on a daily basis, in fact. What she had when I was there was fine and she was enjoying it when I left her. I don't know what happened after I left the room. She was with a young guy I'd met briefly through some modelling acquaintances, called Kevan. They were both pretty out of it, but nothing dramatic. I left the rest of her stuff in the usual place, on the table by her bed, and left the room. That's the last time I saw her. I went down to join the party.

"Bill and Tracy can vouch for me, because I met Tiger and her as they entered the house, and I sat with Bill and about ten other people until I left the party. What happened after I left is anyone's guess. I try not to speculate. Bill leaving England was a bit surprising, but I don't know why," Simone said. "I think we all just assumed he was grieving."

"Is there anything else you can remember that strikes you as odd perhaps, or anyone who you think might have wanted to get rid of Delphine?" I asked.

"I don't think anyone wanted to harm Delphine. I didn't know it at the time, but Bill had already started divorce proceedings against her. She was difficult to handle because of her habit, which I knew he hated. She wouldn't get anything from a divorce from Bill because they had a pre-nup. Delphine wasn't happy about that when they married. She told me about it, but she had plenty of her own money, so it was more a trust issue for her. Bill didn't know about her habit when they met. It's the usual story with heroin addicts— it's often hidden. Actually, Bill's abhorrence of drugs was also the reason he fired Tiger that night," Simone continued as Grandma Blue came into the room and Doris left to use the loo.

"Where did you meet Tiger and Tracy? Was it inside the house?" Robert asked.

"Yeah, I was just coming back down from the bedroom. I'd heard some stuff in one of the rooms and stopped for a short while to listen before I heard Tiger and Tracy come into the house from the garden. He was furious and she was trying to get him to calm down," Simone said. "Tiger was high, as usual, and pissed off at being fired. He kept asking after Malcolm. He was on his way up to the second floor and I had to stop them."

"Was Malcolm having some Triple A action?" I asked and Simone looked at me in surprise.

"Yes. How do you know about that?" she asked.

"I heard Darren ask him if he wanted some triple-A action at the Camden gig. There were all these really young groupies hanging around with Access All Areas passes on their wrists, so I just assumed it meant taking a groupie up to the bedroom," I answered.

Simone shook her head. "That's almost what it means. Access All Areas also means sexual access to all areas—in all orifices. Malcolm and Darren made a habit of sharing girls, and they liked anal sex," Simone explained as we looked at her in shock and horror, realising what she meant.

"That's just nasty!" Grandma Blue exclaimed.

"Malcolm and Darren had a thing for it back then. What can I say, it takes all sorts," Simone continued. "There's nothing wrong with it if it's between two consenting adults, or three as the case may be, and it sounds like they are still enjoying it. When I said I'd stopped outside a door to listen, well, it was those two enjoying some time with a young girl that Malcolm had brought with him to the party. He likes them young."

"This girl was very young and I don't think she really fully understood what she had let herself in for. Tiger and Tracy were threatening to find Malcolm, and have it out with him about being fired, but I didn't think it was the right time or place, so I spent a few minutes talking them out of it before I went into the garden to get a drink." Simone added.

"So this girl, can you remember what she was called?" Robert asked as I sat beside him with my mouth open in shock. I seemed to have led a very sheltered life compared to these people.

"Mandy. I remember it, because it was such a childish name and she was just a child really, very young, but I didn't get a surname," Simone said. "I felt really sorry for the girl. They had plied her with drink and drugs. She was probably one of the most naïve of all the girls that hung around back then."

"Did you try to help her?" Robert questioned.

"No, and I'm not proud of it. When you see all the groupies I've seen hanging around with these guys, you notice that most of them are quite promiscuous and provocative. They sleep with anyone to get what they want, whether it's a concert ticket, backstage passes or drugs. Some of them are very young, but they still know exactly what they are doing. It's a game to them."

Simone looked at each of us in turn, her eyes wide and searching, wanting to be believed. I was still reeling from the shock of what she had told us. I wouldn't be able to look at Malcolm or Darren again without thinking about this. What a couple of tossers.

"Unfortunately, sometimes there will be girls who don't know what's expected of them and Mandy was one of them. By the time I got to the bedroom door the damage had already been done, if you get my drift. It's one of the things I regret most," Simone added.

"Lastly, where were you last Friday? Sorry, but I have to ask. If there is any chance these two deaths

were not misadventure then there is a big chance
they are connected," I explained.

"I was visiting a friend in Glasgow for the
weekend. There were plenty of people there. So, if
you are asking whether I had anything to do with
any of those deaths, connected or otherwise, the
answer is no," Simone answered steadily.

Although Simone was a drug dealer and had
obviously seen the harder side of life's realities, she
was a really likable person. It was not my place to
go around asking these types of questions, I realised.
The police should be doing it, but for them to do
anything at all, I would have to find something for
them to work with. I'd seen how they did it on
TV—eliminating people from their inquiries because
of alibis.

I was a huge fan of Agatha Christie. I'd work
along the same principles and see where it led me, I
decided. It was all quite exciting. Perhaps I was
better suited to being a police detective than a
journalist? We thanked Simone for her time and got
up to leave.

"I like your hair," Simone said to Grandma Blue
as we made our way to the door.

"Thank you. I'm in a band with Rich here and
Doris. Raven is our guitarist. We are going to have a
festival soon. Do you want to come?" Grandma Blue
asked, and the two of them agreed to add each other
on Facebook. I felt like I was living in a parallel
universe again.

Once we were outside, Grandma Blue and Raven
got into my car while Doris and Rich got into

Robert's, and us two drivers stood alone for a couple of minutes talking.

"I think that went rather well, Detective Inspector Hart," Robert said as he gave me a hug and we laughed at his joke.

"Yeah, Superintendent Warnes, now I have to find out who Mandy is. Can we get Proctor on to it?" I asked and he nodded. "Do you think Simone was telling the truth?"

"I can't see why she would lie. Sounds like that Malcolm and Darren are a right pair of charmers," he remarked with disgust.

"Let's say the deaths are connected, I can imagine Malcolm doing it. Perhaps he didn't know Bill was getting divorced and wanted to get rid of the junkie wife," I suggested.

"Okay, but why would he kill Tiger now?"

"Perhaps it isn't Malcolm, but that Mandy who wants revenge for getting sodomised," I suggested.

"But if it was Mandy, why would she kill Delphine and the model? Surely she'd go for Darren and Malcolm? And why would she kill Tiger?" Robert reasoned.

"You're right. It's not making any sense. None of this adds up. Perhaps none of it is connected after all and Tiger really killed himself," I said, deflated.

"Well, that still leaves the question of who removed the drug equipment in 1983 and last Friday. And why anyone would remove it, because somebody did. Now we have to find out who did it and why," Robert concluded.

He smiled at me in amusement as Doris opened the car door and impatiently called out his name. "I'll call you. Drive carefully," he told me. Taking hold of my baseball cap, he turned it around so the brim was facing backwards and kissed me, very gently, before making his way over to his car.

"Oh, put her down, Robert. I want to get back home before the news," Doris shouted. "Yew Tree have picked up another celebrity and I want to see if they say who it is. Dirty old men abusing their position and touching up young girls at the BBC! It's disgusting!"

A little over an hour later, I was so happy to be home again. We drove in silence mostly, Grandma Blue having fallen asleep on the back seat, her Mohican all lopsided and messed up. Once in my room, I checked my messages, found nothing, and crept into bed. It had been a very long day. Just as I was about to fall asleep my mobile rang. I really would have to change that ringtone.

"Hi, Charlie," Brody said warmly. "Sorry for the late call; we've been really busy. How are you?"

"Tired. I just got into bed," I answered.

"What are you wearing?" he asked me, and I laughed, realising it was a joke. "When can I see you?" he added.

I felt my heart leap a little. "I don't know. Soon, I hope. What's happening with Malcolm?" I asked, changing the subject.

"He's been released, for now. But, between you and me, that's a problem that isn't going to go away.

The police are investigating him aggressively. There are some serious accusations flying around."

"Is it a girl called Mandy?" I questioned. "Has she accused him of something?"

The line went quiet for a while before Brody answered, "We don't know any details about it yet and Malcolm isn't talking. He's locked himself up with Darren and I heard them arguing. Who's this Mandy?" he asked in a serious tone.

"I've just spoken to Simone, the dealer from back in 1983, and she told me about her. Apparently, Mandy was very young and not like one of those groupies from the concert. Simone hinted that perhaps Mandy hadn't known what she was getting herself into," I explained and heard Brody take a deep breath on the other end of the line.

"I think you should leave it to the police to find out. There are some really nasty people out there and I don't want you to get into any sort of trouble," he said even more seriously. "I like you, okay?!"

"I like you too," I replied and we hung up.

I slept restlessly with images of Brody and Robert, Doris and Grandma Blue, Rich and Bill, and Tracy and Raven spinning around in my head.

Chapter 12
Danislav Zadravec

I woke up the next morning to the sound of Grandma Blue's drum set pounding and Dad shouting, "Stop, for the love of God!" For a family who don't believe in God, we do seem to call upon him quite a lot, I thought smiling.

Getting up, I checked my messages on my laptop and saw that I had several. One was from Blue, saying that I had been invited to the event 'Newbury Music Festival'. I clicked 'join'. I had a message from Melody asking me why my grandmother had invited her to an event and another from Raven's Nigel. He had sent me a friend request and asked me to talk to Raven for him. He said he could explain 'everything', if she'd just talk to him. And he gave me his mobile number.

No way did I want to get involved in other people's love lives. I had a complicated enough situation of my own, thank you very much. Seeing how I already had an email from Proctor, the private detective, I hoped I'd be paying him by the hour, because he was an extremely fast worker. As before, he just gave me a name and place: Amanda Marshall and an address in Loughborough. I still had no word from the woman at the newspaper, who I'd asked for more information on what happened back in 1983.

I made my way down to the kitchen for breakfast. Raven was already there, talking to Mum. It looked like they were getting on really well. I heard her mention Nigel's name as I entered the room and basically threw myself on the coffee. I'd been woken up by the lyrics 'I've got cocaine running around my brain' by Dillinger, so now it was practically sprinting around *my* brain. You know how that happens sometimes; a song repeating itself over and over, and you just can't get rid of it?

It was a beautiful sunny morning and Raven was going to teach Doris how to play bass. Dad had threatened to make Grandma Blue move out if she didn't find herself some rehearsal rooms, because there was no way he was going to let her use her bedroom; it was driving him nuts. Apparently, she kept forgetting the drum kit was in the middle of her bedroom floor and kept walking into it in the dark when she got up to visit her bathroom, making a lot of noise in the process. I hadn't heard anything, strangely enough.

I had just decided to go and talk to this Amanda on my own when my phone rang—it was Brody again. "Hi, sweetheart," he said, "I can't believe my luck, but I have a few hours off today. How about we meet for a chat? I can meet you halfway."

"Hi, actually can we meet in Loughborough?" I asked sweetly. I got no reaction from him, so he obviously didn't know that the town held the home of the person I had told him about the previous night.

"Yeah, sure, hun, just let me know where and when, and I will be there," he answered warmly.

ACCESS ALL AREAS

I found I liked it when Brody called me 'hun' and 'sweetheart', and I was looking forward to getting to know him a little better. Robert was lurking around in the back of my mind and the last thing I wanted was to start obsessing about him again.

***

I drove over the River Soar in north Loughborough and towards the town centre, passing the lovely medieval All Saints parish church and the Old Rectory that dated back to 1288. There was a sign that said it was used as a little museum. I parked my car on Bridge Street and walked the distance to Loughborough Wharf, where I had arranged to meet Brody. I'd never been here before and had to use my satnav to negotiate the way. It seemed like a nice small, middle England sort of town.

I found a table at a café and ordered a coffee. Brody had the longest drive up from London, and I was just hoping I had time to work out what I was going to say to him when I saw his face smiling at me from the doorway. He was looking exceptionally good in jeans, a T-shirt and a black leather bomber jacket. Brody walked straight over to me and gave me a hug; then, taking my face with both hands, he kissed me very softly before we sat down.

I had been afraid of feeling awkward, but I didn't. Instead, I felt happy, elated even, but I realised that I didn't really know him, so I shouldn't go forward too fast.

"Tell me about yourself, Charlotte. I only know what Bill has told me and that is very little," he said, and I noticed a cheeky glint in his bright blue eyes.

I filled him in briefly on my life so far, leaving out Robert and avoiding Grandma Blue's eccentricities. Well, I didn't want him screaming and running for the hills before I got to know him, did I?

"Now it's your turn. Tell me about you, Brody. I don't even know your surname," I told him.

"Okay, I grew up in the US, California, and my name is Brody McCaine," Brody replied. "My father is of Spanish decent and my mother is from Minnesota of German decent, but that's too far back to even apply to our genes, so watered down as they are. I joined the marines as soon as I could and became very good at what I do. I was a Navy SEAL for a while. Then, one of my best friends, Kurt, who had left the Navy, contacted me. We'd always agreed we wouldn't be in it forever."

"He was having some success with his close protection company, Gresham CPC Global, and asked me if I would be interested in working there. What it involves is basically bodyguard work, but on a higher threat level. I've never looked back. I enjoy it so much. I've been in the UK for a year now, but my work takes me all over the world, although I love living here. That's about it really," he added.

I listened to his voice, which was soft and well spoken. There was no doubt in my mind that my first impression of Brody had been correct and he was a decent guy. "So, no family or children?" I asked him.

"No, not yet," he answered. "It would be really difficult to fit in around what I do for a living."

"How long have you been looking after Bill Graham?" I asked.

"I wasn't allowed to talk about this before. Malcolm muzzled us from the time of our first brief, but I asked Bill and he gave me permission on the condition you don't write anything about it," Brody said. "He's a good guy, unlike his manager and his weasel assistant."

"Of course, yes, those two are dreadful," I agreed. "You won't believe what I've learned over the last few days. Anyway, go on."

"I was hired in for the tour firstly, together with two other guys from the company. Kurt normally puts together a three-man team for round-the-clock work. We were supposed to travel with Bill and keep the fans in check. There was a threat made to Bill specifically, which has been an ongoing thing for many years, so we are prepared to deal with that too," Brody explained.

"I knew you were his bodyguard! What sort of threat was it?"

"Well, after his wife died, he received a letter in the post from someone saying they were going to kill him, basically. He didn't take it seriously to begin with since the letter wasn't specific as to why they were threatening him. A few weeks later, he got another letter telling him to leave the country or he was dead. I believe the letters were handed over to the police. Nobody took them seriously."

"However, a few weeks later a serious attempt was made on Bill's life. They managed to get past his security and into his house. Luckily for him he had a panic room. That was when the police started to sit up and pay attention. From the security camera tapes they saw two darkly clad intruders and they were clearly professionals. I've seen the footage and I agree. They were definitely army trained guys," Brody explained.

"Wow, that's strange though. Did they ever find out why these people wanted to kill Bill?" I asked, shocked.

"They investigated everything. The police questioned the family and friends of Delphine and Kevan, but no one held a grudge towards Bill," Brody replied. "At the time the drug overdoses were being treated as death by misadventure. Then there was a second attack on Bill's house, which led to the death of his housekeeper. Apparently, she caught an intruder as he broke into the kitchen. Her rooms were on the same floor and she disturbed him. This time it was only one person. She managed to press the alarm button before she passed out, but again the intruder got away. I believe she died of a heart attack."

"Bill took the threats so seriously then that he bought a place in the Cote D'Azur in France and moved there. He was only planning on staying there for a little while until the threats stopped and everything blew over, but they didn't. At intervals he would get letters in the post at his house in France, warning him not to return to England. If he did he would be killed. What I understood after reading the numerous letters he got was that the person or persons threatening him were doing it as a form of revenge, but Bill can't understand why or who, or even what they want revenge for."

"The letters basically said that people who have done bad things shouldn't be allowed to live at home. They should be cast out from decent places and made to live in exile. The English was bad and the spelling dreadful. It all sounded a bit nuts," said Brody.

"So why did he suddenly decide to come back now?" I questioned.

"Well, as far as I've been told, Bill is sick of the whole thing. He got the band together to record in France earlier this year, and when Malcolm suggested they go on tour and promised him a tight security program, Bill agreed to it. I believe he's been here on several occasions for short trips without anything happening, so we were brought in to keep him safe once it was common knowledge that he was back."

"What happens if he leaves England and there is no more work for you?" I asked, not looking him in the face and feeling embarrassed.

"I like England and I'm liking it even more now," Brody said, and our eyes met and I blushed.

"I have a confession to make. I haven't been honest with you about meeting in Loughborough," I told him, before filling him in on what I'd found out about Tiger's autopsy report and my meeting with Simone, again leaving out who had been there with me. "The young girl who was raped that night lives here," I added.

Brody shook his head in disbelief. "Let me guess; now you want us to go and talk to her?" he said sternly, but he was smiling, so I didn't think I was in too much trouble.

We left the café together, and he placed his arm around my neck, pulled me close to him and kissed the top of my head. I pulled back a little, because I wasn't ready to have a relationship with anyone yet. Brody seemed to understand and we walked together to his black Volvo, which was parked behind my car. I had to smile as it was not the type of car I had envisioned Brody driving. Seeing my amusement, he clicked the doors opened.

"What?" he asked with a laugh. "It's Bill's car. I borrowed it. Yvette uses it normally."

"Nothing," I said in amusement whilst getting in, "it's fine."

Brody drove us out of central Loughborough, past the university and into a rather humble housing estate on the outskirts of the town where he parked on the street by the number we were looking for. It looked the same as every other house apart from the front garden. Whereas many were paved over, this one was a beautiful combination of lawn and flowerbeds. The window towards the front of the house was curtained and had nets beneath that looked crisp and white.

I rang the doorbell and a small, slim lady opened the door. She had Slavic features and looked to be in her late sixties, with greying hair tied in a ponytail.

When she said, "Hello," I heard a little accent to her English, so I guessed her to be of Russian or Eastern European origin. I noticed Brody shift ever-so-slightly due to this fact.

"Hi, we'd like to talk to Amanda Marshall, please," I said.

"You will have a long wait. Mandy died a long time ago. I'm her mother," the lady replied, and I noticed she looked frail and tired. "What do you want with my Mandy?"

"We are looking into something that happened in 1983," Brody replied.

I noticed him checking things out as he spoke, as if he expected us to be pounced on at any minute. Mrs Marshall shifted nervously, as though considering whether it was safe to let us into her house. At that moment a young man with a large Alsatian dog walked up the garden path to the house beside us and he eyed the old lady menacingly. She stepped back into her hallway and opened the door wider as an indication for us to enter.

"Come in," Mrs Marshall invited, and she led us into a small living room in much the same way as Simone had done yesterday. I sat down on the sofa, as the lady took the only armchair in the room. Brody didn't sit, but stood looking at a few framed photographs hanging on the wall.

"I am Carolina. My husband, Mandy's dad, is long gone. It broke his heart when Mandy died. She was our only child," Carolina said sadly.

"I'm so sorry for your loss," I commented. "What happened to her?"

"She killed herself with drugs," Carolina replied. "Mandy was always so happy and bright; she was my sunshine. Then she started hanging around with people she shouldn't. I know exactly when the trouble started; it was when she started hanging out at concerts. She was raped. Did you know that?"

"Yes, I'm sorry. It must have been really hard for you and your family to come to terms with something like that," I said.

Brody was quietly looking around the room. He studied the photos on the wall of a young, fair-haired girl. There were several snaps of her in school uniform and with her hockey team. There was one of a young man with glasses holding a younger version of the girl on his lap, looking proudly into the camera lens.

"We didn't know. She came back from a weekend at Bill Graham's house—you know, the famous singer—and she was changed forever. Mandy had been an innocent child until that weekend. She was a friend of Bill Graham's manager, Malcolm Reynolds. Malcolm tried to take care of Mandy, but even he couldn't have stopped what happened to her. After that weekend she went off the rails. She was out most nights, never letting us know where she was or who she was with. Sometimes she didn't come back for days." Carolina looked down at her hands and not directly at us.

"Mandy became thinner and more vulgar in her behaviour towards us," Carolina continued. "I could hardly bare to look at her. I contacted Malcolm, but he said he hadn't seen her for weeks. I asked

Malcolm if she had talked to him about anything that happened at the party, when Mandy was raped, and he said she hadn't spoken to him about anything and just wanted to go home early the next morning. Malcolm said he was as baffled by her behaviour as we were. She had stopped going to see him, so he couldn't help her afterwards either. It was such a shame. He's a good man." Carolina said meekly.

"I didn't tell Malcolm about the rape. I didn't want him to feel guilty since he was responsible for her at the party. He said she just disappeared until the next day, but turned up for breakfast and seemed fine. One day she was very high on drugs and she told me what had happened. We cried together. The next morning Mandy was dead. She overdosed on drugs," Carolina finished.

"Was it clear that she overdosed? Did you find the drugs in her room?" I asked softly.

"Yes. I went to wake her up and there she was, bent forward in an unnatural sitting position on her bed, as white as a sheet and still with the syringe hanging from her arm," Carolina replied in a hushed voice as if having trouble reliving the event and seeing the image in her mind's eye. A tear ran down her cheek and she quickly brushed it away with the back of her hand.

Brody walked over to a photograph on the mantelpiece. It was of a soldier in a foreign uniform. "Did Mandy tell you who raped her?" he asked, seeming much more interested now.

"No, she just said they had done unspeakable things to her. Tortured her body until she couldn't

215

take it anymore and passed out," Carolina replied. "Thank God her father never knew about it. His heart was already broken."

"Who is this, Mrs Marshall?" Brody asked, pointing to the photograph.

"That is my brother, Danislav. I am originally from Croatia. His name is Danislav Zadravec," Carolina answered. There was something in her voice that sounded proud, but at the same time there seemed to be an air of determination to her that hadn't been there before.

"Did your brother know what happened to Mandy?" Brody asked.

"Yes, we were a close-knit family and a close-knit community before the revolution. Danislav never had children of his own. He lived here, close to us, and Amanda was the apple of her uncle's eye," Carolina explained.

"How did he react when you told him about Mandy's ordeal and her death?" Brody asked, placing the photo back carefully in its place on the mantelpiece.

"He was angry. I have never seen him so angry. He wanted to kill Bill Graham for taking our sweet little girl from us, but I told him it was pointless, that there was nothing we could do. Danislav said he had his own way of dealing with people like Bill Graham," Carolina said. Her tears ran freely down her cheeks now and she didn't wipe them. "Danislav said rapists and evil people should be exiled or die. He was very passionate about it for a long time."

"So he threatened Bill Graham?" Brody asked calmly, and she nodded.

"Yes, he threatened. Those threats were very real. Danislav wouldn't rest until he had taken his revenge. It was something he had to do for the family," Carolina continued. "Danislav was obsessed with Bill Graham from that day on. He said these rich people didn't care about others. They only cared about themselves and didn't have the decency to keep a young girl safe in their home, because they didn't care. Therefore they didn't deserve to have a home; nowhere would be safe for the likes of Bill Graham."

"Does he still want to harm Bill Graham?" Brody asked calmly, and Carolina hung her head and shook it.

"Danislav said to Bill Graham that if he ever set foot back in Britain, he would know about it. He would hunt him down and he would kill him, and he meant it. It was a very serious threat. Danislav had been a soldier all his life before he came to England. But then there was the Croatian War of Independence and he was called home to fight. Danislav was killed in 1991, when the Yugoslav National Army, together with various Serb paramilitaries, attacked Croatia," Carolina answered, and now she wept openly, the tears rolling down her face.

"So would any other family members take over the revenge after his death?" Brody asked.

"There is only me left now. I have no one. Why would an old woman like me seek revenge?" she

217

asked. "It won't bring my little girl back. I am just thankful that every day I move closer to the end of my life is a day closer to being back with my loved ones. I have no taste for vengeance, only for peace."

"I want you to know that it wasn't Bill Graham who raped your daughter. If Danislav had indeed been successful with his attacks on him, it would have been on an innocent person," I said, getting up to leave. "As it turned out an innocent housekeeper lost her life when someone tried to break into Bill Graham's house."

Carolina looked at me in shock. "No, Danislav would never do that. He was a man of great honour. You are wrong. It must have been someone else. Why are you asking me all these questions? Are you the police?" she asked defensively.

"No, Carolina, we are not the police, but a friend of ours died recently under suspicious circumstances, and we are just looking into it, for our own piece of mind. We thought it might be related to two similar deaths at the party Amanda attended." I said.

I'm really sorry for your loss," I said as I got up from where I was sitting and made to leave. Thank you for your time. By the way, where were you last Friday?"

"Where I always am—here," Carolina answered in surprise.

"Can anyone vouch for that?" I asked.

"I don't know. Yes, the police can vouch for me if it's needed. My neighbour is a vile human being and he was having a big party. I called the police and they came and talked to me before they threw everyone out. It was at about 4 a.m. It had been going on all night," Carolina said. "And his dog kept barking at the noise. It's a nightmare living here."

***

We sat in the car for a few seconds, both in mild shock. Brody started the engine and headed back to where my Range Rover was parked.

"Before we took this job we were briefed on why Bill needed protection. I like to know what I'm getting myself into before I agree to a job," he told me. "Everything Carolina says confirms what I was told. Bill started getting anonymous threats a few months after Delphine's death. That sounds like they coincide with Mandy's death. They were unspecific, but said he would die. They kept on coming to his home in France until they stopped for a few months in 1991. Then they started coming again at the same intervals as before and much the same message."

Brody manoeuvred the Volvo expertly down the winding streets and I looked at his muscular arms holding the wheel when I thought he didn't notice.

"When Tiger died, I was afraid the person making the threats had killed the wrong guy," he continued. "It showed me how vulnerable we were. So the tour was cancelled, but Bill refuses to go back to France, saying he has lived with these threats for so long that he's had enough. If they want to kill him, Bill says they can do their worst, because he's not leaving the UK," Brody concluded as he parked the car behind mine, turned the engine off and turned towards me.

"Well, if Danislav died in 1991 that would explain why the threats stopped for a while. It certainly sounds like he's the guy. Did you notice Carolina used the term 'being in exile'. If it hasn't been Danislav making the threats since then, who is it?" I asked.

"I don't know. I'd think that threatening someone like that for so many years would have to take a certain amount of hatred," Brody answered.

"But if the family members are dead, do you think he would have gotten a friend to continue the threats for him, even after death?" I asked.

"I doubt it. The friend wouldn't have the hatred needed to kill someone in my opinion. I need to think about this carefully. I will tell Bill about our meeting tonight," Brody said.

I thought that was my cue to get out of the car and leave, but as I took off my seatbelt, Brody leaned in and started kissing me. I felt his soft, warm tongue against mine and my temperature went up a few notches from hot to sizzling. He started kissing my neck and nibbling my ear lobe as his mouth moved back to mine and then his tongue found mine again as one hand stroked my neck. Oh my God, I thought. No!

"Stop!" I said between kisses. *"Stop!"*

Brody pulled away and looked at me with amusement.

"I'm not ready for anything like this," I said, feeling breathless. My nymphomania was obviously back in full force.

"On the contrary, you are very ready," he teased.

"Life is about more than sex, you know," I replied in a huff as I started to get out of the car.

"I know that, but it's a nice part of life, don't you think?" Brody said as he waved, and then he was gone.

I got into my car again for the drive back home with a lot more on my mind than I'd bargained for.

***

I checked my messages and email as soon as I got home, and again there were several. There was a second one from Melody: "Can you arrange for me to cover the festival Blue is organising? I want a full interview with her and her band, and the other warm-up band. We can't do The Sticks since we've just done them with a gig review from the Roundhouse, but we could do something about Tiger and weave it together. I'll do the photos and you do the article. Look forward to working with you. Can you recommend a good hotel?"

What on earth was she talking about? I thought this little festival was just something Grandma Blue's little band were doing in our garden and nobody would turn up. I would have to find her or Raven and find out what was going on.

There was finally an answer from the newspaper archives. The lovely lady I had spoken to before had done a great job, and she'd sent me a bill too. Even greater! Anyway, I looked through it and two things immediately struck me about the material she'd sent me. One thing was a photograph of Bill with Yvette, taken over twenty years ago. Under the picture, the caption said 'Bill Graham and Yvette Labyre'.

It was strange that Yvette should have the same surname as Simone. Perhaps it was a common one in France or maybe they belonged to the same family? There was another photo from around the same time with another man in it. He was slim and standing next to the couple, but the image was unclear and I couldn't see his face properly, but there was something familiar about him that I couldn't put my finger on.

Under the picture it said Bill Graham, Yvette Labyre and Christian Labyre. It didn't say anything in the article about who this guy was; it just mentioned the opening of an art gallery belonging to Christian Labyre in Paris. I Googled the name immediately, but there was nothing about him online as far as I could see, yet the guy's face kept niggling me.

I found Grandma Blue and her friends in the shed, sitting around smoking weed and giggling together.

"What's this about The Sticks playing your festival and where are you going to have it? I doubt Dad will agree to let you use the garden," I said, trying to ignore the heavy, sickly smell of marijuana.

"Don't worry about us, Charlie. We have it all taken care of," Grandma Blue replied in a strange voice that sounded like she was talking and trying to hold her breath at the same time.

"I have made the Warnes Group organise the festival. What's the point of owning fifty-one percent of the company if I don't use my right to decide what they do from time to time?" Doris said and she started laughing.

"I've arranged for the festival to be in the field that belongs to our most prominent benefactor of the local church, for a fee, of course, which Warnes have very kindly offered to pay," Mr Heritage added.

"And I've talked to some bands," Grandma Blue said. "I sent that Bill Graham a message and said we could do a tribute concert for Tiger, and that we'd make it a free festival for anyone who wants to come, and my band, The Floozies, will play support. Then Will Hero wanted to be in on it, because he was mates with Tiger. So we've got two support bands and a headliner—piece of cake. Now we only have a week to learn how to play really well. I'm sure we'll be fine."

Grandma Blue took another deep breath on the spliff they were sending around. I must say I was rather impressed with what the old folk had come up with in such a short space of time. The room was beginning to spin, so I left them to their drugs.

Chapter 13
Tiger's Festival – Rig Up

A week before the festival, news of Malcolm's visit to the police station after Tiger's funeral blew wide open in the press. There had been intense speculation in the media about the identification of the person helping the police with their enquiries, but after Malcolm was called in for a second time, the photos from the funeral surfaced in all the national newspapers. He had been called back, so the media were now considering whether the police had cause for arrest and whether the person who had made the complaint against him was believable enough for charges to be pressed.

On the very day of the festival, everyone in our house was tense and nervous, except Dad. He had the idea that Grandma Blue would make a total fool of herself and he was planning on being there to tell her 'I told you so'. He walked around with a strange smile on his face all day.

The riggers had arrived on time the previous day and started to erect the stage. All the instruments and bands would arrive later that afternoon. As it turned out, Grandma Blue and her old friends had managed to get the whole community involved in this festival. The local pub was setting up a stall to sell beverages, and the Women's Institute had organised food stalls, and local arts and crafts for sale.

Warnes Group had even organised T-shirts for sale and all profits from the concert were to go to the Tiger Edwards Charity to help recovering addicts. Tracy had been asked by Warnes Group to be a part of the chairmanship, which she had happily agreed to. I was so pleased this had come together, because it had been Tracy and Tiger's greatest wish to help prevent people from making the same bad choices they had made.

One farmer with a field at the other side of the old parish church was offering free camping, and tents had started to pitch up two days before the festival started. Warnes Group had made a good job of organising the concert, but then they did an annual festival in the area, so they knew what they were doing.

I was in a good mood for two reasons. Firstly, it was going to be a lot of fun and, secondly, I would get to see Brody again. We had spoken on the phone every night since I saw him in Loughborough. Nothing too heavy; we just chatted about what we'd been up to and how Bill was, but there was always this underlying tension and warmth between us. At the same time, I was a little anxious at what Brody would make of my family. I was hoping they had enough weird people in California, so he would be used to it. My Grandma Blue certainly took some getting used to.

Robert had gone quiet, and I was rather surprised that he had not phoned me to ask about my meeting with Carolina Marshall. But then he always was a bit strange in his behaviour towards me. One minute I'd think I knew exactly where I was with him and how he felt, and the next he'd go off and do something completely out of character, like marrying that Alicia, or not talking to me for weeks on end. I didn't understand it, so I decided to try to put it out of my head.

Melody Magazine had arranged to come to the soundcheck and Grandma Blue had brightly coloured Access All Areas armbands ready for us. It made me a little sad to see them, because it reminded me of Tiger. I couldn't get the image of him clutching the AAA armband out of my head and it was bothering me.

Tracy was coming too, as was Simone. I was a little worried about The Floozies' performance, but I hoped people would be kind. They had been practising all hours of the day and night during the week leading up to the concert. I think Raven used it as a way of keeping busy, so she wouldn't have to think about Nigel.

I had tried to broach the subject with her once, but she simply didn't want to talk about him as it was too painful. Raven thought she'd finally met the love of her life only to find he was keeping secrets and lying to her, so she had to move on. I didn't get it. Surely it would have been better for them to sit down and have a conversation to clear the air?

But then, I hadn't done that myself, admittedly. I'd simply gotten into my car and driven out of James' life, so I shut up. It was strange as it felt like years ago that I had lived with James, not just a few weeks.

ACCESS ALL AREAS

The field where the festival would take place was just a little further down the lane from our house on the other side of the parish church. People had started arriving at an early hour, and an adjacent field had been turned into a makeshift parking place. Mr Heritage and his church friends were charging people to park and the money was going to Tiger's charity, so no one complained.

The Sticks' bus arrived at lunchtime and the same little roadie, Digger, whom I'd met in London, was the driver. The Floozies and I got to the stage just as it turned up. Digger parked the bus expertly, as usual, behind the stage and got the other roadies organised. The farmer who owned the field had arranged for fences to be made to seal off a 'restricted area' behind the stage and to the sides, so that the public couldn't mill around there. The backstage area towards the fence was also covered in a thick tarpoleum, so the fans couldn't see what was going on there either. Bill and the rest of the guys would be arriving for a soundcheck later.

I had no idea how many people would come to this concert, but by the look of it so far, it was going to be a busy event. The sun shone from a clear, blue summer sky, so even the gods were favourable.

"Oi, Blue!" Digger shouted to my grandma. "You ain't given me a set list. Watcha' playing?"

"None of your business," Blue answered, but she was laughing. I think she liked his straightforward way of talking to her.

"Well, how can I help you out with the sound if I don't know what song's up next? You tell me that," Digger tried again.

Grandma Blue handed him a piece of paper from the pocket of the new jeans she had bought for the occasion. She had rolled them up as they were a bit too long for her, and now Blue looked like she was expecting there to be spring floods and she didn't want her jeans to get wet. I saw Digger take the piece of paper over to the sound-mixing board and get into deep conversation with another roadie. They kept looking at Grandma Blue and consulting the list, and messing with a phone. I had no idea the sound guy had to have a set list. It sounded strange to me, but I didn't question it.

My phone suddenly sprung to life and I barely heard it above the noise of the rigging and shouting on stage. "Hi!" I said a little too loudly whilst moving away from the stage and the noise.

"Hi there yourself," Brody replied. "I just wanted to let you know we are leaving here soon and will be with you in a short while."

I couldn't wait to see Brody, but at the same time I was a little nervous about it too. I was afraid it would be awkward meeting him and I was scared of what he'd make of my family. We aren't the most normal of people, are we?

"That's great. I'm looking forward to seeing you again. There is just one thing," I said carefully, unsure of how he would take it. "Could I ask you a huge favour?"

"Go on," he said and I heard amusement in his tone of voice. Oh boy, I would have to handle this carefully, and tact was not my strongest point.

"Thing is… you know how when I meet you, we have a tendency to hug and stuff?" I began, trying to work out what to say as I went along.

"Yes?" Brody asked, not helping me at all.

"Well, you know I like you?"

"Yes, and I like you back," he said and then laughed. "Get to the punch line, babe, as we are delaying the flight. What is it you want to say?"

"Thing is, please don't take this the wrong way, but could we tone things down a little whilst we are around my family? I was married until a few weeks ago, and I haven't told my family about you," I explained, and then I waited, holding my breath.

Brody didn't say anything for a few endless seconds.

"Not that there is anything to tell, but… well, you know," I added, feeling really stupid and afraid I'd assumed too much.

"Sure, babe, no problem, but, listen, I've got to go now," he answered and hung up.

I had been putting off having that talk with him for days, so why did it make me feel so downcast now? It wasn't like we were dating or anything. We'd hardly spent any time together, and Brody was not the sort of person who would be a good boyfriend. Not that I was looking for one. He would be gone all the time, jetting off to protect people for weeks on end.

I really needed to pull myself together about this, but he had been on my mind rather a lot. Every evening when my mobile rang and it was him, my heart leaped in my chest a little.

Grandma Blue, Doris, Rich and Raven and I drove back to our house in my car. I was quiet and thoughtful about my situation while the rest of them were so excited about their first gig that they chatted endlessly about what they were going to wear.

"I think I'll put that pink band around my head," Doris said. "I think it suits me."

"You can't wear that," Grandma Blue chided. "You look like a fucking flower-power hippy! We are a punk band, so you need something badass and punk."

"Why do you say badass? It's 'bad arse' in English," Doris replied and I could sense that they were getting a little irritated with each other. Doris suddenly seemed to enjoy winding Blue up. Perhaps the pressure was starting to get to them.

"Saying badass isn't punk either, so you can shut the fuck up too, and I'll wear my flower-power hippy headband if I want to," Doris insisted, to which Grandma Blue just huffed.

They had all taken to swearing since Raven had moved in with us. I made a mental note to have a word with her about it, and perhaps see if she could influence them to tone it down a little.

When we got back to the house, they all trouped into my grandma's room to get ready, and I was pleased they would be out of the way for a while.

Mum was in the kitchen making enough food to feed an army, nervously stirring and tasting, salting and stirring, and tasting again. Bill and the rest of the band, together with Brody, were to arrive soon in their helicopter, which would land at the bottom of our garden! Mum had decided they would all need feeding and that was her cue to get stuck in. I tried to tell her that The Sticks were just people, but she wouldn't listen—totally star-struck. I think cooking was her way of being a part of this concert; her contribution.

The sound of the copter sent her into a frenzy of activity. I went outside to welcome everyone and saw that Malcolm was with them. I had hoped he wouldn't be coming. His presence always seemed to put a damper on everybody's mood. I noticed that Tim Boyce, the bassist with the band Stones Throw, was also with them, which would be a nice surprise for the audience. I had wondered who they would get to fill Tiger's place since Bill had messaged Doris that while he appreciated her offer of playing with them, he had already filled the position with someone else. She had been quite disappointed about it.

Brody smiled at me warmly as he, Bill, Keith and Marianne, Ronnie, Tim and Malcolm all entered our house by the back door from the garden. My parents greeted everyone heartily and a bit excitedly, as the helicopter whizzed off into the air.

Yvette had not come with them and I was told she would be arriving later. She was another one I would have been pleased to see the back of. Bill seemed

much more at ease when Yvette wasn't with him,
but to be fair, they had been together for quite a long
time, so it was only natural for her to attend this
concert.

"Would you all like something to eat?" Mum
asked nervously.

"No thanks, no time for that." Malcolm almost
brushed her away like some annoying fly, as he
looked around our living room and kept glancing at
his watch. "When does the car get here?" he asked
no one in particular.

"It's here already. We will go in two cars. I'll
drive you over, and so will Dad," I answered curtly,
seeing the hurt expression on my mother's face.

"Actually, thank you very much, Mrs Hart," Bill
said steadily. "We need to go over to the venue and
get the sound right. When that is done, I, for one,
would love something to eat. Whatever you are
making smells delicious and I'm starving."

I smiled at Bill for his kindness, and then Dad
and I drove the guys over to the stage, parking
behind the bus in the restricted area. Malcolm was
acting like he usually did; nagging Darren, who had
arrived with Yvette, for an envelope of 'green stuff'
and getting on the wrong side of almost everyone.

The Sticks went on stage to check their
instruments and mics to shouts from the
neighbouring field. Although people couldn't see the
stage from the parking place over there, they could
hear it very well indeed. The security around the
field was tight. High fences had been built all around
the area, making sure people entered and left via one

place to control the crowd. No one apart from the people working at the event had been let into the field yet.

Towards one side, several stalls had been set up, selling food and drink, T-shirts and all manner of stuff. Mr Heritage had been running back and forth between them and the parking area, as this was obviously his organising responsibility. I must say, I was pretty proud of the work they had all done.

Yvette turned up with a friend, who had his back turned to me. She stood by the front of the stage to one side, looking bored and checking her watch every five minutes or so. Brody made his way over to me and drew me aside backstage when he thought no one was looking and he gave me a long kiss that seemed to last forever.

I pulled away and suddenly felt shy. Taking a quick look around to see if anyone had seen us, I noticed Yvette glance at us with contempt and say something to the guy she was with. He turned and looked at me with a snigger on his face, and I suddenly recognised him. Not only was he the man in the photo taken of Bill and Yvette over twenty years ago in Paris, but I now recognised the bushy eyebrows of the guy in a hoodie who had tried to steal Raven's lens. I drew in a sharp breath.

"Brody, who's that man standing with Yvette?" I asked.

Something in my tone of voice obviously alerted him to the fact that I was excited about something, because he looked at me with concern. "That little toad is Christian, Yvette's brother. Why?"

"Well, remember the first day I met you, and we got mugged outside the Sticks and Stones restaurant? That was the guy who tried to steal Raven's lens," I replied.

Brody looked calmly over to Christian and then back at me. "Are you one hundred per cent sure? It's a very serious accusation to make if you are not."

"I am one hundred and fifty per cent sure. I got a good look at his face when I was sitting on you. He turned around and looked straight at me. Then he smiled as he put the lens on the ground and ran. It was him. I recognise the bushy eyebrows and those beady eyes," I insisted.

Brody very calmly made his way over to the stage and positioned himself in the place where Bill would leave it. He spoke into his earpiece, which he always seemed to have perched behind his right ear, turning away from Yvette as he did so. I'm guessing it was so as not to alert her to the fact that he was mentioning her name.

I watched intently as Bill walked to the right-hand side of the stage, intending to leave. Brody stopped him and spoke to him for several minutes before leading him back the way he had come. Yvette and Christian watched them both with surprise, but they made no move to go after them. I turned and made my way to where Brody had gone, further backstage.

Bill motioned me to come over. "Are you sure it was Christian you saw in London?" he asked me.

"Yes, I am positive," I answered truthfully and I saw the anger in his eyes; white hatred burned there, which I'd never seen before.

Suddenly, Yvette was standing next to us, and I felt the air become ice-cold with tension. Her brother was no longer around. Brody spoke once more into his earpiece and nodded to Bill. "They've got him," he said. "What do you want them to do with him? Get rid?" Brody added and Bill nodded.

Taking my hand, Brody led me away from Yvette and Bill, but we couldn't avoid seeing the blinding row that took place between them or help hearing what was being said, shouted and screamed back and forth. Actually, Bill seemed quite calm. It was Yvette who was doing the hysterical screaming.

"It was you, wasn't it?" Bill accused her and she went pale, seeming to know what he was talking about straightaway.

"When that Zadravec died and the threats stopped in 1991, it was you who carried on sending them. Why?" Bill's tone was calm and emotionless.

"When the threats stopped, the first thing you talked about was going back to England. I didn't want you to leave. I didn't know the man was dead, only that the threats had stopped. I was afraid, you have to believe me," Yvette said, weeping. "I was just thinking of your safety."

"You knew how terrified I had been. How could you do that to me?" he asked. His voice was still calm, but there was a dangerous edge to it.

"Because I didn't want you anywhere near her!" Yvette cried out shrilly.

"So your selfish jealousy made you carry on the façade that haunted my life for thirty years? All because you thought I would see your sister? How pathetic! As for Christian, has he known about this all along?" Bill asked and Yvette nodded slightly.

"Then when we came back, you decided to stage that theft of the camera lens to scare me into cowering back to France with you again, yes?" he continued.

"I didn't know what to do," Yvette replied. "It was only a matter of time before Simone would hear of your arrival and do what she always does—swan in and take you away from me. I couldn't let that happen. I thought if you saw the threats were still real, you would want to leave as fast as possible."

Bill shook his head in disbelief. He motioned to Brody to join them, but I stayed where I was.

"Get rid of her!" Bill said coldly. He turned his back on Yvette as she cried loudly and fought Brody, who had to carry her off the stage. She screamed Bill's name and I almost felt sorry for her.

As Bill's face was bright red with anger, I thought it best to leave him alone to calm down. Mel had arrived and was taking a few shots of the stage. She smiled at me as I went to greet her in a restricted area at the front, which was also a makeshift mosh pit.

"Hiya, what was all that screaming and shouting about?" she asked, but added quickly, "Never mind, I don't want to know."

Mel was carrying a heavy camera bag and an overnight bag. I had offered her one of our guest rooms, which she accepted. It meant we had a full house, but it didn't matter to anyone. The more the merrier was my mother's comment when I told her. I think we were all joyous at the prospect of being a little part of this festival. It wasn't often that exciting things like this happened in our neck of the woods.

Tracy arrived just as the Floozies took to the stage to check their instruments, much to my delight, and after I had introduced her to Mel, the three of us made our way back to the house on foot. Rich had promised to drive my car back carefully, following my dad in his, so we didn't have to stand around and wait for the Sticks and Floozies' sound check to end. Nobody knew when Will Hero would arrive.

Mum had made the dining-room table the longest I'd ever seen it in a long time. I think there were about twenty chairs set around the thing, which had those extra panels in the bottom to make it longer. She had laid the table with our best china and cutlery. I heard frantic activity coming from the kitchen and Mum bossing my father around, asking him to get some good wine from the cellar, much to his annoyance as he was unwilling to share it.

The French doors leading from the dining room out onto the porch were open wide, letting in a light breeze and the sound of instruments being checked at the festival in the distance. I could hear Grandma Blue's voice shouting, "One, two; one, two. Che, che," into her microphone before the opening riff to something was played for a couple of chords and then discarded. I really hoped people would be kind, because if the soundcheck was anything to go by, the Floozies seriously sucked as a punk band.

***

Grandma Blue had changed into her stage outfit for dinner, which was a pair of black faux leather trousers and one of Raven's black T-shirts with 'WANKER' emblazoned across the front in bold yellow lettering. The trousers looked PVC or plastic—seriously skin-tight and leaving little to the imagination—and they swished every time she moved. Blue completed her gear with a pair of brand new Doc Marten boots, which actually looked good on her and must have been quite comfortable by the way she was strutting around.

"Hey, Charlie, how do you like my stage outfit? Cool or what?" Grandma Blue asked me as I entered the kitchen with Melody and Tracy, whose mouths gaped open in surprise. "Mind you, I don't know what these trousers are made of, but I keep getting static electricity zapping me every time I touch anything metal," she added, trying to demonstrate, but finding it didn't work on command.

"I think you've overdone it with that T-shirt, Blue," said Rich, dressed head to foot in black.

"No, I haven't. That's the whole point. It's supposed to be shocking. If you say it enough times, it doesn't mean anything," Grandma answered.

"No, I've looked at it several times and it still holds the same meaning to me," Rich answered.

"Can you imagine Fat Jean in those trousers?" Doris cut in from where she was standing by the door. "The chub rub at the top of her legs could get dangerous on stage. I mean she could start a fire!"

Melody and Tracy looked at Blue and Doris, and tried to suppress a giggle, not wanting to be rude, but obviously not sure how to handle this. Doris was dressed in a pair of flared trousers with flowers all over them, a flowing kimono-type top and a pink headband. I could see why Grandma thought she was too hippy looking and not very punk.

Brody and The Sticks were given a lift over by Dad and Rich. When they arrived, Bill and Simone stood outside our house, taking a few minutes to talk alone, while everyone else entered and trouped into the living and dining room area. Brody, however, had seen me in the kitchen and he now stood in the doorway, looking at the two old ladies with an amused look on his face.

"Hey Blue, you better not have any baked beans for dinner. Keep away from anything that can make you gassy" Digger said and my grandma doubled over with laughter.

"Yeah, Digger, where would the excess air go? These trousers are so tight and plastic—one fart and I would launch myself into the air with such a force, you'd have to send out a search party to find me!" Grandma Blue answered and then giggled hysterically.

This sent everyone, including Brody, into a fit of laughter that I thought I wouldn't survive. Grandma Blue nudged me in the ribs and pointed her blue Mohican in Brody's direction while raising her eyebrows to indicate that she thought him a hot guy.

I shook my head at her in amusement and walked towards the hall just as Bill and Simone entered the house. I was pleased to see that she was with him, and Malcolm and Darren were not.

"Hello, again," Simone greeted me.

She was looking very stylish in jeans and a black leather biker jacket. I noticed she had touched up the colour of her hair and it made her look ten years younger, or it might have been the bright glow that her complexion seemed to have right now. Something was obviously agreeing with her.

I pulled her aside as the others went into the dining room. "Why didn't you tell me you were Yvette's sister?" I asked.

Simone shrugged. "I didn't think it was relevant. Besides, we are sisters in blood only. We share the same father," she explained. "Yvette and Christian are results of my father's third marriage and we have never spent time together. They are over ten years younger than me and we have never bonded, or even liked each other. Yvette has always been in fierce competition with me about every aspect of life. I introduced her to Bill. That was a big mistake."

"Why?" I asked "Did you fancy him yourself?"

"Yes, I had known Bill for many years, even before he met Delphine, but we never got together, much due to the line of business I'm in. But there was always this vibe between us. So, when he got together with Yvette, I decided to keep away. Bill just told me what she's done. I can believe it of her. She is shallow and cold. I never understood what Bill saw in her."

"Have you asked him?" I said.

"Yes, I did. Just a couple of minutes ago, and he said she reminded him of me," Simone replied, and I could see she was very pleased about that.

I placed my hand on her arm in a gesture of support and we walked together into the dining room. Bill seemed to have calmed down, and Simone and he fell into a deep conversation.

Mum had made various types of pasta. Lasagne, spaghetti, fettuccini—you name it, it was there. They were served with an array of sauces to cover every dietary need, from vegan to vegetarian to basic carnivore. Everything came with a huge salad and garlic bread. The smell of the food was amazing and everyone around the table helped themselves quite a few times, to Mum's delight. It was great and I know she had spent several days worrying about whether there would be enough food and pondering what people would like or dislike.

Grandma Blue sat between Rich and Doris, and tucked in heartily. You wouldn't think they were the least bit nervous about playing their first ever gig on a huge stage in front of thousands of people. Raven seemed to be the most anxious, only picking at her food.

"What's up with her?" asked Mel, who was sitting beside me, after we had finished the first course.

Mum and Grandma Blue had gone into the kitchen to get dessert. Simone, Brody and I collected the dinner plates and carried them into the kitchen, and I saw Mum look at him with a knowing smile. I can't seem to get away with anything in this family.

"It's either stage fright for the gig or she's missing her ex-boyfriend," I told Mel when I got back to the table.

"Well, I've got a surprise for her. Nigel contacted me, asking for help in getting Raven to talk to him," Mel said, smiling slyly. "He told me all about the silly argument."

"Has he been cheating?" I asked quietly, so Raven wouldn't hear us talking about her.

"No, but he's been a right silly sod though," Mel revealed. "He would never cheat on Raven. Thing is the social services threatened to take Jason into care. He's only fourteen. Anyway, Nigel asked what needed to be done for Jason to be allowed to stay with them, and they said they wouldn't accept him living in a squat. They said his future was unsure as the owners of the house might come back and evict them at any time.

"So Nigel, being a man of means, bought the house and has been scared stiff of telling Raven. She's been into this nostalgic, punk squat lifestyle shite. Nigel kept putting it off and not telling her, and the lie seemed to grow, as he had to make sure he got to the post before her in case there was anything there to give him away. It's all really silly.

"Anyway, I've invited him to come to the concert. Blue sorted him out with a backstage pass, so we'll just push them together when we get over there and force her to listen to him. He should have arrived by now, I think," Melody said, conspiratorially, and I laughed. Yes, it was a really good plan.

"Just make sure you wait until The Floozies have had their fifteen minutes of fame before you do anything, because if Raven doesn't fall into his arms, she's going to be mad as hell, and I don't want anything to go wrong," I replied.

Mel nodded. "Trust me," she said, unconvincingly. "Hey, what happened to Will Hero?"

"He hasn't arrived yet. Has he done that nude photo shoot with you yet?" I asked.

"No, he hasn't answered. I sent him an email, but he's on tour. I have no idea if he's even seen it or if I have the right address."

Grandma Blue looked up from her second serving of dessert. "I can give you the right one, Mel," she offered, and Mel nodded in thanks.

"I can't believe it, but your grandma is better connected than me," she joked. And we both laughed. "And who's that dark haired guy sitting over there with Bill and Tim Boyce? I haven't seen him before," she asked, nodding in Brody's direction.

Before I had time to answer, Tracy, who was sitting on the other side of me cut in, "That's Brody. He's Bill's bodyguard. Hot or what?"

"Yeah, I can see why you keep throwing yourself at him," Mel teased, which resulted in my face heating up as Brody, appearing to have radar to the fact that we were talking about him, looked over at me and smiled warmly.

Grandma Blue, clearly possessing the same type of detector, glanced up, shifting her interest from her pudding to what was being said around the table. She looked at me in surprise and then cast her eyes towards the end where Brody sat amidst the Sticks members before casting her toothless, knowing grin in my direction, which only embarrassed me further.

Chapter 14
Tiger's Concert

It was time to interview The Floozies, so Melody took a few photos of them together. I got my nice new Dictaphone out of my bag and once again realised that I still had no idea how to turn it on. I called to Raven, who looked at it closely, flipped a switch and there it was, all working well. Apparently, you have to hold the switch in for a few seconds before it connects and then you have to follow the instructions on the tiny screen to record or play, because it is a digital Dictaphone. All this technology was way over my head.

"Okay, so you have started this punk band. Tell me a little bit about how it came about," I asked Raven, Blue, Rich and Doris as the first question in the interview. We were sitting together in the garden, away from the others.

"You know how it happened," Grandma Blue answered.

"Yes, I know, but the readers don't," I replied, patiently.

"Well, it was because we came up with the idea of a festival and we didn't know any bands, so we started our own. It had to be punk because that's the only music you can be really bad at and still sound good, which is handy, since we are bad," Doris answered.

"No, we're not!" Rich cut in. "We are a really good punk band. We are the worst punk band there has ever been, and in punk terms that's good."

"Well, you've totally confused me now," I told him.

"I just really want to meet men," Grandma Blue announced. "Doris and I started the band with Rich because everyone knows that people in bands get all the action. It's a well-known fact. So we are in it for the groupies."

"I can't write that!" I said, shocked. "What are your ambitions for the future?"

"I'm sixty-nine, for fuck's sake. The future isn't interesting any more. We live for today," Grandma Blue said. She was closer to eighty.

"Yeah peace and love is the future," Doris said, making the peace sign, to Grandma Blue's annoyance. "The punk movement is about peace and love too," Doris added.

"It's not a movement!" Grandma Blue shot in. "That's another hippy expression. You haven't understood the concept, Doris. It's all about doing stuff."

"I do stuff!" Doris answered, and the two of them started a discussion about who did what when, and I totally lost my train of thought.

I had to give up on the interview, which was quickly turning into an argument. I dropped the Dictaphone into my handbag as it was now time to leave.

When we reached the festival, I could not believe how many people had made their way to our little village. Tracy tried to talk to Malcolm, who was so high on his spliff that it looked like he had no eyes, so she soon gave up.

Will Hero had thankfully arrived with his band in our absence and Mel took her place in the mosh pit with her camera, waiting for the first support band to take the stage. My stomach churned with excitement. I would definitely be doing more gig reviews for Melody, I decided. This was fun.

My best friend, Camilla, and her husband, Peter, were there to support his grandmother, Doris. I couldn't see Robert, and I was quite surprised he hadn't accompanied them. I made a mental note to ask Camilla about him later. She had brought both of her children with her and they were wearing headphones, so as not to damage their hearing. They ran around backstage making a nuisance of themselves until she herded them towards the stage, so they could watch. Camilla and I stood together, holding hands in excitement.

"Blue is in for a surprise," Camilla confided in me. "Doris has been planning this for weeks."

"Planning what?" I asked.

She smiled secretly. "Don't worry. You'll see."

There was a roar from the audience as Peter Warnes took the stage to address the crowd, and thank them for coming to honour a great musician and a great guy who had left this world way too soon.

"What does he mean way too soon?" Grandma Blue whispered in my ear. "He was seventy-two, for fuck's sake." She had taken to swearing just as much as Raven and I made a note to have a word with her about it and definitely not swear in front of children.

Peter introduced Tracy to shouts and clapping from the crowd, and she stood there alone, staring out over the fans who had shown their appreciation so loudly. "Thank you all for coming here tonight, and supporting Tiger and his charity that was so kindly set up by the Warnes family," she said as the crowds cheered once again.

Grandma Blue, Doris, Rich and Raven waited to one side of the stage, looking out on what could only be described as a sea of people; the field being that tightly packed with fans. I stood with them and Peter and Camilla, who were excitedly waiting for Tracy to introduce the first support band, The Floozies. I noticed Camilla was holding a spray can, which I thought was strange, but I didn't comment.

Malcolm, who was sitting on a box a little further back stage, looked unsteadily at Grandma Blue's Mohican hairdo with an arrogant laugh. He said something to Darren, which made him turn and look at the band with a snigger. Malcolm stumbled towards me with Darren in tow.

"I see you took a leaf out of my book and hired the worst band you could find as warm-up," he said with an ugly grin on his face while Darren nodded in approval.

"Shut the fuck up, Malcolm, you fucking moron," I said angrily, hoping Camilla's kids weren't listening and deciding that I'd let Blue get away with her colourful language a little longer.

Grandma Blue and Raven were too excited to hear anything that was going on; their attention was fixed on the stage, and they were ready and raring to play. Rich, however, turned and looked thoughtfully at Malcolm, who was walking unsteadily and grudgingly back to the box he had been sitting on backstage.

Rich followed him and I watched as he walked past him on his way back to us and nudged him slightly. Malcolm dropped the spliff he was just about to light up and groaned in annoyance. Rich apologised, bent down to pick up the smoke from the ground and handed it back to him.

"...so without further ado, here is the first support band. Please give it up for the punk band The Floozies!"

At Tracy's announcement, Raven, Rich and Grandma Blue leapt out on stage. Doris stayed behind, quickly removing her kimono to reveal a black T-shirt with the words 'BADASS BASSIST' in gold lettering and a hundred different safety pins attached to it. She whipped off her headband and flared jeans to reveal the same faux leather trousers as Blue was wearing.

Camilla laughed as Doris bent forward and she sprayed her hair bright pink with the aerosol can. It was now as pink as Grandma's was blue. She messed it up, so it was standing on end, before running on to the stage and doing the duckwalk, Chuck Berry style, for the last few yards. It was the coolest thing I'd ever seen. It was also such a sight to see Grandma Blue's jaw drop when she realised she'd been tricked.

Rich hit the drums and Raven played her riff, but Blue was too shocked to do anything. She just stood there, staring at Doris in surprise. Digger strode past and almost ran me over in his eagerness to get to the mixing desk. "Steady on, Digger!" I said. "What's the rush?"

"That flaming band is the rush. I can't let them go out there without help. The crowd will slaughter them if they play anything like they did at the sound check," he called back.

There was a loud, if somewhat surprised, roar from the crowd, and it seemed to be what Blue needed to compose herself. She took the mic and shouted, "Are you all right?" and the fans roared back at her. "It's not about how old you are in this business, it's about how good you are," she went on. "So let's show you what we're made of after just a few weeks of rehearsals. RIP Tiger, let's fucking rock!"

Rich hit the drums again, Raven set out with a brilliant riff, and this time they blasted out the Sex Pistols' 'Pretty Vacant', followed by 'God Save the Queen', and lastly, Grandma Blues' hoarse voice sang 'Seventeen' to a jubilant crowd.

I actually had goosebumps, and the audience screamed and whistled in appreciation. I couldn't believe how good they suddenly sounded and then I got it. Digger, who was in charge of the sound, had managed to edit much of the things that had gone wrong in their gig with background music taken from original Sex Pistols' tracks. The Floozies rocked out and loved every minute of it. Before they all left the stage, Grandma Blue shouted into the mic, "Thank you very much. This is what punk is all about—getting off your backside and doing something. And if we can do it, you can too."

"Peace and love!" Doris shouted into the mic as she passed it while making her way offstage.

Grandma Blue, Raven, Rich, Doris and I all hugged each other in excitement at what they had achieved when they came backstage again.

"Don't you know it's dangerous to trick people my age, Doris? I was so shocked I forgot the words to the song," Blue said and then she was laughing. "You look fucking amazing! And that Chuck Berry dance was brilliant. This has been the best day of my life so far."

"Yeah, Blue, you rocked out. I think we should go on tour!" Doris replied, and I noted the look of utter horror on Diggers face at that remark.

Robert had been standing behind me, but I'd had no idea, being too engrossed on what was going down on stage. He looked as proud as punch as he kissed his pink-haired grandmother. Rich passed me and whispered in my ear whilst discretely pointing a thumb at Malcolm. "Watch him tonight. I think he's in for a surprise."

"What have you done?" I asked.

"Let's put it this way, he's going to be getting a bit more than he bargained for," Rich replied and laughed wickedly. "I switched his smoke with something a little stronger."

I could tell that Malcolm was extremely high as Robert made his way over to greet me with a big, soft kiss right on the lips. Looking up, I saw Brody flinch where he was standing on the other side of the stage, staring straight at us.

"Hello, stranger," Robert said warmly.

Yikes, this was not good. I hadn't thought about what I'd do if I ever had Brody and Robert in the same place at the same time. I became a little flustered.

We had to wait a little while to talk, however, because of the roar made by the crowd when Will Hero and his band took to the stage. I glanced down into the mosh pit to see Melody spring into action, eagerly focussing her attention on Will Hero, who, in turn, played up to her camera. He was dressed in black leather from top to toe. There were screams from some giddy girls as he'd entered the stage and I could see what they found attractive. The man oozed sex appeal. The music was loud and the beat was almost the same as my heartbeat, as I felt it shake and bang in my chest.

"Have you got time for dinner any time soon?" Robert asked me between two songs.

The music blasted out again and the audience screamed, so I didn't answer him straight away. I was glad of the noise because it gave me time to reflect on how I should answer him. At any other time, before I'd met James, an invitation to dinner with Robert Warnes would have been accepted with excitement. I'd have spent a whole day getting ready for it and built up so much nervous tension that I'd be a wreck. Now, however, it didn't feel right. My whole life was a mess at the moment. I really needed certain aspects of it to end before I could even begin to contemplate starting other parts.

Malcolm, who had been sitting on a box, seemed to lie down on his back and gaze up at the stars. Darren kept nudging him and trying to get him to sit up, but Malcolm was totally out of his skull. Rich watched him with interest and gave me the thumbs-up. I wondered what he had managed to give him to have that effect.

Raven and Nigel had found each other, and were having a hefty chat behind the stage. It looked like it was quite heated for a while, but then she fell into his arms, so I guessed everything had worked itself out and that she would be going back home. I would miss her.

Finally, there was a lull between songs again and I leaned towards Robert's ear. "I would love to have dinner with you one night," I replied and he nodded in approval. "We are friends and go back a long way," I added, trying to make it a meal between friends, as opposed to an actual romantic date.

You can have dinner with a friend even though you're kind of, sort of, perhaps getting involved with someone else, right?

"About that, I have a confession to make," Robert said, but then the music was once again too loud for me to hear anything. He mouthed the word 'later' to me and I nodded, wondering what it was he was going to tell me.

When Will Hero came off stage there was a break before The Sticks were set to play. There was a lot of activity in the stage area—guitars were carried off stage and mics were moved around to suit the next band. Digger worked fast and ordered his team of roadies here and there.

I turned to Robert again and asked, "What was it you wanted to tell me?"

He shrugged. "Not now. It will keep for later."

Melody was now backstage with me, waiting for The Sticks. She had been in the pit with her camera for the whole of the support act and was the only photographer who would be allowed to take pictures all the way through The Sticks' performance. The others would be turned out of the pit after the first three songs, as was usual.

I noticed Will Hero acting a little strangely. He was normally quite subdued and quiet, but now he was messing about and kept glancing in Mel's direction. Looked to me like he was showing off and trying to impress her. She, in turn, flirted by sending him smiles and long looks. When I nudged her, Mel turned her back to Will and mouthed 'What?' without actually saying it. I laughed and shrugged my shoulders.

As The Sticks took to the stage to another loud roar from the fans, I made my way back to the band bus and half expected to see a bunch of groupies hanging around. There were none, just the roadies. Seeing Digger standing with two other men having a quick smoke, I asked him for a word in private. We stepped a couple of yards away from the others.

"Hi, Digger, thank you for what you did for The Floozies. You are the head roadie, aren't you?" I asked.

"I'm the road *manager*," he replied a little indignantly.

"Well, Digger, I remember you from the Camden gig. Can you tell me if you helped anyone get any heroin that night?" I asked, half expecting him to refuse to talk to me.

"I might have done. What's it to you?" he asked defiantly.

"Well, Tiger overdosed and I am trying to work out how he got the gear, because he was with Tracy all the time," I explained.

"You are not going to pin that on me! I never got no heroin for Tiger. I wouldn't. He was a mate. Nah, you got it wrong, mate."

"But you got some heroin for someone? Can you please tell me who it was? I promise I won't breathe a word to anyone. I just have to know it wasn't you," I lied.

If it was him, I was going to phone that Detective Jack Baldwin straight away and cart his sorry arse off to prison without a second thought.

"Too fucking right it wasn't me. Only one person asked for heroin and that was Darren. I don't know who he wanted it for, unless Malcolm's started getting new habits."

"Why would Darren ask you for the heroin?" I asked, not understanding. "I thought he was the one who supplied Malcolm with marijuana."

"Listen, love, Bill says you are alright, so I'll tell you how it works, but if you repeat anything I will deny it. Are we agreed?" he said and I nodded.

"Darren can't go out and get drugs himself. He's far too well known. So they use a roadie or more often, one of the groupies. Sometimes it's me, sometimes someone else. We don't attract a lot of attention and we know where to look. It's the same in every town or country we play. You can't take the drugs with you across the borders, so we get new stuff in every place we play."

"So, was it usual for someone to want heroin? Have you been asked for it before?" I asked, trying to understand.

"It happens," Digger answered. "We get asked for a lot of things. It depends on who we playing with and what they are into. Ain't no one in The Sticks that uses heroin though, so I just assumed Darren was catering for that Will Hero or one of The Sleuths. In Camden, I got the heroin for Darren before the concert. He doesn't tell me who it's for and I don't want to know, but I doubt he'd get any for Tiger. No way! I don't care what them doctors were saying, Tiger was clean!" Digger insisted, and then he turned his back on me and wandered back to the other roadies.

Darren was standing right by the stage staring at me and not in the direction of the band. His eyes looked full of hatred as he made his way towards me, and I suddenly felt a little frightened. I moved further away from the roadies, the bus and the semi-darkness, and towards the fence separating the parking field from the stage. Darren came after me.

"It was you who gave Tiger that heroin," I challenged him and he sniggered arrogantly.

"Nobody's going to believe a story like that," he replied, confidently. He moved very close and I realised that no one had noticed us leave the stage area.

"But it *was* you. Why?" I asked.

"You can't prove it was me. There is no evidence, remember?" Darren said, glancing around to make sure no one was nearby. He sniggered again. "It will be your word against mine if you talk to anyone about this."

"Relax, I know that," I answered, trying to make him believe I wasn't a threat. "I'm just curious why you would get Tiger heroin."

He laughed again. "You still don't get it, do you? Tiger didn't ask me to get him any drugs. I planned it."

"I'm still not understanding; what is it that you planned?"

"Tiger was a loose cannon; I couldn't let him go around talking about what he'd seen," Darren said, sounding proud.

"What had he seen? Was it something that happened back in 1983?" It was a stab in the dark, but I hoped he would open up to me. "You must have been very clever; much cleverer than the police and everyone else."

"It was an accident. I didn't mean to hurt Kevan and Delph. She was a good sort really. That stupid

257

Aussie idiot heard me enjoying myself with that girl. The bitch kept screaming," Darren continued.

"Was this the girl that you and Malcolm raped?"

"Malcolm and I enjoyed her company," Darren corrected me. "She was keen to be with us in that room to begin with. We gave her a few lines of coke, got her in the mood, but then she didn't want to, and said she was leaving. So we stopped her and Malcolm had his way with her, which was only right. Then it was my turn and Malcolm suddenly decided he couldn't be bothered listening to her screaming anymore, so he sodded off to find a smoke." Darren said.

"So there I am, enjoying myself and the door is ripped open and that Aussie idiot, Kevan, comes falling in, saying he's going to rescue the girl. He threatened me with the police and God knows what. But he was very slow, because he'd been taking heroin with Delphine in her room. I managed to get him off me and back into Delph's room, and then I saw the pouch with the gear inside on the bedside table. So I very nicely offered him some more and he was too drugged to protest. Quite the opposite, he wanted a little top-up."

Darren was standing close to me and talking directly into my ear. I could smell Malcolm's spliff on him and he had the smell of stale beer on his breath.

"It was really very easy. I've seen junkies shoot up often enough and sometimes even helped, so I put some of Delphine's drugs into his vein. I had no idea how much it was. I just wanted him to shut up

258

and leave me alone. Delphine started to stir, so I put what was left into her arm. Then I picked up the gear, so they wouldn't take any more and top themselves by mistake, and I left the room. What a stroke of luck that turned out to be." Darren laughed dryly.

"In the hallway I bumped into Tiger ranting on and on about being fired and he wanted to talk to Malcolm. I told him I had no idea where Malcolm was and gave him Delphine's gear to shut him up. He and that bird of his were already out of their skulls, so I promised to talk to Bill and Malcolm about him getting his job back, and they left. The girl I'd been messing with had passed out on the bed, so I went back and picked up where I'd left off," Darren boasted, and I looked at him in disgust.

"You could have blown me over with a feather the next day when they told us that Delph and that Kevan overdosed. I was just glad I'd taken the drugs, so they didn't have my fingerprints on there," he added.

"So that was an accident. I get that. But why give Tiger heroin now? It doesn't make sense," I said, trying to keep him talking and beginning to worry about how this would end. That I was going to tell the police was a definite plan, but how I was going to get Darren to leave me alone for long enough to call them was another problem altogether.

He laughed. "I didn't just give him the heroin, my dear. I planned it all in detail, because you are right, I'm cleverer than the lot of them. Not that Malcolm or anyone else appreciates what I do for them. They seem to think that things take care of themselves by magic. I even left a little calling card, but no one got it, stupid fuckers," he added.

"Do you mean the Triple A armband?" I asked.

"Ah, so you did see that," Darren remarked, laughing loudly. "I wanted it to look like Tiger was sending a message from beyond the grave, just to see if anyone was the least bit suspicious about his death, but no one picked up on it."

I sensed a rustle in the atmosphere close by, but couldn't see anyone. It was dark and there was only a dim light reaching us from the stage. I clutched my handbag tightly because I was scared stiff, but I couldn't stop now; I had to know what happened.

"When we got the band back together, after Bill stopped shitting himself over those threats, Tiger came and thanked me. The stupid sod thanked me!" Darren continued. "He told me he'd used every last bit of the gear I gave him that night over the next four days, and he'd overdosed. Tracy managed to get him to hospital and then into rehab. Tiger was there for a few weeks and they didn't learn about Delphine's death until much later, when they went to Crete. And still he didn't put two and two together. It made me think that perhaps one day he would and I couldn't risk it. When we were at the Dublin gig, I heard him telling the roadies how fantastic I was and how I'd been instrumental in getting him off drugs."

"So you decided to kill him?" I asked softly and he nodded slightly.

"You see, Tiger would one day put it together," he said. "He wasn't stupid. Or he would tell someone else who would start asking questions about where I got heroin from at the party where two people overdosed. So I played a little game. I put a strong sleeping pill into Tracy's wine. I'd gotten a friend to make Malcolm some hashish brownies and I gave a few to Tiger before he went up to his room, and he thought I was being nice and giving him a cake. He was carrying a cup of tea from the ballroom and I slipped a couple of Valiums in it when he wasn't looking, just in case he didn't eat any of the cakes."

Darren sniggered now, appearing to be quite proud of his achievements. "After a little while I knocked on his door and there was no doubt that Tiger was high as a kite. Tracy was passed out on the bed. He was laughing and saying he was afraid he'd had a relapse, because he was feeling strange. It didn't take long to get him to have a drink with me. We got talking about old times.

"As soon as I got him to take a little drink there was no stopping him. Tiger drank vodka like it was water and told me how good it felt to be able to drink again. He said it set him free, ironically. As soon as he passed out on the bed from the drink, I made sure I put a good dose of heroin into his arm," Darren concluded.

"But why not leave the heroin equipment in the room?" I asked. "The police would have written it off as Tiger having a relapse; death by misadventure."

"I couldn't do that in case something I hadn't thought of led to the police looking more closely at the equipment. It had my fingerprints all over it. I took everything—the drug gear, the drink and the food—to my room before I went back down to the party, and I'd only been with Tiger for an hour. It was too easy," Darren recalled. "You know it's really rather good to tell someone about all this. I was bursting to tell someone, but I couldn't. Not even Malcolm would understand what I had done for him. If that Kevan guy had called the police, we would both have gone to jail."

"What now?" I asked him, a little frightened.

Before I realised what was happening, Brody was alongside me, suddenly appearing out of the darkness. I felt my body jerk backwards as he leapt forward and took Darren down hard, face down in the grass, and sat on his back. It was another guy with the same build as Brody whom I hadn't seen before that pulled me backwards, away from Darren. Everything seemed to happen at once.

"I can answer that question, Charlie," said Brody. "Now Darren will get what he deserves."

"How did you find me?" I asked.

"Digger said you might need help. I think he was more afraid you'd get raped though, since he knows what these guys are like," he answered. "Say hello to my partner, Glen."

Chapter 15
Revenge

I was shaking badly when the police arrived to pick up Darren. Two cars screeched to a halt in the parking area in the field adjacent to the festival one. Brody and Glen frogmarched Darren to the waiting officers just as the last song in the tribute concert to Tiger was being sung, and the crowd shouted and whistled their appreciation once again.

The police were filled in on what had happened, and what Brody and Glen knew of my conversation with Darren. They had both heard him admit to killing Tiger, but nothing regarding Delphine and Kevan. I gave them a short statement and also the name of the detective who had been running Tiger's case, Jack Baldwin.

I felt shaken and my blood sugar levels were through the floor when I heard a text message click on my phone. Opening my handbag, I pulled out my Dictaphone instead of my mobile by mistake. I looked at it in surprise and then suddenly realised exactly what it was I was looking at.

The green 'record' light was still on. Unable to work the damn thing, I'd just thrown it in my bag after interviewing Grandma Blue and her Floozies. It was still running. My hand started to shake with excitement when I realised there was a good chance that the Dictaphone had recorded the whole conversation I'd had with Darren.

"Hey, here's his confession," I announced to the police, handing over the Dictaphone. "You'll have to turn it off yourselves. I have no idea how to work that thing," I added as the policeman closest to me looked at it closely and switched it off.

"You will need to come to the police station and make a thorough statement as soon as possible," he told us, and we agreed.

I really didn't feel up to it straight away though. Brody put his arms around me and held me for several minutes while I tried to pull myself together, but all I could do was tremble. I felt really weak and silly. We walked back to the stage where The Sticks were making a jubilant exit and Malcolm was starting to come down from his 'trip'. I felt cold and tired, and Bill's face resembled a huge question mark when he saw me. I just wanted to go home.

Remembering that I had received a text message, I took my mobile phone out of my handbag and turned it on. It was from James. That was the last thing I needed right now. It said, "Meet me at your house after the concert. We need to talk." That was it. Speaking to James was the last thing I wanted to do.

By now people started to make their way out of the field. A few stayed behind in groups sitting on the grass talking and drinking. Grandma Blue and the rest of the Floozies were nowhere to be seen, except for Raven and Nigel who stood closely together, their arms wrapped around each other. Digger and the roadies were working to get the instruments into the bus, and there was a bustle of activity on and around the stage.

It was late and very dark, apart from the lights that were still on around the stage area. I watched as bats zig-zagged in the bright light and my mind was numb. All I could think about was how they managed to fly so fast in the light and not bump into one another—amazing. I made a mental note to Google it later.

Brody led me by the hand to the bus where Bill and Simone were sitting together, talking and waiting for the crowd to disperse. Malcolm was there, as were the other members of The Sticks. Everyone else had already left.

Raven and Nigel sat down, tightly wrapped together, and I felt pleased they had worked things out. I was also glad that Tracy had already left, because I needed to get my head around everything before I could fill her in on all the details surrounding the death of her husband. It was something I dreaded, but I knew I would have to do it at some point soon before it broke in the news. It would be better for her to hear it from me.

"Mel said to tell you she won't be needing that bed tonight after all," Raven told me, sounding tired. "Last time I saw her she had locked lips with Will Hero and they wandered off into the sunset, if you know what I mean."

"Wow, I know she has a soft spot for him," I answered, happy that at least someone was getting some action.

"Can Nigel stay in my room tonight?" she asked.

"Of course, you are welcome to stay for as long as you like," I answered.

"Thank you, but I miss Jason badly. Tomorrow it will be time to get back to the squat—sorry, I mean our house," Raven said with a smile, and Nigel kissed her.

Brody and Glen, together with Digger, spent half an hour filling Malcolm and Bill in on what had gone down with Darren, and they were both shocked and disgusted.

"Darren isn't a bad sort really. He was just trying to protect me," Malcolm said and everyone else protested.

"Well, he killed my wife and my best friend, so you need to decide whose side you are on, because I can't have anything to do with anyone who takes Darren's side in all this," Bill said sternly.

He was sitting beside Simone with his arm around her shoulders, so I concluded that Yvette's fear of her sister and boyfriend having feelings for each other had been correct.

"Steady on, I'm not taking sides. Darren will have to answer for what he did," Malcolm replied slyly. "I feel really rough tonight. I don't know what was in the green stuff today, but it sent me on a right wobbly."

I was wrapped in a blanket that Digger had found for me, with Brody sitting alongside. It wasn't cold, but I was feeling shaky. Digger handed out chilled bottles of beer to anyone who fancied one and then he gave me a large glass of rosé from a bottle tucked in a plastic bucket of ice at the front of the bus.

266

"I remembered you liked this stuff in London, so I got you some," Digger said as he handed me a plastic cup.

I smiled at him in appreciation and took a large sip. I was beginning to understand why Digger was so popular with Bill and the rest of the guys. Brody accepted a beer, and I once again remembered that I hadn't told Bill about my situation with James.

"I have to tell you something," I said to him. "James and I are not together. We haven't been for weeks. I left the week before I interviewed you. I just don't want you to get the wrong impression."

"I know that. James contacted me, asking what was going on with you," Bill answered and smiled reassuringly. "He tried to give me the impression everything was fine and didn't realise that I understood he was trying to get information about you. Needless to say, I didn't tell him anything. Lately he has been a bit of a pain in the arse."

"He just texted me that he is here," I added.

"I know he's here. He tried to get Digger to let him into the backstage area, saying he was your husband and my best friend. Of course, Digger wasn't born yesterday," Bill answered, grinning.

"If you are not on the list, you are not on the fucking list," Digger added. "That woman he was with was a right tart. Stacey, he called her."

Oh my God, James was here with Stacey in tow? I wondered what he wanted to see me about in the middle of the night, miles away from home.

"You don't have to see him, you know. I have enough security around here and your house to make that problem go away. Like Digger said, he's not on the list. It might be about time you sorted yourself out when it comes to James. What are you planning to do?" Bill asked me.

"I'm going to divorce him," I replied. "I'm sure it will come as no surprise to him."

"Funny you should say that, because a lot of the questions James has been asking were about what sort of frame of mind you were in, and whether you were ready to come to your senses and come home. He seemed very confident. I'll give you a number for a good divorce lawyer, if you like. I'm sure it's just a question of sorting the paperwork out since I'm guessing you have a pre-nup," he suggested.

"No, we never got around to having one of them drawn up," I answered and Bill started to laugh loudly. "I think the overconfident James believed he could bully you into doing just about anything," he added.

"Well, dear girl, I can understand why he's so anxious to get you back. If you divorce him you are going to be a very rich lady indeed," Simone stated, and she and Bill laughed at my shocked expression. Money had not even crossed my mind.

An hour later, we drove several cars to my parents' house where Grandma Blue was hosting a jubilant after-party, totally unaware of what had gone down at the concert. Even Dad was celebrating.

The old iron gates opened slowly, reluctantly allowing us to drive into the parking area in front of the house. We spilled out of the cars and Malcolm, being a little unsteady on his feet, was the last person out.

"Do I really have to attend this after-party?" he grumbled arrogantly. "I'd much rather get the helicopter to take us right back to civilisation. Don't you think we've hung out with the bumpkins for long enough, Bill?" His lips were pointing downwards and he was, as usual, very unimpressed with everything. Bill didn't even bother to answer.

The house was lit up and there was loud music coming from the ground floor windows, which were wide open. Steps lead up to our porch, which is paved with stone, and covers the entire back and left-hand side of our house, leading straight into the dining room via a pair of large French doors. We normally use the porch as an outside eating area during the summer months. As the doors were wide open, it was in that direction that I led everyone as we left the cars.

Glen had picked up the blanket I discarded in the car and carried it politely for me as we all walked towards the porch. Malcolm held back at the rear, as if wanting to avoid entering our house. He had his mobile out and was phoning the helicopter people about getting picked up. He was just stepping on to the first step to the porch when we heard a loud boom, sounding like a small explosion.

I turned in shock to see Malcolm sprawled on his stomach on the steps. Just behind him, standing among the parked cars was Carolina Marshall, holding something that resembled a rifle, but the end section looked to be missing. Malcolm whined in pain. His entire bottom and back looked like it had been pebble-dashed with a million tiny wounds.

I realised that Carolina was carrying a sawn-off shotgun and she'd shot Malcolm in the buttocks! Brody leaped over the stone railing of the porch and was quickly by her side, closely followed by Glen.

"Bill Graham didn't rape my little girl, Malcolm, you did! You've just been questioned by the police for abusing young girls, so it didn't take me long to work out who raped my Mandy," Carolina said, weeping. "We trusted you with the most precious thing we had and you abused her. The police can't do anything to put you away for what you've done. Prison would be too good for you!"

As Carolina spoke, we all stood and stared at her in horror, except for Brody and Glen, who had both reached her side before anyone else managed to react. We were all too shocked to move. Brody pulled the shotgun from Carolina's hands and there was no resistance. She just stood there weeping as he emptied its contents on to the grass.

Glen ran back to the porch and grabbed the blanket from where he had left it. He threw it to Brody, who caught it with one hand while still holding the shotgun in the other. We all watched in amazement as Brody used the blanket to clean off the weapon expertly. I realised it was to make sure there were no fingerprints on it. Then he threw it as far into the field beside our house as he could. Malcolm was still lying face down on our steps whimpering and asking for someone to help him.

"You have your revenge. Now go before the police come, and don't tell anyone about this or you'll be in big trouble," Brody told Carolina sternly.

She looked at him as if she didn't understand what he was saying. "But I killed him. I shot him."

"No, you've only wounded him. That is just buckshot. What you've done is fire hundreds of small pellets into him. Whoever sold you that shotgun was ripping you off, because this thing can't kill anyone, but he will be hurting for a long time. Now go!" he insisted.

Carolina seemed to suddenly understand what Brody was saying. She nodded to him thankfully through her tears and then walked away slowly towards the gate. Brody turned around to face us. Strangely, no one inside the house had reacted to the blast as they were playing the Sex Pistols very loudly.

Rich Brewer appeared on the porch carrying a bottle of beer and a cigarette he was about to light up when he saw us. He glanced down at the bleeding figure that was Malcolm, who was unable to move. "Oh, Malcolm seems to have slipped. Did anyone see how that happened?" he asked loudly and a little drunkenly while making no move to help him.

"No, I didn't see a thing," I answered, and the rest of the people standing outside shook their heads in agreement.

"Somebody should call an ambulance," Brody remarked as he carefully stepped over Malcolm.

271

"Yeah, someone should. Did anyone see what happened just then, because I was looking away?" Raven said.

Bill shook his head and put his arm around Simone's neck. "Nah, I was too busy hugging an old friend," he replied, laughing.

"Help!" Malcolm called out weakly from his place on the stairs, as we entered the party through the French doors.

Grandma Blue was dancing with Mum in the dining room. The music was pumping and everyone seemed happy and upbeat. If I wasn't mistaken, I would have said that my grandma was quite tipsy.

"Hey, Charlie, where have you been?" she called out, letting go of my mum and coming over to hug me. "That Brody is a really hot guy. You should go and talk to him. Remember, life's too short. Enjoy it while you can," she added.

I made my way towards the hall. I was planning on going into the kitchen to get myself some more wine when I was suddenly pulled aside by a strong arm, which drew me into the downstairs bathroom. Brody's lips found mine and we shared a long kiss before I eventually pulled away to catch my breath.

"I have been longing to do that all night," he whispered into my ear.

"Me, too, but there's something bothering me though," I said, and Brody looked at me with a twinkle in his blue eyes. "Now that Bill doesn't need a bodyguard any more, what will you do?"

"Well, I think I need to take some time out to relax," he replied.

"So you are not planning on going back to the States any time soon?" I asked.

"Babe, I'm not planning on going anywhere. I'm staying right here," he answered and kissed me again, this time more intensely.

"Stop, Brody! This is moving too fast. We need to slow down," I said, feeling a full-on attack of my nymphomania hit like a seizure.

"We can take it as fast or as slow as you want. Like I said before, I like England and I'm not going anywhere. And I like it a lot more now I've met you."

My body ached, but we pulled apart as Mum opened the door that we had forgotten to lock. She looked at us with raised eyebrows and then smiled. I guess that let the cat out of the bag. I knew the family would have found out about Brody at some point, so now was as good as any.

A little later, my mother phoned the police to report a strange man lying on the steps of our porch. She told them she'd been tipped off that he had been taking drugs, and that he seemed to be under the influence and bleeding from superficial wounds. Mum asked that he be removed from our garden, which they did two hours later.

Karma? You tell me…

Project Polina

As the daughter of a mega-wealthy Russian oligarch, you would assume Polina Averyanov has everything money can buy. When eighteen-year-old Polina aspires to be a pop star, her wealthy father does what any well to do magnate would—he does his best to make his daughter's dream come true and starts Project Polina, but quickly discovers pop stardom cannot be easily bought.

When Polina competes in a small song contest in the Ukraine, her existence comes to the attention of her father's worst enemy, Boris Korzhakov. Boris has reached the higher echelons of Russian politics to head the FCB, which is concerned with internal security of the Russian State, but is also involved in the fight against espionage and organised crime, formerly a faction of the KGB. Boris Korzhakov was Stanislav Averyanov's business partner until Averyanov was arrested for crimes against the state. After bribing his way out of prison, Averyanov moved the major part of his assets to London, without a second thought of his partner's share.

Polina's career isn't taking off, and when there's a direct threat to the Averyanov family, Gresham CPC Global are called in to protect the spoilt young girl. Brody McCaine and his partner, Glen, are asked to guard the girl on a twenty-four-hour basis. Her parents try to work out what they need to do to stay safe, after an arrest order is issued for Stanislav and his assets that remained in Russia, seized by the state. Project Polina suddenly changes from making her a pop star to keeping her alive.

Charlotte Hart is still living with her dysfunctional family and struggling to make a career for herself as a music journalist while divorcing her husband, who is making life difficult for her. It isn't made any easier by Grandma Blue and her best friend, Doris, who are pushing Charlie into the arms of Doris's divorced grandson, Robert, whom she had a schoolgirl crush on, disregarding the fact that Charlotte and Brody have become close.

It all comes to a head when Brody and Glen turn up at Charlotte Hart's family home, in need of a safe house. Brody's feelings for Charlie become evident to Polina, who has developed a deep crush, bordering on obsession, for Brody. Charlie's dysfunctional family finds itself in the middle of a bitter feud that has international implications and isn't helped by the fact that the band The Sticks road manager, Digger, turns up with problems of his own.

Loyalties are tested as the need to escape from the Hart family house, which is surrounded by FCB agents, becomes imperative. Polina has to leave, or they will all die.

The second book in the Charlie Hart crime series will be released in spring 2014.

A Vicious Love Story: Remembering the Real Sid Vicious

Teddie was 16 years old in 1977, when she was asked to be the translator for the Norway leg of The Sex Pistols Scandinavian tour. The book tells the inside story of the romance between Teddie and Sid Vicious. Instead of the self-destructive caricature of popular myth, Teddie reveals a troubled, vulnerable and generous young man. She gives a first-hand account of four young men at the eye of an international media storm, labouring under the sudden weight of expectation at the height of their fame. We are given a closer look into the dynamics between all the band members and their associates. The last chapters are written in part by Eileen Polk (ex-girlfriend of DeeDee Ramone) and Peter Gravelle, who were in New York at the time of Sid's death.

Fast Living: Remembering the Real Gary Holton

"Be proud of everything that you do, or have a fucking damn good reason for doing something which you're not proud of." (Gary Holton to Danny Baker, NME, November 1984, a year before his death)

A true rock 'n' roll casualty, Gary Holton packed a lot into his thirty-three years, including fronting proto-punk legends, Heavy Metal Kids, and playing a leading role in one of the most revered TV dramas of its day.

Drawing on her own recollections and first-hand accounts of others who knew him, Teddie Dahlin completes the picture of a man who never outran his demons but who, in the process, gave a lot of pleasure and some little anguish to those who surrounded him.

Born in East End London, Holton became a member of the Royal Shakespeare Company at an early age before joining a touring production of Hair, prior to pursuing long-harboured musical ambitions. While Heavy Metal Kids never did reach the heights predicted for them, there was a number one solo single in Europe and an invitation to front AC/DC that was declined.

He would, however, become a fixture of British TV as the first actor cast in the hugely successful 'Auf Wiedersehen, Pet', his portrayal of the flamboyant, womanising Cockney carpenter Wayne Norris drawing heavily on his own experiences and outlook.

Before he succumbed, in murky circumstances, to a cocktail of alcohol and morphine, brought low by unpaid tax bills and bankruptcy proceedings, he would be a key part of an incestuous and hedonistic social circle in London, his propensity for alcohol and drug consumption sadly unchecked by wiser counsel.

This is an unflinching account of a life lived in haste, without hesitation, and of those he touched, both personally and professionally.

Alex Ogg Writer and journalist and the author of more than a dozen books, including The Art of Punk, The Hip Hop Years, Independence Days, No More Heroes, and many more.

About the Author

Teddie Dahlin lives in Oslo, Norway and in addition to writing books, is a freelance music journalist who has written a string of interviews and articles in the UK.

ACCESS ALL AREAS

ACCESS ALL AREAS

Lightning Source UK Ltd.
Milton Keynes UK
UKOW03f2046060114

224087UK00009B/101/P

9 780957 517042